Michael Moorcock is a
includes around fifty no
a rock album. Born in
of *Tarzan Adventures* at
Sexton Blake Library. H
editor ever since, and
most popular and mo
compared with Tennyson, Tolkien, Raymond Chandler,
Wyndham Lewis, Ronald Firbank, Mervyn Peake, Edgar
Allan Poe, Colin Wilson, Anatole France, William
Burroughs, Edgar Rice Burroughs, Charles Dickens,
James Joyce, Vladimir Nabokov, Jorge Luis Borges, Joyce
Cary, Ray Bradbury, H. G. Wells, George Bernard Shaw
and Hieronymus Bosch, among others.

'No one at the moment in England is doing more to break
down the artificial divisions that have grown up in novel
writing – realism, surrealism, science fiction, historical
fiction, social satire, the poetic novel – than Michael
Moorcock'
Angus Wilson

'He is an ingenious and energetic experimenter, restlessly
original, brimming over with clever ideas'
Robert Nye, *The Guardian*

By the same author

The Cornelius Chronicles
The Final Programme
A Cure for Cancer
The English Assassin
The Condition of Muzak
The Lives and Times of Jerry Cornelius

The Dancers at the End of Time
An Alien Heat
The Hollow Lands
The End of All Songs
Legends from the End of Time
The Transformation of Miss Mavis Ming (Return of the Fireclown)

Hawkmoon: The History of the Runestaff
The Jewel in the Skull
The Mad God's Amulet
The Sword of the Dawn
The Runestaff

Hawkmoon: The Chronicles of Castle Brass
Count Brass
The Champion of Garathorm
The Quest for Tanelorn

Erekosë
The Eternal Champion
Phoenix in Obsidian
The Swords of Heaven: The Flowers of Hell (with Howard Chaykin)

Elric
Elric of Melniboné
The Sailor on the Seas of Fate
The Weird of the White Wolf
The Vanishing Tower
The Bane of the Black Sword
Stormbringer
Elric at the End of Time

The Books of Corum
The Knight of the Swords
The Queen of the Swords
The King of the Swords
The Bull and the Spear
The Oak and the Ram
The Sword and the Stallion

Michael Kane
The City of the Beast
The Lord of the Spiders
The Masters of the Pit

The Nomad of Time
The War Lord of the Air
The Land Leviathan
The Steel Tsar

Other Titles
The Winds of Limbo
The Ice Schooner
Behold the Man
Breakfast in the Ruins
The Blood-Red Game
The Black Corridor
The Chinese Agent
The Russian Intelligence
The Distant Suns
The Rituals of Infinity
The Shores of Death
Sojan the Swordsman (juvenile)
The Golden Barge
Gloriana (or, the Unfulfill'd Queene, a Romance)
The Time Dweller
Moorcock's Book of Martyrs (short stories)
The Entropy Tango
Heroic Dreams (non-fiction)
Byzantium Endures
The Laughter of Carthage
The Brothel in Rosenstrasse
The War Hound and the World's Pain
Letters from Hollywood (non-fiction)
The Opium General (short stories)

MICHAEL MOORCOCK

The Adventures of Una Persson and Catherine Cornelius in the Twentieth Century

A Romance

GRAFTON BOOKS
A Division of the Collins Publishing Group

LONDON GLASGOW
TORONTO SYDNEY AUCKLAND

Grafton Books
A Division of the Collins Publishing Group
8 Grafton Street, London W1X 3LA

Published by Grafton Books 1980
Reprinted 1986

First published in Great Britain by
Quartet Books Ltd 1976

Copyright © Michael Moorcock 1976

ISBN 0-583-13101 8

Set, printed and bound in Great Britain by
Cox & Wyman Ltd, Reading

Set in Linotype Pilgrim

All rights reserved. No part of this publication
may be reproduced, stored in a retrieval system,
or transmitted, in any form, or by any means,
electronic, mechanical, photocopying, recording or
otherwise, without the prior permission of
the publishers.

This book is sold subject to the condition that
it shall not, by way of trade or otherwise, be
lent, re-sold, hired out or otherwise circulated
without the publisher's prior consent in any
form of binding or cover other than that
in which it is published and without a similar
condition including this condition being
imposed on the subsequent purchaser.

For
Miss C. Malone,
Aviatrix

I shall not say why and how I became, at the age of fifteen, the mistress of the Earl of Craven. Whether it was love, or the severity of my father, the depravity of my own heart, or the winning arts of the noble Lord, which induced me to leave my paternal roof and place myself under his protection, does not now much signify: or if it does, I am not in the humour to gratify curiosity in this matter.

Harriette Wilson, *Memoirs*

INTRODUCTION

A note concerning the principal characters and sources of this book

The unpublished memoirs of Miss Una Persson, the temporal adventuress, have been the chief source for the story which follows. These memoirs, entrusted to me some time ago and constantly added to and modified by Miss Persson, exist partly in the form of notes in her own hand, partly in the form of tape-recorded interviews between myself and Miss Persson, partly as notes taken by me after one of our many conversations. The memoirs, therefore, are discursive and unorganized, but are remarkably consistent in their details and I have used them indirectly in several novels where I have needed to write about the earlier years of this century or, indeed, the last years. Occasionally I have used them to check certain facts found in other published accounts concerning important moments in recent history and in all cases where there have been inconsistencies it has been proven that Miss Persson's record was the most objective, the most accurate.

Only when the subject of her method of time-travel is raised does Miss Persson become a little vague. That the time-travelling often works profound and subtle changes on her character is undeniable (and there are sometimes physical changes, too) but how she achieved the ability to move easily through the years and centuries and why the changes take place are mysteries I can only hope that one day she will choose to explain. There is no doubt that a few other people share her ability (she has described it as a 'talent') including at least three members of the ubiquitous Cornelius family, that stranger figure Karl Glogauer, Lord Jagged of

Canaria, and the doomed Oswald Bastable (whom my grandfather knew so well) and it is fair to assume that she has been responsible for helping some of these develop the talent – Catherine Cornelius quite obviously learned the knack from Miss Persson, with whom she has had a close friendship since adolescence. Most of my knowledge of the Cornelius family comes from Miss Persson's accounts, received in turn from Miss Cornelius; most of my information about that peculiar period of the far future known as the Age at the End of Time also comes from Miss Persson.

Needless to say, I have often inquired about the reason for Miss Persson's rarely revealing her marvellous talent or, indeed, using it to obvious advantage, and again I have found her answers a trifle numinous; something to do with the creation of 'alternative' futures, with unwanted paradox and the tendency of Time itself to resist anachronistic events by 'spitting out' any time-traveller who might seek radically to change the course of history. This, I gather, is why a good psychic and physical disguise is necessary to the committed time-traveller; and the result is often a form of temporary amnesia where the traveller sinks so thoroughly into the spirit of the age that he or she forgets any other identity or having existed in any other period (indeed, Miss Persson has suggested to me that the ability to achieve this state might even be a crucial factor in the make-up of those who have found it possible to travel through time).

As for the question of 'alternative' versions of our history, I am afraid that I have neither the intelligence nor the information from which to speculate; I can merely repeat in good faith what Miss Persson has told me – that a very few people are also able to cross from one 'alternate' age to another and that few of those do so of their own volition (here I must cite the two volumes edited by my grandfather, published under the titles The Warlord of the Air and The Land Leviathan, for anyone wishing to consider further evidence).

One last point: the narrative which follows is fiction in so far as I have taken liberties of interpretation, organization and speculation with Miss Persson's records, moreover the *selection and therefore the bias is mine. My simple intention has been to make from the material entrusted to me an entertaining book which can be enjoyed as a work of fiction is enjoyed, and I hope that the reader will judge it in that light alone.*

Ladbroke Grove
London

MICHAEL MOORCOCK

November 1975

PART ONE

DEPRESSION DAYS: TAKING IT EASY

This may be hard to believe... but when you're looking at this little sweetheart you're looking at Miss World. True enough, she hasn't got a proper crown – it's only an old cake decoration. And she is just eight months old. But her Mum, Pauline, will support little Layla's claim that she was born to be Miss World. That is largely on account of her Dad being Mr World... Well, a girl has to make the most of her assets.

DAILY MIRROR, 3 November 1975

ONE

In which we are introduced to our heroines and learn that, having rested and recovered sufficiently from the experiences of their previous adventures, they are prepared to embark upon a new series of excursions into the twentieth century

It was light at last.

Jars of cosmetics rattled and perfume bottles clinked on the dressing-table, pushed back towards the white-framed oval mirror by Una Persson's breakfast tray, heavy and steaming, as in some relief she let go of the handles. She crossed to the wide bow windows and jerked a cord, sending the white and black art-deco blind whizzing on its roller to reveal the sunlit shrubbery, the sloping lawn, the broad, shallow river and, beyond it, the green wooded Pocono Mountains. Two days ago the boy scouts had set up their camp on the far shore of the river. The camp was invisible from the house; Una could hear one of the scouts practising dawn bugle calls from somewhere behind the elms near the bend where the muddy Delaware was at its widest. The sun rose over the Poconos: another cloudless day. Naked, Una stretched her fine, strong arms and fluffed at her short chestnut hair, yawning. The bugle call faltered, became a series of brief, desperate discords, then collapsed and did not begin again. The birds resumed their interrupted chorus.

Una turned to look at Catherine Cornelius who was peacefully asleep in the midst of the white sheets and primrose pillows; she was undisturbed by the sunlight which fell on her fair skin, reflected in her gleaming, near-white hair, the silver filigree rings on the fingers of her exposed left hand.

Reflecting that she was pleased with the world this morning, Una concluded that she must be bored; then she smiled: she was becoming far too interested in the minute details of her momentary states of mind. She opened the windows and took a deep breath. The air was already very warm. In the bed Catherine stirred, drawing her hand under the sheets, awake but unwilling to wake up. Una went back to the breakfast tray, lifted it and carried it to the bed, placing it carefully near the edge, climbing back in, pulling a sheet up to her waist, reaching forward and taking the tray again to lower it on to her lap. She began to pour herself a cup of coffee, noticing how its smell blended so well with the smell of Catherine's skin. She unfolded the *Briggstown Examiner* and without glancing at the headlines turned at once to the funnies page.

By the time Una had read 'Krazy Kat' and 'The Katzenjammer Kids' Catherine was on one elbow glancing over her shoulder to see how Tarzan and Flash Gordon were doing (Una had known that this would draw Catherine out of her sleep – Tarzan and the smell of coffee).

'Coffee?'

Una smiled as she poured another cup. Catherine rubbed at her head and sighed, trying to focus her eyes on her favourite strip. She nodded and then kissed Una's shoulder before taking the offered coffee in an unsteady hand. The cup rattled in the saucer. Catherine sat up and began to drink, her large blue eyes staring bleakly at the window. The sheet fell away from her breasts. She opened her mouth in a wide yawn.

'Is it Tuesday?'

'Yes.' Una looked at her watch. 'It's early. Not seven.'

'Oh, shit.' The tone of despair was profound.

'You were asleep by eight,' said Una good-humouredly. 'You've had eleven hours.'

It took Catherine a short while to make sense of this statement but when she did understand it she was relieved. 'Oh, well...'

'You missed the boy scouts.'

Catherine licked her lips. 'What?'

'They were playing their bugles. Do you want the paper?'

Catherine accepted the *Examiner*. Her expression was rapt as she followed the adventure strips (she could only rarely see what was amusing about the joke strips). She sipped her coffee. She relaxed; she came to life. She finished the coffee and handed the paper back. 'That's better.'

Una folded the pages slowly, glancing at the news. 'They had a fire yesterday, in town. The general store. Not a lot of damage. There's a German rival to Ford. A popular car within the reach of everyone's pocket.'

'Bullshit,' said Catherine, and then, self-consciously, 'life's too bloody short for bullshit.'

Una had not really been listening. 'Go back to sleep, if you like. I've . . .'

'Sorry, but it is a bit early.' Catherine hugged her, kissed her cheek. Una scarcely flinched. She returned the kiss.

'Have you any plans for today?' Catherine swallowed the remains of her coffee.

'Not really. Maybe finish off the bit of writing I started.'

'Your "memoirs"?'

'And you?'

'I don't know. Read, I suppose. Lounge on the lawn. Improve my tan.' Catherine held her arms in front of her and inspected them. She was already very brown. 'Are you all right?'

'A trifle bored.'

'You're sure that's it?'

'Yes. Why?'

'You seem distant.'

'I am. But it's just boredom.'

'As long as you're not brooding. Proper holidays always are boring, of course. That's what they should be, shouldn't they?'

Una laughed. 'I know.' She was grateful for Catherine's common sense which so often saved her from her moods of morbid introspection. Una hugged her friend, this time with spontaneous affection. Catherine looked vaguely surprised, but she was pleased. She sighed.

As Una got up Catherine asked, 'Do you feel like another Adventure, then?'

'I suppose I do. I'm trying to curb the impulse. I swore I'd have a good long rest.' She opened the door to the landing. 'I'll see what a lukewarm shower does for me.'

The landing was bright with light from the huge window which ran almost from roof to floor on two levels of the big wooden house. The bathroom, pink, black and silver in a local decorator's idea of art deco, was comparatively dark. The plumbing began to groan as Una turned on the hot tap for the shower; a spurt of steaming hot water was immediately followed, as usual, by a gush of tepid, rusty liquid. Philosophically, Una stepped under it. The businessman who had originally bought the place as a summer retreat had crashed with all the others in 1929, before he could make the improvements he had planned. As his chief creditor, Una had inherited it and had left it pretty much as she had found it. If he hadn't made his thirty-storey jump a little ahead of the fashion Una would have given it back to him. She felt it was only right, therefore, not to make any radical changes. The poor man had no other monument.

She finished her shower and began to dry herself with a large brown bath-towel, singing a song which, in another of her roles, she had made popular. This led her to wondering what had happened to her old lover and manager Sebastian Auchinek who, by now, must have become mixed up in the Zionist politics that would cause him so much anguish in the years to follow. She considered this mood of sympathy a dangerous one for her at the moment and tried to stop the process of association which brought memories of other lovers, other romantics, other victims. It would be much healthier, for one thing, if she considered herself a victim; after all, so many had betrayed her. On the other hand it was rather difficult to sustain that attitude of defensive bitterness, although it was an attitude which had enabled her to make her last escape to this haven. She must be in a healthy state of mind, of course, if she was thinking in these terms; it meant that the holiday had done what she had intended it to do – it had restored her sense of perspective. As yet, though, she was not sure that she welcomed the restoration. It would mean giving up that comfortable ambience of conspiracy which she had been sharing with Catherine, who had taken this holiday for the same reasons as herself – because she had become, as she put it, pissed off with men. It was probably more important for Catherine to maintain her cynicism, since there was far less of it in her character than was sometimes good for her. There again perhaps it was equally unhealthy to take towards Catherine an attitude of maternalism which surely indicated a lack of respect for Catherine's own identity. Checking herself before she went any deeper into such questions, Una burst again into song, this time a bawdy revolutionary ballad concerning the inadequate sexual proficiency of some soon-to-be-forgotten Mexican general. It never failed to make Catherine laugh and now, as Una swept grandly back into the bedroom, Catherine enthusiastically joined in the chorus with an accent which only Spaniards found charming. She was standing by the window, wrapped in a silk kimono tied around the waist with one of the ex-owner's yellow cravats. Una donned pants and bra with a flourish, climbed into a pair of jazzy lounging pyjamas, still singing, and strode to where the tray lay upon the bed. Picking up the tray she marched out of the room, down the curve of the stairs and through the long, wide living-room to the kitchen, washing the dishes under the impetus of what remained of the final verse and was able to dry the last cup with an 'Olé' which was decidedly off-key.

Her notebook was on the kitchen table where she had left it the night before, having written a couple of pages after Catherine had gone to bed. She controlled the slight sense of panic she felt on realizing that she had left the clasp unlocked. She went to the cupboard where she kept the key, took the key down and locked the book. Through the kitchen window she could see the dusty Duesenberg parked near the back door. The Duesenberg was also part of her inheritance. Later, in the nineteen-fifties, she would give it to Catherine's brother Jerry. She considered a drive in the hills, but the thought produced an agoraphobic twinge and she decided that it would not be a good idea. It was not really agoraphobia at all, she told herself, but an unwillingness to meet anyone, no matter how briefly; an encounter with one of the residents of this period and place would require a disguise and she still did not feel fit enough to relish such artificiality for its own sake. At this, she became reconciled to enjoying the rest of her retreat and she wandered back into the living-room to take down one of the late-nineteenth-century bound volumes of *Life* magazine (in those days a sort of American *Punch*) and continue through the french windows, out on to the sweet-smelling lawn where butterflies were already at work on the bright assortment of roses, hollyhocks and sunflowers. There was a movement in the shrubbery: she caught a glimpse of a deer galloping through the broken fence and into the forest on the other side. And that, thought Una with satisfaction, was what 1933 had to offer that you wouldn't be able to get in 1983 (indeed, by 1980 this particular stretch of the valley would have been flooded to make a boating resort and nearby Briggstown itself would be under water). She sat down on the battered wrought-iron bench in the middle of the lawn. The bench's white paint was peeling to reveal a more durable layer of green. As she leafed through the dusty pages of *Life*, Una picked unconsciously at one of the larger blisters until the grass beneath was littered with little white spots, like confetti.

From inside the house came the sound of the pianola being pedalled, a Strauss waltz which lasted only a few bars before Catherine became bored. There was silence, then Una heard the familiar sounds of selections from *The Merry Widow*, Catherine's favourite. Una realized that she had left her cigarettes in the kitchen.

For some reason Una chose not to go back the way she had come and instead walked right round the house to the kitchen door, getting her cigarettes and lighter from the table and leaving again, passing the windows of the living-room where Catherine, still in her kimono, sat with her knees pumping up and down at the pianola, her lips soundlessly forming the words of the song she was playing.

Life lay open on the bench, but she ignored both as she wandered on down to the river bank, lighting a cigarette and looking to see if there were any signs of the scouts' tents, but they were well camouflaged. Save for a glimpse of khaki, they remained invisible. Something organic and tangled went past, drifting swiftly on the current. Una shivered and refused to look at it. She took a deep drag on the Sherman's and then threw the thin brown cigarette into the water. The music had stopped.

Turning, Una saw Catherine come wandering down the lawn towards her. So that Catherine should not catch sight of the disappearing refuse on the river, Una walked rapidly back, calling, 'Hello!' She said: 'I saw a deer!'

'Where did it go? Through the gap?'

'Yes.'

'Phew! I think it's going to be hotter than ever today, don't you?'

'Seems likely.'

'You picked a nice time, Una.'

'Thanks.'

Catherine frowned. 'Am I repeating myself?'

'I don't think so.'

Catherine sat down on the grass, pulling back the kimono to expose her legs. 'Can the boy scouts see us from here?'

'I haven't noticed a glint of field-glasses.'

'I rather like the idea...' Catherine peeled off the kimono to reveal her shoulders and breasts. 'I wonder what American boy scouts are like. Even primmer than the British ones, I'd guess...'

'Very probably. But there's always the odd black sheep,' said Una. 'Or is it wolf?' She frowned, adding: 'Boy scouts, indeed! You're bored too, by the sound of it.'

'How long have we been here now?' Catherine stretched herself out in an attitude of crucifixion. 'A month?'

'A bit longer.'

'We said a month, didn't we?'

'Or two, we thought.' Una tried to keep her tone neutral.

'Where was it we jumped from? 1960—?'

'1975.'

'That was a heavy year. For me, anyway. I thought next time I'd go back a bit, to somewhere nice and early, where there's not quite so much happening on what you'd call an international scale. Fewer people, too. 1910 or sometime like that. It would be a good way of leading into a new cycle – starting with a fairly easy period, you know . . .'

'A bit *too* dull for me, 1910. I'm not sure why. It depends, I suppose, on the place.' Una hoped that she wasn't manipulating Catherine. 'Russia might be all right.'

'There should be brochures,' said Catherine. 'Come to Sunny Bali in 1925g, and so on.' Her eyes were shut against the glare. 'I'd like to see my rotten old mum again, anyway.'

'It takes all tastes.' Catherine's mother terrified Una. Catherine, however, had never lost affection for her.

'And Frank. And Jerry.'

Una raised her eyebrows, returning her attention to the river.

She did not have a lot of time for Catherine's family, though she suspected that this could be because she saw them as rivals. Catherine's boyfriends (those she had met, at any rate) did not arouse the slightest feelings of jealousy in her, merely dislike. She had once admitted to Catherine that she found her friend's taste in men bewildering.

The bundle in the river had disappeared.

'I've known some good, brave lads,' Catherine was saying, sentimentally.

'And a lot of cunts,' said Una, but she spoke affectionately.

'You're thinking what I'm thinking, aren't you?' Catherine sat up.

'What?'

Catherine laughed.

'Oh!' Una turned so that she could see their jetty, where the little white motor-launch was moored. 'Yes.' With a sigh she went and sat down beside Catherine. She stroked Catherine's hair, picking out one or two pieces of grass which had stuck there.

'Christ,' said Catherine. 'It seems a long while since I heard some good rock music. I suppose it's a craving, really. I tried that book you recommended, but I'm not much into books, as you know. I liked the title. *The Amazing Marriage.*'

'There's no reason why you should enjoy it.' Una regretted what might have been taken for a note of condescension in her tone; she had meant exactly what she said. 'It would make a better film, probably. I'd love to play the part.' She was relieved and did not continue in this vein when Catherine seemed to accept the statement without interpretation. Catherine yawned; she shrugged off the kimono and rolled over to let the sun get at her back. Absently, Una stroked her bottom. A little later she heard soft snores and realized that her friend was asleep again.

Una now felt much more relaxed. She rose and entered the cool of the living-room, replacing *Life*, then moving from bookshelf to bookshelf, finding little but children's books and adventure stories and obscure humorous novels from the previous century (whose humour, like that in *Life*, seemed almost wholly based on the fact that the characters spoke in thick dialect and did not understand very much about North American society). A few unbroken records in the electric phonograph's cabinet had been heard too often to be entertaining. She began to wish that it was lunch-time. She considered playing a practical joke on the boy scouts, but was unable to think of anything suitable.

She had become depressed. Perhaps she had been depressed all morning and had only now admitted it to herself; but then boredom easily led to depression. She wondered if her period was early.

She went upstairs and changed into a swimming costume.

Instead of going immediately to the river she allowed herself to lie down on the unmade bed. She stared at the cracks in the ceiling, studying them as she might study the map of a familiar country. She chose part of the ceiling as a military objective and planned how best to move the troops and artillery along the cracks and visualized her forces so well that when a cockroach walked slowly across the ceiling she was shocked, seeing it as a grotesque monster which threatened to crush her tiny army underfoot.

Her spirits much improved, she swung herself off the bed, ran down the stairs, through the living-room, through the french windows, down the lawn (jumping over a still sleeping Catherine) and into the river.

Deliberately, she chose to swim against the strong current, so that she would not be carried too far down. Slowly, with a patient breast-stroke, she swam towards the far bank.

TWO

In which Catherine Cornelius and Una Persson receive a visitor and reach a decision

A young man in a soft brown hat was standing on the lawn at the side of the house when Una, having startled a party of paddling scouts, returned. The young man was quite goodlooking, rather scrawny, dirty and shabby, and his redrimmed eyes showed that he was either insane or had not had much sleep. He had not yet noticed Catherine, though he could now see Una as, dripping, she waded through weedy mud to the bank.

'Good morning,' said Una. The young man had some sort of haversack over his shoulder. 'Are you on the run?' she asked.

'Oh, no . . .' His grin of understanding was embarrassed. 'No, ma'am. The bum. I'm looking for work.'

'Work? Here?'

'What!' Catherine looked up suddenly. 'Ah!'

The young man saw her and he blushed. He lowered his head. 'Gee, I'm sorry. I'll be . . .'

'That's all right,' said Catherine. She stood up, tying the kimono round her body. 'I'm nearly burned as it is.'

'Oh, dear,' said the young man to himself and then, as he looked up. 'I can see I'm intruding. I'm not quite myself, you know. I forgot my manners. This house is the first I've seen all day and I hoped . . .'

'You're hungry?' Without thinking, Una put her hands on her hips. Catherine folded her arms under her breasts. They stared together at the young man.

'Hungry! You bet!' He sniggered. 'I'm on my way to California, to work for my uncle, I hope. I lost my job in New

York about a month ago, so I decided that California was the place for me. Anyhow, I've been on the road a week...'

'A week?' Una calculated the distance.

'I'd gotten almost to Washington when I jumped a train which took me back to New York,' he explained. 'I guess I make a lousy hobo, don't I?'

'A what?' said Catherine.

'A tramp,' said Una.

'A what?' said the young man. He blushed again. 'Sorry.'

'I'll do you an omelette,' said Una. 'Will that be all right?'

'That'll be fine. I'll work for my bread, though. You must have some odd jobs you need doing. Although I suppose your husbands fix most things.'

'No,' said Una. 'We do everything ourselves.'

'Oh.'

'We haven't any husbands,' said Catherine. She winked at Una who grinned back.

'Ah.'

The two women advanced up the lawn. The young man seemed to consider bolting, but a combination of hunger and good manners made him hold his ground.

'Through the door, there.' Catherine pointed.

He went into the living-room.

They followed. 'Sit down.' said Una.

He sat on a sofa covered in worn chintz. 'Oh, this is *very* comfortable,' he said. 'You have a nice home.'

'What would you like to drink?' Una asked.

'I'm not sure I—'

'With the omelette? Milk?'

'Milk! Oh, fine!' His laugh was hollow and it pained them both.

'Please relax,' said Una. 'It won't take a minute.'

Catherine sat down in an easy chair on one side of the sofa. She stretched her legs in front of her; she stretched her arms over her head.

'What do you do, Mr – um?'

'Bannermann – William Bannermann – Billy...' He added 'Junior' under his breath. 'I was working in this office

– advertising agency. I wanted to be a copywriter. I've been there four years, since I was fifteen. I was working my way up.'

'What happened?'

He laughed at a joke he had evidently told a number of times. 'I was working my way up to the top of a scrap-heap, as it turned out. The agency collapsed. We were all laid off. My uncle isn't doing bad. He's got a store in Berkeley there. I'm going to handle his publicity and displays – among other things. I've got plenty of ideas. And the weather's so good out there, isn't it?'

'I've never been there,' Catherine told him. 'This is really my first time in America.'

'Oh, it's great weather.'

Catherine was only half-aware of the effect she was having on Mr Bannermann. It had been so long since they had had visitors that she had become used to following her impulses. And while she had not set out to embarrass him, she couldn't help relishing his discomfort. He blushed as she crossed her legs.

'The weather's been very nice here,' she said.

'In New Jersey?'

'In Pennsylvania, I think. I'm sure this is Pennsylvania.' She was pleased to be able to name the hills. 'And those are the Appalachians!'

'Well, you'd know where you live, eh?' He drew a deep breath and looked at the books in the shelves. 'I've been travelling a bit erratically . . .'

'So have I,' she said.

'You've been travelling?'

'Until recently.'

He lifted his hand to his head and realized that he still wore his hat. He snatched it off. 'This is your home.'

'Not really. I live in England most of the time.'

'You're English?'

'Yes.'

'I wouldn't have guessed.'

'Don't I look English?'

27

'Not what I think of as English.' His neck reddened still more. 'I mean – you don't seem typical. I mean, I always think of English ladies as – I mean, well, you know, *English*.' He added, lamely, 'I *like* English people.'

'I like Americans. They're friendly. Easy-going.' She pushed her hair back from her cheek. 'Relaxed.'

'The English are very polite.' He struggled in the depths of the sofa, trying to sit closer to the edge.

'Thank you.'

'I used to read a lot of, you know, Jeeves.' He managed to get to the edge at last and sat there breathing heavily. 'In the *Saturday Evening Post*. Gee, I *am* tired.'

'What? Jeeves?'

'Right!'

Una came in with a tray. She had made a huge omelette and there was some salad left over from last night. She had put a glass of milk on the tray. As he reached for it he spilled it. He moaned helplessly while Catherine stifled a snort. Una put the tray on a table and went to get a cloth. Mr Bannermann took a dirty handkerchief from his pocket and began first to mop at the milk in his lap, then at the milk on the carpet.

'Don't worry about it,' said Catherine.

'Gee, I really am sorry. My reflexes aren't what they should be.'

'You're tired.'

'Yes sirree.'

Catherine got up and took the tray over to him. 'Eat it while it's hot, Mr Bannermann.'

He wolfed the omelette.

Una came in and cleaned up the milk.

'Best omelette I've ever eaten, ma'am.' He spoke with his mouth full; his eyes held a feral glint.

Una smiled. 'It's because you're hungry. Thank you.'

She glanced at Catherine and then glanced away again, smirking. They were both staving off a giggling fit and neither wanted to make the young man any more uncomfortable than he was. Indeed, Catherine felt sorry for him and was sure that Una did as well.

Carefully, Billy Bannermann picked up the fresh glass of milk and sipped it. His caution was so exaggerated, his hand so shaky, that Catherine gave up her efforts and, spluttering, ran from the room. The young man looked up in surprise and for an instant stared full into Una's grey eyes. He coughed and put down the glass of milk. Una said gravely: 'Bladder trouble.' She sat down in Catherine's place and stretched languorously.

'Oh, yes?'

'Would you like to bathe?'

'If it isn't any trouble.'

'The bathroom's upstairs, along the landing, second door on the left. The water's only warm.'

'Oh, anything, anything!'

He fled.

Catherine returned. 'We shouldn't laugh,' she said. 'He's tired and hungry and dazed. Isn't he delicious, though?'

'I wonder what he makes of us.' Una lit a cigarette. 'Just imagine his fantasies!'

'Oo-hoo,' said Catherine and uttered something very close to a belly laugh.

Una lifted a recent copy of *Vogue* from the floor and began to turn the pages. 'We must seem pretty glamorous to him. You're right. I was thinking of leaving tomorrow.'

'So was I. For 1910?'

'Or thereabouts.' Una studied an advertisement for riding boots. 'I thought 1917. Would that suit you?'

'Fine. If you could drop me off in London.'

'Of course.'

'Shall we ask Mr Bannermann to stay the night?'

'What do you mean?'

'Just to stay. Nothing else.'

'I suppose he could do with a rest and a bit of feeding up. All right. But I don't want to . . .'

29

'No. Neither do I.'

'I'm not sure it would do *him* any good.' Una grinned. 'You know how clinging lads like that can be.'

'Well, he couldn't very well follow us back to 1917.'

'You never know.'

'He's an antidote for boredom, anyway.'

'He wouldn't last very long.'

Catherine showed her teeth. 'Long enough.'

With pursed lips Una chuckled. 'We're being very childish, you know.'

'Why not?'

'Ah!' Una stretched once more. 'I feel so good all of a sudden.'

'Me too. Awake.'

Una was glad that her analysis seemed to have been correct. With the advent of Mr Bannermann and a break in what had become a monotonous routine her fears and her worries were gone, although she was still determined to leave, to get back into what she would have called 'real life'. It was dreadful, she thought, how one went round and round, experiencing the same succession of moods and never quite being able to do anything about them: did everyone have this almost schizoid cycle of intense activity followed by periods of equally intense lethargy? Most people, she supposed, were not free to experience the extremes: the more you had of what was called leisure, the more you were inclined to lose the centre. And was the centre worth holding? She had, in her time, made a virtue both of holding it and of leaving it behind. At this moment, however, she felt merely irresponsible – she would have used the word 'naughty' if it didn't have such awful associations with infantile sexual fantasy and the kind of role-playing whimsy she abhorred. And 'wicked' was far too strong. 'Irresponsible' would have to do. She winked at Catherine who appeared to be in an identical mood.

'It's silly really,' said Una. 'We're like a couple of excitable old maids, no matter how you look at it – no matter how innocent our intentions are.'

'I quite fancy him,' Catherine said, 'but he's not really my type. I prefer old foreigners, as you know.'

'You wouldn't have fancied him before we arrived here,' Una reminded her.

'You have to take what you're given,' said her friend.

'That's the sort of attitude which has got you into so much trouble,' said Una.

'You mean them knocking me about. Well, that could be my fault, couldn't it?'

'Don't let's go into that one. You blame yourself too much. Avoid people who make you feel guilty, that's my motto.'

'I seem to bring out the worst . . .'

'Stop it! You just happen to like childish, ego-bound, flashy little sods who always want more than anyone can give them. I'm not going to say it all again.'

'Don't,' said Catherine, 'because I might resent it, Una, at the moment. We all make mistakes.'

'True.' Una was anxious to avoid tension.

The two women fell silent, though it was a perfectly friendly silence, and when the spruced-up Mr Bannermann returned he found them both looking at him through sleepy, half-closed lids. Una thought he shivered so she said kindly: 'The shower's done you good.'

'It was very welcome.'

'We've a spare room, if you'd like to get some sleep.'

'Well . . .' The idea was attractive to him, but he was still nervous.

'Come on,' said Una rising, 'I'll show you where it is. Are there any sheets on the bed, Catherine?'

'I think so.'

Showing Mr Bannermann into the rather dark room on the opposite side of the landing to her own, Una resisted any further impulse to embarrass him. She looked in briefly, to make sure the bed was made. She smiled a neutral smile. 'There! Sleep as long as you like, Mr Bannermann. Sleep tight!'

'You're very kind . . .'

'These are bad times for everyone.' She found the conventional phrase useful now.

'Yes sirree!' He brightened at the familiar sound.

'I won't wake you, but if you should get up after we've gone to bed, help yourself to anything you find in the icebox.'

'You're very kind...'

'We've all got to pull together nowadays.'

'Yes, sir!'

Glad to have given the young man the reassurance of this Depression dialogue, that most comforting of all ideas, the idea of the 'common struggle', Una hummed to herself as she descended the stairs and rejoined Catherine in the livingroom.

'What are we going to give him for dinner?' asked Catherine. 'All we've got is a lettuce.'

'I hadn't thought. I'll go into town and get some meat. Or a chicken. What else, do you think?'

'I'll do the cooking, if you like. Shall I write out a list?'

'Okay.' Una was amused by the transformation in Catherine who, up until this moment, had been content to let her prepare the small amounts of food they had been eating. 'He might sleep on, past dinner.'

'We'll wake him up. I could do with a good feed myself.' Catherine pushed herself out of the chair. 'Perhaps we'll both go into town. I've only seen the place once, and that was at night.'

'What if Mr Bannermann is a thief?'

'What is there for him to steal?' Her eye swept the room.

'The boat. But it wouldn't do him much good.' Una smiled. 'You'd better dress carefully, if you're coming. Nothing out of period.'

'You should know me better!'

'Sorry.' Una swung her arms as she followed Catherine upstairs and into the bedroom.

'This is a bit too chic for Briggstown, I suppose,' said Catherine, holding up a blue and yellow Chanel tunic dress, 'also it's four or five years out of date, but maybe one offsets the other.'

'It'll do. Put it on.' Una donned an incongruous gingham over her bathing costume.

Catherine wriggled into her bra and pants. 'These do feel strange.' She pulled the dress over her head and straightened it on her body. 'There!'

'Fine.'

They found shoes for themselves and tottered downstairs and out to the Duesenberg. Catherine sat beside Una as she turned the engine over and put the car into gear. 'It's really falling to bits,' said Una. 'All it needs is a service. Maybe I'll book it for one while we're in town.'

'I thought we were leaving soon.'

'The car can't.'

The engine growled; the body lurched backwards as Una reversed; gravel crunched and spattered. Una hauled on the big steering wheel, changed, and drove down the path towards the iron gate which had hung by only one of its hinges since they had arrived. She was able to squeeze the car through the gap without Catherine having to get out to open the gate further, and then they were bumping down the track towards the road. 'I wouldn't like a car like this to rot,' Una said. 'I mean, think how much they're going to be worth in thirty years' time.'

'You sound like my brother.' Catherine sighed.

'I'll say that for him. Frank made himself a rich man by thinking ahead.'

'But who wants a family fortune based on old copies of the *Wizard* and *Hotspur*?' complained Catherine.

'He couldn't do much else. You know the dangers of people like us manipulating the stock market, or even buying gold. He kept a low profile. He invested in cheap, trashy comic books.'

'It's a bit vulgar, though, isn't it?'

They turned on to the Briggstown road; here the hills were gentler and unwooded; in drowsy fields cows and sheep panted and the countryside was broken only by the occasional Pennsylvania Dutch farmhouse or National Recovery billboard.

'It's very peaceful,' said Catherine as she brushed her hair. 'What a pity they don't have stereo yet.'

THREE

In which Mr William Bannermann comes into an unexpected inheritance

Catherine leaned towards the full-length mirror; she puckered her lips; she dabbed delicately with the lip-rouge brush; she fluttered mascaraed lashes. Una grinned. There was no response from Catherine, who was concentrating.

'The black chiffon, I see!' Una fingered it.

Catherine gave an affirmative grunt.

'Well, it always suited you better than me.'

Catherine had not heard her. She was stepping back from the mirror with a dissatisfied sigh, shaking her head. 'It doesn't take long to lose the knack, does it?'

Una shrugged and made a humorous face. She already had on her dark blue costume. 'You're really giving our guest the works,' she said. 'He might be shocked – by the make-up.'

'I'm doing it for the fun of it.' Catherine was defensive. 'I mean, it's been such a long time . . .'

'I'm only taking the piss.' Una lifted a calming hand. 'Can you take him in a cup of coffee and wake him while I go and look at the dinner?'

Absently, Catherine nodded, her attention drifting back towards the mirror. 'Are you sure this is all right?'

'It's simple and elegant.' Una patted Catherine's bare shoulder. 'You look lovely.'

'But do I look lovely *enough*?' With a snort of self-mockery, Catherine put her lip-rouge away. 'You know what a perfectionist I can be.'

'Poor Mr Bannermann's going to be overwhelmed. He saw a pair of scruffy slags and he wakes up to find us transformed into fancy harlots.'

'He seemed pretty overwhelmed to begin with!' They went out on to the landing, dropping their voices. 'Are you sure you don't want me to do my salad?'

'It isn't worth it. You be the hostess. I'll be the cook.'

'Don't tell me I've got the easiest job this time.'

They crept downstairs. In the kitchen Una opened the oven and looked at her chickens. Catherine smacked her lips. 'Oh, that really smells delicious. And all the trimmings, too. It's like Christmas. Did you have Christmas, Una, when you were a little girl?'

'Oh, yes.' Una carried the dishes to the table and began to baste the birds. 'Oh, yes. Trees and tinsel and so on.' She spoke vaguely, as if she could not really remember; as if it had occurred to her that her memories might be false, based on films she had seen and books she had read rather than on direct experience.

'Is that your amnesia?' Catherine asked tentatively. 'Can't you—?'

'Just a minute.' Una replaced the chickens in the oven. She took the lid off a saucepan and studied the contents. 'What did you say?'

Catherine heaped coffee into the filter pot; she filled it with cold water and put it on the stove. She lit the gas.

'What were you saying?' Una stepped aside.

'I was saying about your amnesia. You know – those areas of childhood you find hard to recall. You've told me about them . . .'

'Have I? Yes?'

'Christmas . . .'

'Oh. Yes, maybe you're right.' Una rinsed her basting spoon under the hot tap.

'Am I in your way?' asked Catherine.

Una kissed her. 'I hadn't thought about it, but, yes, you probably are.'

'You're feeling a bit solitary again, aren't you?'

'It's only temporary.'

Catherine wandered out of the kitchen and into the living-room. She was whistling to herself as she stood looking through the windows; it was not yet sunset; a breeze had sprung up and was moving the tops of the elms; birds of some kind wheeled in a flock over the boy scout camp. Catherine fancied they were vultures and the boy scouts had all been wiped out by Indians, but a distant blaring assured her that at least some of the scouts had survived. Then she saw two canoes, filled with small green- and khaki-clad figures paddling hard against the current, come slowly round the bend, heading for the camp. All at once she felt self-conscious, as if she were wearing an imperfect disguise. She wondered if one only wore clothes for reasons of disguise not, as she usually thought, to emphasize one's 'personality'. She shrugged and moved away from the window, entering the small dining-room where the table had already been laid. It would have been nice, she thought, to have had some good wine, but the California rosé wasn't all that bad. She was tempted to open a bottle and try some; instead she turned to the sideboard behind her and poured from a decanter half a glass of Madeira (the last of the businessman's supply). Feeling a little guilty, for she didn't like the Madeira very much and knew that it was supposed to be very good, she knocked it back. A snort of fine cocaine had the effect on her which others claimed for favourite wines. She resisted the temptation to pour herself another glass and returned to the kitchen where Una was bending over a salad, picking delicately at some cucumber and tomatoes. The water had boiled and Una had already turned the pot over. Catherine could hear the water dripping through the filter. She took a cup from its hook and put it in a saucer; she filled the cup, put it on a tray, found sugar and milk and placed them beside the cup.

'I'll take it up,' she said.

'Fine,' said Una without turning.

Catherine carried the coffee to the top of the stairs, pausing outside the spare room and balancing the tray on one hand while she knocked on the door. There was no answer, so she went inside. It took her a few moments to make out Mr Bannermann in the bed. His head lay awkwardly against the pillow; his mouth was open and he was snoring quietly. Catherine thought he looked more attractive now. She leaned forward and shook him gently by the shoulder. He grunted, opened his eyes, licked his lips.

'Coffee?' she said. She put it on the bedside table. 'Dinner's almost ready. We're making a special one. In your honour.'

Mr Bannermann's mouth moved, but he said nothing. His expression was almost ludicrously puzzled.

'Quarter of an hour,' said Catherine. 'For dinner?'

'Oh, right . . .'

'It's chicken.'

He began to wake up. 'Chicken!'

Pleased by his response Catherine left him with his coffee and his bewilderment.

When Mr Bannermann came down, his hair carefully combed, his eyes betraying an eager appetite, a neat tie at his throat, Catherine Cornelius was jigging about the living-room to the scratchy strains of 'Livin' in the Sunlight, Lovin' in the Moonlight' by Paul Whiteman. Outside, the sky was spread with the oranges and purples of an Italian religious lithograph, almost incredibly lurid, and no lights burned indoors as yet. 'Feeling better, Mr Bannermann?' The chiffon swished. 'Can I get you a drink?'

'A beer, if you have it. You're very kind.'

'We all have our parts to play.' She swayed to the table where she had already laid out the drinks. 'Whisky?'

'Well, if . . .' He nodded.

'Soda?'

'To the top. I'm not really used . . .' He took note of her perfume as she handed him the glass. She saw his Adam's apple give a convulsive movement.

'Do you like Paul Whiteman?'

'He's the tops.'

'He is here,' she said mysteriously. She skipped a few more steps, doing a kind of modified jitterbug which was interrupted by the thump and click of the record ending. She lifted the lid, selecting another record. 'It's almost all Paul Whiteman. What about "My Suppressed Desire"?'

'Your—?'

' "Suppressed Desire". Bing Crosby vocals, too.'

'He's great. Have you seen any of the movies?'

'I might have done,' she replied vaguely. She had probably seen some on television.

Una entered as the record started. She lit a cigarette and smiled at Mr Bannermann. 'It's almost ready,' she said. She sank with a sigh, on to the sofa. 'I hope you like fowl, Mr Bannermann.'

He leaned forward to show that he had not quite caught the remark.

'Fowl,' she hissed. He blushed.

'Do you dance, Mr Bannermann?' Catherine opened her arms.

He cleared his throat. 'Uh.'

Mockingly reproving Una said: 'Mr Bannermann's only just woken up, Catherine.'

'I'm a bit drunk.' Catherine excused herself. 'Oh, I feel smashing!' She continued to dance.

'Sit down for a second, Mr Bannermann.' Una patted the sofa. He obeyed, sipping his Scotch. 'You must forgive us if we seem rude,' continued Una. 'We haven't had a visitor here before. You can imagine, I'm sure, how a pair of spinsters, with only one another's company, can get a bit strange...'

'Oh, no! Miss—?'

'Persson. You see, we haven't even thought of introducing ourselves. I'm Una Persson and this is Catherine Cornelius.'

'It seems an odd place, ma'am, to find two English ladies living alone. Aren't you ever scared?'

'I think we can look after ourselves when we need to, Mr Bannermann. And there aren't many dangers to worry about in this part of the world, are there?'

'There are stories of roving gangs, looters, hobos...'

'I'm sure they're exaggerated.' She rose to her feet. 'I'll get dinner. Catherine, would you like to escort Mr Bannermann in?'

Catherine took Mr Bannermann's arm.

'It's through here.'

'My, that looks good,' said Mr Bannermann. He eyed the cucumber salad, the mushroom salad, the tuna fish salad, the dish of roast potatoes, the sweetcorn, the squash. He stared reverently at the chickens as Una carved. 'A real country meal.'

'Help yourself to some tuna fish salad,' said Una. 'I'm sorry there's no soup. Treat the tuna fish as an *hors d'oeuvre*. Pour Mr Bannermann some of that rosé, Catherine. Do you prefer breast or leg, Mr Bannermann?'

'As it comes, ma'am.'

'There you are.' She handed him the plate. He put down the spoon with which he had been about to take some tuna fish salad. He accepted the plate. 'Gravy's there,' she said, 'and cranberry sauce, if you like it. Have as many potatoes as you like. We don't eat them.'

'You must let me do some work around the house for you before I go,' he said. 'Just to repay your kindness.'

'We're better off than you, Mr Bannermann. It's our duty to do what we can,' said Catherine piously. She put out her fork and impaled two potatoes. 'Besides, we're leaving tomorrow.'

'Oh, which way are you heading?'

'We're going up-river,' said Una. 'I'm sorry we can't give you a lift.'

'It wasn't – I didn't mean . . .'

'You haven't had the cucumber yet.' Catherine handed him the dish. 'Take a lot. It's lovely.'

'Squash?' said Una.

'Well, if you don't mind . . .'

'You don't like it.' Catherine winked at him. 'Neither do I. I never did. Of course, we don't have it in England. Do we, Una?'

'No, not squash. Swedes.'

'Something like it,' said Catherine. 'Parsnips are okay, though.'

An expression akin to terror came and went in Mr Bannermann's mild brown eyes.

They fell silent as they ate.

'Phew!' said Mr Bannermann, after a while. He put down his knife and fork and sipped his wine. The alcohol had made him relax more; for the first time his smile was not nervous. 'I think this is the best dinner I've ever had.'

'It makes a nice change for us, too,' said Una. 'Would you like some more chicken?'

'Not just yet, ma'am, thank you.'

'Do you like the house, Mr Bannermann?' Una became thoughtful.

'Very much. And the country.'

'Do you drive?'

'Yes, ma'am.'

Catherine filled Mr Bannermann's glass to the brim. She touched his wrist as she steadied herself. Open-mouthed, he turned to look at her. He shut his mouth.

'There!' she said, settling back. She lifted her own glass. 'Here's to you, Mr Bannermann. To your improved fortune!'

'Well, I will drink to that, if you don't mind.' He grinned and clinked his glass against hers. Pink wine spilled on the cloth. He offered his glass to Una and she put down her own cutlery to join in the toast.

'To your improved fortune, Mr Bannermann.'

He downed the wine in one enormous swallow. 'This is so strange. It's like a dream. Like a story.' He became enthusiastic. 'You're like goddesses, both of you. Diana and Venus. I'm sorry. I'm drunk.'

'Carry on, Mr Bannermann!' This time Una filled his glass for him. 'It's lovely.' She glanced at Catherine who uttered a luxurious sigh. 'Who would have guessed you had a penchant for poetry.'

'You're making fun of me, ma'am.' He was flattered.

'Not at all,' Catherine told him.

Una frowned. 'We must get an early start.'

Catherine and Mr Bannermann stared at her without speaking.

'In the morning,' said Una.

'It can't be that late.' Catherine cast about for a clock. 'Can it?'

'Well.' Una smiled apologetically at Mr Bannermann. 'After dessert and coffee – that'll take us to eleven.' Having suddenly developed a lust for Catherine and seeing Mr Bannermann as a rival she was having a hard time controlling her manners. 'We ought to try to get as much sleep as possible.'

Catherine, who had taken a fancy to Mr Bannermann, felt that Una was being a bit of a killjoy. She considered making this observation directly to Una but contented herself with: 'You've had a tiring day, really, Una – and then doing all the cooking.'

'Actually, I feel very fresh.' Una was anxious to make it clear that she was motivated only by commonsense. 'But we had agreed...'

Mr Bannermann, having taken another half-glass, began to tell a joke about two Jewish stockbrokers which was not improved for Una by the fact that she had read that morning an almost identical story in an 1897 number of *Life*. She began to collect up plates. Catherine, unable to sustain as much interest in Mr Bannermann's joke as she would have liked, helped her. Una, with a slightly malicious wink at her friend, carried the plates to the kitchen.

Mr Bannermann finished his joke and began to laugh. Catherine did her best to join in and was very glad when Una returned with the dish of trifle. Mr Bannermann was also pleased. It had dawned on him that his story had not gone over well. Una felt that a relaxed Mr Bannermann lost much of his charm. She offered him the bowl and the serving spoon.

'I could trifle with some trifle, I think,' he said.

It surprised Una when Catherine found this amusing. Mr Bannermann winked at Catherine in recognition of her appreciation and Catherine added with drunken archness: 'I hope you're not *trifling* with my affections, Mr Bannermann, when I have entrusted you with the *custardy* of my heart.'

Una found it difficult to remain silent. She ate her own trifle with surly steadiness.

Becoming conscious of a change in the atmosphere but unable to identify its source Mr Bannermann complimented Una on the dessert. 'It's very sweet,' he said. 'I love sweet things.'

'You're very sweet, too, Mr Bannermann.' Catherine, giggling, helped herself to more wine. 'Isn't he, Una?'

'We're not being very polite, tonight, I'm afraid, Mr Bannermann.' Una put down her spoon.

Mr Bannermann half-rose, steadying himself with one hand on the table as he lifted his glass. A little indistinctly he said: 'Nonsense! I give a toast to the two most charming ladies in the whole US of A!'

Una's mood passed. She could see that Mr Bannermann was very drunk and she blamed herself. She should have realized that he had not eaten any proper food for days. She had overwhelmed him.

He staggered against the table and Catherine reached up to help him. He apologized. He blushed. He collapsed into his chair and began to cry. He said something to the effect that no one had shown him such kindness since his mother had been prematurely taken from him. He said that he had given up hope of ever finding it but now his optimism was restored, that he could face life again, that if it had not been for them he might have followed the example of so many New Yorkers and ended it all. There had been times, he said, when he had been known far and wide for his cheerfulness, his ability to console others less fortunate than himself, but, when his own need for consolation had materialized, there had been no one to offer that which he had given so freely and with such goodwill. Wasn't this, he asked them, always the way – or so he had thought until now.

The two women listened: Catherine with sympathy and Una with disapproval bordering on cynicism – until with a sudden sigh, like a locomotive reaching its destination after a long and difficult haul, he subsided. Catherine and Una began to clear away the dishes while Mr Bannermann toyed with his glass and murmured general apologies for his outburst.

'We're all a bit tired,' said Una kindly.

'I think we ought to get him to bed, don't you?' Catherine said when they were both in the kitchen.

'We?' Una lifted a nasty eyebrow.

'Oh, Una! You know what I mean. Don't you fancy him, though?'

'I think you've been too long away from masculine country.'

'You do sound bitchy!' Catherine laughed without much rancour. 'You're probably right. But he does make you want to mother him a bit.'

'That isn't quite the same thing as fancying him,' said Una. 'Or maybe, in your case, it is.'

'Off and on. Shall I wash?'

'Don't you want to continue mothering Mr Bannermann?'

'I'll ask him if he wants coffee.' Catherine departed.

By the time she returned Una had almost finished the dishes. 'He kissed me,' Catherine told her, 'and then he went to sleep.' She sighed as she picked up a cloth to dry a plate. 'Actually, I'll be glad to get away. Should we leave him there, or what?'

'We'll have some coffee and then see what he looks like.' Una felt dislike for herself as she detected in her tone an increased friendliness, now that Mr Bannermann was no longer a potential rival. She hated to detect signs of jealousy in her behaviour.

Catherine kissed her. 'Let's have a really nice time tonight,' she said.

Una brightened. She indicated a sealed envelope on the kitchen table. It had *Mr William Bannermann* written on it. 'I'm letting him have the house and a loan of the car,' she said. 'They might as well benefit somebody.'

'I thought you didn't like him much.'

'That's hardly the point.'

'You're genuinely good-hearted, Una. Much more than me. I'm so selfish, really.'

'I'm practical, that's all. And you have more to protect. Selfishness is just unrationalized instinct in your case.'

They sat in the kitchen and enjoyed a cup of coffee together.

Later, as they lay in each other's arms in the big bed, they heard Mr Bannermann stumbling up the stairs and they grinned, wondering what he would make of Una's letter when he woke up in the morning and found them gone.

FOUR

*In which our heroines give themselves up,
once again, to the Tides of Time*

Una, with an expertise Catherine always admired, got the little white motor-boat going and they began to move slowly out into the water. They picked up speed where the river widened at the bend. For the first time Catherine had a good view of the boy scouts. Some of them had come crawling from their tents at the sound of the engine. 'It's a pleasure to wake them up, for a change,' said Una. One or two of the scouts whistled and waved. Carefully, Catherine waved back. 'Take it easy, boys,' she called.

Una wished that she could get a better sight of Catherine, standing there with her hand on her hip, her scarf fluttering in the wind. Catherine looked at her most beautiful in the white dress with the red, green and blue embroidery. 'It's funny.' She gave the wheel a quarter turn. 'I don't feel like going at all now. Still, I expect I'll get into it.'

Catherine looked up at the sky. 'I know what you mean.' She added, 'Can you feel jaded, even when you've nothing, as it were, to be jaded about?'

'Is that how you feel?'

'Not now. I didn't like to bring it up before. It would have sounded as if I were complaining.'

'You're only talking about boredom again.' Una straightened the bottom of her khaki fatigue jacket, keeping one hand on the wheel. 'That's all.' The water began to run faster as they neared some easily negotiated rapids. The boat bounced. 'Are you sure 1917's okay?'

'Oh, yes. Fine.'

'At least you won't meet any rock-and-roll musicians there.'

Catherine considered this a bit unfair and she replied a little sharply. 'It doesn't matter where you go, Una – you'll always find politicians.'

'True.'

'God,' said Catherine. 'I really need to hear some good music.'

'Well, you're going to hear some in a minute,' said Una. 'Unfortunately.'

They went past a poverty-stricken town which looked as if it had been deserted.

'Don't you get cravings for music, Una?'

'Not that kind. Music hall and musical comedy's my first love. It's a different sort of sentimentality.'

Catherine laughed. 'You couldn't call Mick Jagger sentimental.'

'Couldn't I just.' Una pursed her lips and concentrated on the rapids.

Catherine settled herself on the port-side seat, humming in time to the roar of the water, but the rhythm was too erratic and so she stopped. She yawned. It had been a long while since she had got up this early. She wondered if she were wise to go back as far as 1917, when really she would have preferred what she considered to be her own period, the mid-seventies. The hills on her right had become gentler and were giving way to blackened fields. In the distance, near the horizon, black smoke boiled. She stared, without curiosity, at the smoke until another stretch of forest obscured it. The boat entered calmer waters. Una removed the canvas cover from an instrument set close to the wheel. The instrument looked a bit like a large brass ship's chronometer; engraved on the dial, where the maker's name was usually found, were the words *Cornelius and Co., Ladbroke Grove, London W*. It was, in fact, the work of Catherine's brother and it would help them to get to the period they had selected.

'It's beautifully made, isn't it?' Catherine was proud of her brother's craftsmanship. 'You'd think it was a hundred years old.'

Una made adjustments to the controls just below the rim. 'I sometimes wish he could produce a machine to take us right back – say to the nineteenth century. It would save so much energy.'

'He did get to 1870 once.' Catherine was almost defensive. 'But he didn't like it. He always says he's a twentieth-century person at heart and he might as well accept it.'

'Well, I'm no conservative,' Una brought an outer dial into alignment with two of the inner ones, 'but I find that remark a bit prissy. I'd love to go back, say, to St Petersburg around 1890.'

'You couldn't leave well alone.'

'I agree, it is dangerous. It becomes harder and harder to acclimatize, too.' The motor-boat's engine began to complain as the current flowed with increased pressure against the hull. Its note rose to a high whine. 'We're approaching the real rapids. Are you ready, dear?'

'Ready,' Catherine gripped the seat with both hands. The boat began to bounce dramatically, the water became white and up ahead she could see a wild, undulating spray. Gradually, the river began to shout.

Una had been through these rapids a hundred times, but she still liked the feeling of danger they gave her. A glance to her left showed her that Catherine was not enjoying the sensation at all. People sought different kinds of danger, physical or emotional, and Catherine tended to prefer emotional dangers which Una would go to almost any lengths to avoid. 'This is it!' she called. She felt an intense surge of love for her friend as she turned on the sound. The Deep Fix began to play their version of *Dodgem Dude* at full volume (why had that bastard geared everything to cheap rock-and-roll vibrations, and his own rotten band, at that?). The boat plunged into the spray which gradually became a white, muffling mist.

'We'll give ourselves up to the darkness and danger...' began Catherine, quoting some popular song, but the rest was obscured by the echo of a nameless vowel.

PART TWO

GOING TO THE FRONT: WOMAN'S ROLE IN WARTIME

This girl has a mission in life ... to kill. She is one of the women soldiers in a private army fighting a civil war. The battlefield is a street in Beirut ... It is a bloody religious and political conflict tearing the country in half. On the one side are the right-wing Christians – to which the girl in the picture belongs. On the other are the left-wing Moslems, who include Palestinian guerrillas ... BEAUTY IN BATTLE: Two girls man a barricade while another takes up a strategic position.

DAILY MIRROR, 3 November 1975

Bursts of small-arms fire and the intermittent explosion of mortars and rockets continued to paralyse Beirut's seafront hotel district today. The St George, Phoenicia, Holiday Inn, and Excelsior hotels remained in the hands of the right-wing Phalangist militia, despite mounting pressure from an array of left-wing groups who now control the Vendome and Palm Beach hotels.

GUARDIAN, 3 November 1975

FIVE

In which Miss Una Persson encounters a Hero of the Revolution

Una glanced down through the tall french window, through a broken pane, at the street. In the dusk a line of her former comrades was being marched along Lesnoye Prospekt towards the Finland Station. Dumpy and downcast, most of the women made no attempt at maintaining military step. Una had heard rumours of ill-treatment after they had been captured during their defence of the Winter Palace on the previous day, but for the most part there were no signs that they had been so much as involved in the fighting; save for their rifles, they retained their uniforms, insignia and accoutrements, and the attitude of the Red Guards escorting them was humorous; kindly rather than brutal.

'Well,' said L. Trotsky from behind her. He was in a languid, sated mood. 'So much for the Women's Battalion of Death. I thought better of you, Una. A Kerenskyite. Oh, they won't be shot. Just disbanded quietly.'

'After they're raped?' The accusation came without force.

Trotsky spread his hands. 'Which do you think they'd prefer?'

He remained attractive, as relaxed and controlled as ever, but Una was disappointed by his attitude. One such piece of easy cynicism, she thought, and a revolution was as good as lost. One act of treachery (and there had already been many) and the ideals themselves became worthless. She felt in the pockets of her black greatcoat for her cigarettes and matches. Trotsky handed her one of his, yellow and long, a Latvian brand; she lit it herself, holding it gently between her teeth so that when she spoke her words were slightly slurred. 'It wasn't merely a propaganda stunt, you know. Those women wanted to fight for the revolution.'

'Yet they allowed themselves to be mobilized against it.'

'Against your counter-revolution. Can it last?'

'We've been very successful so far.'

'Because you've been prepared to sacrifice everything for the short term,' she said. 'How many allies have you?'

'Surprisingly, quite a few, if temporary.'

'Whom you intend to betray?'

Trotsky shrugged and sat down on one of the bare desks of the office. 'Anarchists, nihilists, opportunists, bandits ...'

'Whom you'll sacrifice?'

'They're naïve. They'd betray *us*, many of them without realizing it. We use them. We direct their energy.'

'They're innocent and naïve, at least. You're a much more depressing spectacle. You're depraved and naïve. You used to be so charming. In London. This revolution will last no longer than Kerensky's.'

He considered her criticism. 'I think you're wrong. You want a bourgeois Utopia. Sweetness and light are no substitute for bread and cabbage, Una Persson. Perhaps it's the difference between weeping for the people and soiling one's hands for them. Between dying for them and killing for them. Committing their crimes for them. Taking the moral responsibility, if you like. Which is the bravest deed? Which is the hardest?'

Her smile was thin. 'All ego – a politician's logic. Very masculine and high-sounding. Very romantic, too. But one need neither die nor kill. The hardest thing to do is patiently to nurse the wounded. This war has made you as simple-minded as the rest.'

'Wars do that. But the war gave us the revolution!'

'Because it robbed us of our subtlety, our humanity. Look what a general you've become. Are you any different from Kornilov or Haig now? Where is your old voice, comrade? Do you ever listen to it these days?'

'This is merely rhetoric, Una. I'm disappointed. You're overtired. How much sleep have you had in the past few days? You must consider your nerves.' He paused. 'I must say you're not at all grateful. You could have been marching to the Pavlov Barracks with your friends.' He shook his head. 'I'd never have expected you to join anything so ludicrous.'

'I thought it had possibilities.'

'The daughters of merchants, armed with a few old rifles?'

St Petersburg was dark. Electric lights burned in some buildings, others were lit by flames. The power supply to the Winter Palace had been restored. Occasionally a shot sounded or a motor-truck or a horse-drawn cart would rush urgently through the street below.

'I'm letting you leave,' he said. 'For old time's sake.'

'I don't want to leave. I worked for this revolution.'

'No. You worked for the other revolution. The wrong revolution.' His dark eyes were sardonic.

'The same one you were working for until you thought it might fail.'

He laughed. 'Well, it did fail.'

'Do you think that if I stay I will try to sabotage what you're doing?'

'I hadn't considered that. You're not Russian, after all. We're facing purely domestic problems at present.'

'Your problems aren't even domestic any more, Leon. They're entirely personal.'

He scowled at this. 'I don't really need your criticisms, Una. Not on top of everything else. I *do* accept certain responsibilities, you know.'

'You saved me, because you needed my moral support?'

'Scarcely.'

'Because you wanted to make love to me?'

'You won't allow me any expression of altruism?'

'Is that it? Sentimentality. I'm not sure I like being free, if it's merely to let you salve your conscience a little.'

'Una, you're trying my patience.' He removed his spectacles. It was a threatening gesture. She refused to acknowledge it. 'It would be easy to make out a case for your being a foreign spy.'

'My record's too well known.'

'You overestimate the memory of the people.'

'Oh, maybe.' She had indeed had very little sleep in the past few days and felt too tired to continue this silly argument. 'I think I should have stayed in 1936.' The scene before her began to flicker. She became alarmed.

'What?' he said.

'It doesn't matter.' The scene stabilized. 'Are you kicking me out of Peters, then?'

'Out of Russia,' he said.

'All my friends are here.' The words sounded feeble to her own ears.

'Cornelius and his sister?'

'And the others.'

'They're leaving, too, if they haven't gone already. The train should be on its way to Germany by now. I signed the safe-conduct papers myself.'

It was her turn for self-pity. 'After all I've done...'

'You can't change history,' he said.

He rang a bell.

SIX

*In which Mrs and Miss Cornelius hear some
news of the past*

Mrs Cornelius was flustered, and the weight of her overloaded hat, with its feathers, ribbons, lace and imitation flowers, had caused sweat to gather on her broad, red forehead and run between her eyes and down her nose; but in spite of this she was able to set her features in the expression of prim disapproval she always reserved for her encounters with authority (in this category she included doctors, dentists, postmen and anyone employed by the Town Hall). Catherine was beginning to regret her impulse to visit home. She had found her mother in a state of unusual agitation, having that morning received a letter from Whitehall telling her that if she could call at the Ministry's offices she might learn something to her advantage.

'About bloody time,' Mrs Cornelius had said. 'You'd better come along, too, Caff.'

Catherine had said that she was tired and that, anyway, she hadn't been sent for. Secretly she knew that her mother wanted her moral support and refused to admit it.

'Yore comin', my gal.' Mrs Cornelius had insisted and, to make things worse, had found her an off-white old-fashioned linen frock with a sailor collar, a boater with a broad, faded ribbon (which looked and felt as if it had been cut from deckchair canvas) and a pair of brown boots which, with some polishing, looked fairly respectable. The underwear, stiff with starch, had not been worn for years, and she was sure to discover patches of red, rubbed skin when she took it off. The spring weather was bright, but hardly hot, and she shivered as she sat beside her mother in the waiting room.

Mrs Cornelius had given her name to the uniformed man at the desk. Now they sat on a dark mahogany bench in a draughty green-tiled hall opposite the desk watching the uniformed man pretending to check a type-written list while actually reading the racing page of the *Daily Sketch*.

Catherine, with her hair brushed back at her mother's insistence and pinned under her hat, remembered that she had felt a bit like this when she had appeared in court, several years before, when they had sent her to the Reform School. She had almost forgotten those days; she had run with an all-girl gang in Whitechapel until her mother had moved to Notting Dale. They had all worn more or less the same clothes in the gang – dark blue coats and skirts trimmed with red ribbon. They had worn grey in the Reform School. They had been training her to be a housemaid.

A messenger boy, with bright, silvery buttons securing his navy-blue serge, a pill-box cap precisely positioned on his brilliantined head, appeared from the far end of the hall.

'Mrs Cornelius?'

'And Miss Cornelius,' intoned her mother significantly. She rose like a cast-off airship. 'Come on, love.'

Mrs Cornelius kept a firm grip on Catherine as they followed the boy down another green-tiled passage, up a short flight of wooden stairs, along another passage, to arrive outside a plain green door at which the boy knocked.

A man of military bearing opened the door and smiled graciously at them. 'Good afternoon, ladies. I am Major Nye.'

Momentarily won over, Mrs Cornelius gave a kind of half curtsy.

'It was good of you to drop everything,' said Major Nye as he stepped aside to let them enter his office.

'Eh?' said Mrs Cornelius brightening. Her mask returned almost at once as she realized that no innuendo had been intended. 'Oh, yeah. See wot yer mean.'

Catherine was in an agony of embarrassment. Not only was her mother, true to form, putting the most vulgar interpretation on this man's statements but, worse, she was using her 'posh' voice: a grating tone that was nearly twice as loud as usual.

'Will, is it?' added Mrs Cornelius.

'Um.' He crossed back to his big desk, indicating a leather armchair and an ordinary chair with a basketwork bottom. Catherine took the ordinary chair. Her mother, with an expression of some satisfaction, settled herself in the leather one. Major Nye waited until they were both at ease before he sat down behind his desk and picked up a file with a smile.'Well. It's um ...' He paused, glancing, for no apparent reason, towards the window on his right. A little daylight showed between the dark green blind filling the top half of the window and the grey net curtaining at the bottom. He looked at the file.

'The procedure. Well, I'm going to follow the book – insofar as there is a book for this sort of occasion.' He smiled as if he had made a joke, noted their expressions, tapped the file and cleared his throat.

'If it *is* a will,' said Catherine's mother, 'you can skip all the 'ows and wherefores, Major. We don't mind.'

'Well, there are formalities,' he said. He seemed to be ashamed of himself, thought Catherine. She studied him.

'Oh, netcherelly.' Mrs Cornelius drew her knees together and placed her handbag in her lap. 'Hi was only suggesting, in case ...'

'Appreciated. Do you mind if I begin? I want to read something to you for a few minutes. It might seem a bit dull, but we think it might be important.'

The fact that her mother showed no impatience made it evident to Catherine that Mrs Cornelius found Major Nye attractive, that she was beginning to feel at ease in the office. Mrs Cornelius glanced at the picture of the King on the wall behind Major Nye, at the highly polished wooden filing cabinets near the door. She winked comfortably at Catherine and Catherine knew her mother had recognized the ceremony as Tradition. Tradition always cheered Mrs Cornelius up. 'Please continue, Major,' she said in her poshest accent.

'This is a report.' Major Nye raised his voice a little.

'We've held it for some time. A bit dry, I'm afraid. Well, here we go, eh?' Major Nye began to read but Catherine did not catch the opening words because her mother was leaning over and whispering, as if they were at the theatre: ' 'Asn't 'e got a lovely speakin' voice? Almost like music.'

Major Nye had not, apparently, heard. His head was bent over the report. '... Frederik George Brown. He was born in 1874. His father was, so he later claimed, an Irish merchant sea captain and his mother was Russian. After being educated in Petersburg on purely Russian lines he obtained what appears to have been his first post with the Compagnie de Navigation Est-Asiatique. He seems to have acquitted himself well so that in 1900 he was appointed the chief agent for the company at Port Arthur. He remained in Port Arthur for four years, evidently familiarizing himself with political conditions in the Far East and obtaining a degree of personal influence and connection which, in a few years' time, was to be of the greatest use to himself and to the Russian government.'

Mrs Cornelius blew her nose. She might have been at a funeral.

'In 1904 he returned to St Petersburg, appointed to a good post with the house of Mendrochovitch and Count Tchubbersky at 5 Place de la Cathedrale de Kazan. This house was, of course, the most important Russian firm of naval contractors and, in the Russian capital, also represented the great Hamburg firm of Bluhm unt Voss. At the conclusion of the Russo-Japanese War, Bluhm unt Voss acted as agents for the Russian government in the repatriation of Russian prisoners in Japan and, in this connection, the experience and personal influence of Frederik Brown made his services invaluable, much enhancing his reputation in Russian official circles. More than this, he was able to use the influence he had gained with the Russian government to place with Bluhm unt Voss large orders in connection with the restoration of the Russian Navy, on which that nation was then engaged. It may be assumed that his commission was large ...'

Mrs Cornelius looked up from where she had been inspecting the quality of the leather on the armchair, but since it was evident that Major Nye had not yet finished she nodded and gave her attention back to the chair.

'Except for two or three very intimate friends,' said Major Nye, frowning as he read, 'Brown never entertained at his own home. Hardly anyone could boast of being his friend. Always a little sombre; serious, elegant, Frederik Brown was greatly admired at St Petersburg but, naturally enough, the mystery in which he shrouded his personal affairs made him the subject of innumerable whispered stories and rumours.'

Major Nye rubbed his left eye. He had a plain gold ring on his left hand. 'On his passport he was described as a British subject, but he neither knew nor cared for the English colony there. Russians regarded him as an Englishman who had become to all intents and purposes Russian. He was known in a dozen European capitals and was everywhere at home. He wrote and spoke English, Russian and German irreproachably, but each one, it was remarked, with an accent equally foreign.

'In 1909, the year of the greatest exploits of the brothers Wilbur and Orville Wright, some of the leading spirits of Petersburg decided to launch an Aeronautical Club. A committee was formed and the club, *Les Ailles*, came into being. Then, following a general council meeting of all its members, a letter was addressed to Frederik Brown, asking him to join them. Frederik Brown consented, joined them as a respected and much admired active member, and very soon had become the leading spirit of the club, flying his own aeroplane. For the next two years all his activities seemed engrossed in *Les Ailles*. He was recognized, we gather, as a loyal friend, a good companion and as a man who dominated his company.'

Catherine thought that the account sounded like a private report, probably requested by the Ministry from one of its contacts in the business world. She had no idea who Brown might be or why her mother, who was plainly unaware of the man's relevance to her own affairs, was being read to from the report. 'In the year of the foundation of *Les Ailles*,' said Major Nye, and then, looking up, 'I really must apologize for the style. It isn't mine.' Another smile, with no response from either Catherine or her mother.

'In that year he was appointed to the council of his old firm, the Compagnie de Navigation Est-Asiatique. By this time he was recognized as one of the leading figures in the Russian business world, and circumstances were soon to provide a field for his talents in commercial diplomacy. This was his position and reputation when in 1914 war broke out between Russia and Germany.

'There came a demand for munitions to which he, more perhaps than any other man in Russia, was in a position to attend. He immediately proceeded to Japan to place contracts for military equipment in the name of the Banque Russe-Asiatique. From Japan he went to America and placed large orders with the chief engineering firms there. During this period he returned twice to Petersburg but was in America when news arrived that the revolution had broken out, that Russia's continuance of hostilities was unlikely and that, in any case, her need for munitions had come to a sudden stop.

'Brown seems to have been at a loose end. There was nothing left for him to do in America and little purpose in his returning to Russia. The orders which he had placed in America were taken over by the British government and he himself came to England to put his services at the disposal of his father's country. His particular value to the British Intelligence Department became immediately obvious. Evidently a man of the greatest courage and resource, he had the added advantages of flying experience and perfect mastery of the German language, and in a very short space of time he had become one of those who undertook the difficult and hazardous task of entering Germany (usually by aeroplane via the front line) in quest of military information. His services in this direction were of undoubted value and his exploits in Germany have become legendary, so much so indeed that it is practically impossible to sift the true from the false in what has been told of his adventures there. He certainly made a number of trips to Germany and brought back information of the greatest value to the Allies and, with the complete breakdown of Russia and the working there of influences inimical to the Allies, he was sent to Petersburg to work against the German agents in Russia. Shortly thereafter, he disappeared.'

Major Nye closed the file. Catherine, who had become absorbed in the story, felt disappointment. The Major was looking expectantly at Mrs Cornelius.

Mrs Cornelius looked from him to her daughter. 'Oh, yes?' she said vaguely.

'These details are, by and large, familiar to you, I suppose, Mrs Cornelius?' Major Nye stroked the file with two fingers.

'What?' Mrs Cornelius glanced furtively about, seeking, as if by occult means, the right answer, but she failed and gave up, asking weakly: 'Whatcher want me ter say?'

Major Nye frowned. 'That is your husband, is it not?'

A sly, conspiratorial look crossed her face. Then her expression changed to one of cool appraisal. Catherine shivered with embarrassment. Her mother pursed her lips. 'Well,' she began, 'it could be, couldn't it?' Mrs Cornelius thought she had scented money. Major Nye, leaning across the desk, showed her a photograph. Catherine did not recognize the rather heavily built, sombrely dressed man. Mrs Cornelius, however, grinned in relief. 'Blimey!' Her recognition was genuine. 'That's my 'ubby orl right! Wot yer say 'e's bin up ter?'

'Didn't you hear anything at all, Mum?'

With the knuckle of his right index finger Major Nye smoothed his moustache away from his upper lip. 'Is that the name you knew him by, Mrs Cornelius? Brown?'

'Nar!' She found this outrageously amusing. 'Cornelius 'e was corled. Obviously.' She stopped grinning and became horrified. 'Blimey! Don't say we wasn't legally married! There's free kids!'

Major Nye was sympathetic. 'You seem to be properly married, Mrs Cornelius.'

'Phew!' Turning to Catherine her mother raised a relieved brow.

'For all we know,' said Major Nye, 'his real name is Cornelius. What I have read to you is everything we could find out about him. When we were considering employing him for the work in Russia. There were no lady-friends, if that reassures you. No personal friends at all, so far as we could discover. There is, however, evidence that he had several names, indeed that he worked for several governments. He might, it emerges, have been Dutch, his mother not Russian but part-Chinese or Javanese. There is a little evidence that he was of Greek-Albanian extraction. There are many conflicting stories.'

' 'E was a bit on the dark side,' confirmed Mrs Cornelius. ' 'E's not dead, is 'e?' She was trying to disguise the urgency in her tone. She was eager to know if she was in for some money. She had been speculating on the amount since she had received the letter.

'That's what we're trying to discover,' said Major Nye. 'It's more likely he changed sides – and changed his name. When was the last time he visited you?'

'It'd be a while back now,' she said. 'Ten years?'

Catherine could not remember anyone visiting them who had looked like the man in the photograph but, aged eleven, she hadn't been in very much.

'You can't be exact?' Major Nye was coaxing Mrs Cornelius.

'Year o' the Corernation?'

'1910?'

'Sounds right. 'E said 'e'd be gettin' me an 'ouse, aht Peckham way, but nuffink come of it. Is this abaht me entitlements?' She had lost patience at last.

Major Nye glanced at Catherine, as if for an interpretation. 'Your—?'

Catherine was fairly certain that she must be blushing. She gathered her courage. 'Money,' she murmured.

'Money,' said her mother warmly. 'Was you 'is boss, then?'

'We worked for the same department for a while. I'm afraid there's no pension, Mrs Cornelius. And, indeed, we've no idea of your husband's private assets, though they must have been considerable.'

'But you said "to my advantage" in the letter!' Mrs Cornelius reminded him. Even Catherine felt the pathos.

'Yes.' Major Nye drew an envelope from the file. 'I'm sorry it's opened. We had to, you see. I'm afraid it was mislaid here and only recently came to light. That's how we were able to contact you.' He passed the envelope to her. She withdrew a sheet of yellowed paper. Attached to it by a pin were two large white five pound notes. She folded them back so that she could let Catherine see the letter as she read it.

Dear H,
Sorry I couldn't make it Friday after all. Just passing through. Be back next week and hope to look in then. In the meantime, here's a little present for you and the kids. Get yourselves something nice.

Lots of love,
J

'When did 'e write this?' asked Mrs Cornelius.

'We think 1914.' Major Nye cleared his throat. 'He asked someone in the office to post it. They put it in the file by mistake.'

'Cor!' said Mrs Cornelius feelingly. 'I could 'have done with a tenner in nineteen bloody fourteen!' She put the note and the money in her bag. 'An' that's orl, then?'

Major Nye stroked his small moustache with the tips of the fingers of his right hand. 'We'd appreciate hearing from you if he turned up again, Mrs Cornelius.'

' 'E done somefink?'

Major Nye drew a deep breath, but did not speak.

'Y'wan' me ter turn 'im in?'

'We're not the police. There are no criminal charges involved.'

'A wife can't testify against 'er 'usband,' she reminded him gravely. 'Y'know that, dontcha?'

'Quite.'

'An' Caffy 'ere wouldn't know 'im if she saw 'im!'

Suddenly Catherine became aware of the Major's own embarrassment. It was much more intense than hers. She caressed her lower lip with her front teeth, studying him again. She thought he might be reddening. She almost smiled. She lowered her eyes and studied her hands which rested in her lap.

'Of course,' said Major Nye. 'But you are legally entitled to demand maintenance from him. It could be back-dated, if necessary. He was, as I said, a rich man.'

'I've managed to keep them kids on me own, wivaht an 'usband . . .' Mrs Cornelius began proudly.

Catherine was not as impressed by this as the Major. It was not her father who had married bigamously. Her mother was rising awkwardly to her feet. 'Oops!' She steadied herself. 'I'll be off, Major, if yer don't mind. If there's nuffink else . . .'

'I cannot keep you, Mrs Cornelius. I can only say that there might be money in it – a sort of reward – services to your country. Something of that kind.'

'Yeah?' Mrs Cornelius straightened her hat, considering, reasonably, what he said. Then she shook her head, 'Nah. I couldn't. I advise *you* ter keep a sharp eye aht fer 'im, though. An' if y'find 'im, let *me* know. I wouldn't mind 'avin' a word or two wiv 'im.' She laughed, her confidence returning now that the end of the interview was in sight and the pubs were about to open. 'Still, that's life, innit?'

He moved across the room and opened the door for her.

'Come on, Caffy, dear.'

Obediently, Catherine followed her mother from the room.

'Thank you, Mrs Cornelius. At least you've cleared up one mystery,' said Major Nye. 'I regret, um . .'

Her mother had paused so that Catherine had to stop directly in front of Major Nye. She studied his neck. It was a definite pink. She resisted the urge to touch the sleeve of his tweed jacket. She loved the sensation of tweed against the palm of her hand, although she couldn't wear wool herself.

'Mystery?' said her mother.

Major Nye laughed. 'Goodbye, ladies.'

They moved forward, into the passage. The boy was waiting for them. The door closed.

'I 'ope I didn't say anyfink to incriminate 'im,' whispered Mrs Cornelius as they walked behind the boy.

'I don't think so, Mum.'

' 'E was a funny bloke. I wonder if 'is real name was Brown.'

'He was a bastard, whatever his name was,' said Catherine feelingly.

'Wotch yer language, gel.' Mrs Cornelius nodded primly at the back of the messenger.

'He was stinking rich,' said Catherine. 'And what did we have? Three rooms in Whitechapel! Frank getting TB. Jerry...'

'Oh, well.' Her mother hadn't heard her. She patted her bag. 'We made a tenner aht of it, anyway.'

SEVEN

*In which Miss Una Persson begins to witness
the first signs of World Anarchy, the inevitable
result of the Bolshevik Revolution*

The sea was rising; there were black clouds gathering to eastward; the ship swayed rather than rolled; a big liner, she was fitted with the latest stabilizers. Una drew her chiffon scarf tighter about her face and turned up the collar of her coat. Her companion's hands tightened a little on the rail of the first class recreation deck, but the movement of this ship did not interrupt him.

'To see them wilt before the brute power of the proletariat,' he continued enthusiastically, 'to see their authority snatched from them as a strong animal snatches meat from a weaker one – to hear the loud authoritative voice, used to being obeyed, falter and grow mute before the demoralizing silence of the mob – oh, there is my relish, Una Persson.' He spoke in Russian although a moment ago he had begun in French.

They had come aboard at Marseilles and were going all the way to New York. From the ballroom below came the faint strains of a dance band. 'Well, you should have a good time in America.' She was feeling pleasantly melancholic; the grey sky and the broad grey sea always had this effect, particularly if, as now, the wind was gentle and cold.

'We.' His eyes were intense behind his spectacles. 'We can be married formally in America.'

She was amused. 'Your principles...'

'I thought you'd be pleased. Women need these evidences of security.'

'Men don't?'

She was flattered by the notion but, of course, she had no intention of marrying him. When they reached America, she would tell him. There was no point in spoiling his voyage when he was enjoying himself so much. Also, she could not face a cross-examination. Let her leaving him, in Chicago or San Francisco (she had not quite made up her mind at what stage of his lecture tour she would abandon him) be his first and smallest disappointment. There would be worse to come.

'I am unworthy of you,' she told him. It is what he would think, in a month or two. He would think the same of the United States for that matter.

'No. If anyone is unworthy...'

A slim finger on his lips silenced him. He looked sheepish. This expression was so rare these days that she had almost forgotten it. When he had worn it often she had been most in love with him. When he had been a revolutionist without a revolution. Responsibilities ruined an idealist so. Power might make men attractive to some women, but it made rotten lovers of them. She recalled him when he had been hesitant, gentle, when his words had seemed more like poetry than rhetoric, when Utopia would be achieved through goodwill and self-discipline, when the reins of power would be taken gently but firmly from the hands of the misguided ruling classes. He had seemed impotent then, his dreams so unrealistic as to be no more than fairy tales to which she would listen, dismissing her dim, disturbing memories of the future, of filth, blood and the rationalization of brutality.

'Is it too cold for you out here?' he asked.

She shook her head. 'Not yet.'

'I was going to make some notes this evening.'

'You go to the cabin. I'll join you soon.'

'I can't leave you here.'

'I'm not likely to be washed overboard.' She smiled. 'Make your notes, my dear.'

'I'll stay.'

She accepted this, though she knew that he would soon condemn her for keeping him from his work. This knowledge made the melancholia all the sweeter. She felt guilty. 'Well, perhaps I'll come down now.'

'You're sure? If . . .'

'It is getting cold,' she agreed. 'Could we possibly have a hot drink brought to the cabin?'

'Why not? It's all paid for by the Americans.' He grinned, happy that she had decided to go with him, although she knew that once he had begun to write he would be disturbed by the slightest movement she might make, that she would have to find some dreadful novel from the ship's library and pretend to read it. If she did not, he would decide that her restlessness was a sign that she wanted attention from him. She linked her arm in his as they crossed to the companionway. She hoped that he would decide to practise one of his lectures aloud to her; it would be preferable, certainly, to the novels. She sighed to herself. In a situation of this kind it was so hard for her not to fall back on easy cynicism. After all, she had agreed cheerfully enough when, in Paris, he had suggested they make the trip together, that his expenses allowed him to bring his wife. It was a way out of the plague ghetto, where she had been working as an auxiliary nurse and where, as a result, she had been confined when the Commune voted to quarantine the area.

As they entered the warmer air of the corridor she began to cough. An officer saluted them, speaking English. 'Good evening, madam. Evening, sir.' They nodded to acknowledge him. He turned the handle of the cabin door. 'I can never tell if they're using English or German,' he complained. 'I'm so rusty on languages. I'll have to improve. You must give me lessons, Una.'

'Your lectures sound all right.'

'The accent is good?' He turned a light switch. The cabin was untidy, scattered with his clothes and papers. Apart from a few cosmetics on the tiny dressing-table there was hardly any sign that she also occupied the room.

'Well, perhaps you could do with a refresher course in pronunciation.'

'I want them to understand every word.'

'They will.'

He was nervous of America. It seemed that he was anxious to win the approval of the workers there, more than anywhere else. He regarded them as more sophisticated, more articulate, more politically educated than workers in any other country. 'To win America,' he murmured to himself. Here was a return to the unrealistic idealism which had first attracted her to him when she had met him at the International before the War, in London. 'They want me. They have sent for me. Oh, I know I am one of many speakers contracted by the agency, but if they didn't wish to hear me, they wouldn't pay, would they?'

Una nodded. She peered through the porthole at the ocean; the horizon moved upwards and disappeared. She drew the tiny curtains.

Una awoke at dawn. She was cold. There was fresh, sharp air in her nostrils and she thought at first that the porthole had come open; then she wondered if the book, crushed between her body and the side of the bunk, had been the cause of her early waking. The book's edges were pressing into her ribs. She moved it, leaning over to place it on the floor. In the opposite bunk he was asleep, half-dressed, one leg hanging free, characteristically. She was about to turn on her side and go back to sleep when she realized that what had actually disturbed her was a series of loud noises, shouts, thumps, possibly gunshots. She rose, went to the porthole and looked out. The sea had vanished. In its place was the side of another vessel, painted a creamy white but covered in large patches of rust where the paint had peeled. Craning her neck she looked up. She could see the ship's rails and parts of her superstructure. She appeared to be a battleship.

The sea was very calm now. If there had been a storm then it had passed in the night. She went to the wardrobe and took out a slightly crumpled morning frock in green silk. As she dressed she listened, trying to interpret the sounds. It seemed as if the ship was being commandeered, possibly for provisions, as sometimes happened in wartime.

She was not aware of any international war taking place at that moment. She had unpacked very few of her clothes, since they had to appear in public only once or twice on the voyage. Thoughtfully, she put everything into her suitcase. Experience told her that it was as well to be ready for flight in this sort of situation. Another shot: clearly identifiable. It was closer. It had probably come from one of the nearby passages.

Men in heavy boots could be heard running along companionways towards the cabins. There were more shouts: orders. She heard angry voices, exclamations, banging doors. The passengers. There came a rap on her own door. He stirred in his sleep, feeling for his spectacles even before he awakened. Una lit a cigarette while the knock was repeated. She heard a man say in Spanish: 'Give me the passenger list.' A moment later she heard the same man laugh.

She opened the door.

He was swarthy, looking Jewish rather than Spanish, and the barefooted sailors grinning behind him were mainly Negroes, some very black, some quite pale. His uniform was of the same cream colour as his ship and the jacket and the left leg of his trousers had large brown blood stains on them, like rust. It was almost as if the similarities between ship and uniform were deliberate. He was very tall, his head almost touching the ceiling. He saluted cheerfully. 'Good morning, Comrade Persson. There was a rumour that you were aboard. And this comrade, also.'

He was grumbling, sitting on the edge of his bed and rubbing at himself. 'Are we sinking?'

'Your ship is perfectly seaworthy, if that's what you mean, comrade. If you are speaking symbolically . . .'

'Get out,' he growled. 'What do you want?'

'We are requisitioning stores and personnel for the use of our navy,' replied the tall man.

He was buttoning up his shirt. Now he recognized the voice of the newcomer. He looked up. 'Good God! Petroff! I thought you were dead.'

'I know that my services were no longer useful to your

particular struggle, comrade.' Petroff handed him his tie. 'However, I am now employed in another cause and seem to be appreciated better.' He spoke, Una guessed, not without bitterness. Petroff had been regarded as something of an opportunist in Moscow, but she had always thought him nothing more than a well-intentioned realist. She was as surprised as her companion to discover that Petroff was alive.

'Your own cause, eh, comrade?' Polishing his glasses he glared at the intruder. 'What is it? Simple piracy? How do you dignify it?'

'I support the principles of World Revolution and I am presently representing the Cuban Revolutionary Council. I am an officer in the CRC Navy. I hold the rank of Commander.'

'You will hardly get British recognition for your council,' he said, 'by committing acts of piracy against her civilian shipping.'

'We aren't interested in British recognition,' Petroff told him frankly. 'We want your food and your women.'

'What?'

'You're kidnapping the women?' Una felt a stir of interest at last.

'The young and the beautiful only.' He bowed to her.

'For ransom?'

He smiled. 'Certainly not. For pleasure.'

From over Una's shoulder there came a braying laugh. 'Thieves and rapists! Well, Petroff, you are revealed in your true colours. You are one of those who uses the vocabulary of revolution to justify acts of the grossest criminality . . .'

Petroff sighed, saluted again, but addressed Una. 'You will come with us willingly, comrade?'

'You intend to take Mademoiselle Persson? This is ridiculous. She is a comrade. An important and respected worker . . .'

'She is young and very beautiful.' Petroff drew a long-barrelled Colt revolver from the holster at his belt. 'We have orders to shoot anyone who resists. We have already shot fourteen members of the crew and five passengers.'

'I am horrified.' Vigorously he knotted his tie. 'We executed men for less during the revolution.'

'Perhaps that is where you went wrong, comrade. Cuba is primarily a Catholic country. Rather than learn to be puritans, renouncing our humanity, we intend to follow our instincts and achieve, as a result, a healthy and vital revolution. We are seizing only the First Class passengers and taking food intended for the First Class galley.'

'Your logic is ludicrous. If there is no food for the First Class passengers, the other food will be shared.'

'Requisitioned from the less fortunate. Exactly. An excellent moral lesson. Thus we sow the seeds of World Revolution.'

He turned away in disgust.

'I'll get my bag,' said Una.

'I'll die before they'll take you!' He moved to put himself between Una and Petroff.

Una kissed him. 'Your work is too important,' she told him. 'You must go to America. You know what it means to you — what it could mean to the American workers. The revolution is more important than the feelings of a couple of individuals.'

He hesitated. 'But I love you, Una.'

'And I love you, Lew.' she whispered: 'I will find you again, as I have found you before.' She picked up her suitcase.

This satisfied him. With an expression of contempt, he watched the sailors escort her from the cabin.

Petroff was the last to leave, casually waving the revolver. 'I suspect, Comrade "Brown", that it was you who signed the order for my liquidation. Happily for you, I am proud of the fact that I am not a vengeful man. Besides, to shoot you would carry no weight. Much better that I should take the only human being for whom you have any natural affection.'

'Brown' screamed at him. Quickly, Petroff closed the door. He seemed upset.

Una joined the other women in the line in the corridor. One or two of them were in shock but the others (about ten) appeared to be either amused or angry; most of them were in nightclothes and dressing-gowns but a few had managed to do their hair and make-up. Not one resisted as the party was herded on the deck, into the mild dawn air. There were only a few bodies in evidence. A crane had been swung out from the pirate battleship and jutted over the liner's bottom deck, where they were now gathered. From the crane ran a heavy chain attached to a makeshift wooden platform which was lowered to the deck as they emerged.

In pantomime the sailors indicated that the ladies should step on to the platform. Nervously, they complied. Una settled her suitcase on it and turned as she heard a scuffling near the rail. They had the Captain, a small, round-featured Irishman. There was a flesh-wound in his left arm. He had been handcuffed. 'Piracy,' he was saying with an almost romantic relish. 'Nothing but old-fashioned piracy!'

Petroff approached him and saluted, offering him a piece of paper which he accepted with both hands, wincing at his wound. Petroff explained. 'It is your receipt, Captain. The cases of food have been itemized. The fourteen passengers have also been itemized. There will, of course, be no compensation.'

The Captain raised his head to stare at Petroff. 'Hum.'

'Your company is insured against acts of piracy, presumably,' said Petroff.

'I don't know...'

'It would be wise of you to remind them, when you get to New York.'

'Yes.' It was obvious to Una that the Captain was only dimly aware of what was happening. The platform swayed as the crane began to crank it up and swing it over the side. One dark-haired girl of eighteen cried out as her little bag fell off the edge.

'I think it would be better if we were all seated down.' They accepted Una's suggestion and the platform steadied itself Looking down, Una caught the captain's astonished eye. She waved.

Una noted that grappling lines had been secured between the ships. Already the pirates were using these to cross back to their own vessel while their comrades, at the battleship's rails, brandished light machine-guns and rifles, covering them. Though all the pirates adopted a style of rakish villainy there was amongst them an almost childish good-humoured ambience, as if they knew they were being bad. Una saw that Petroff remained on the liner's deck, chatting to the Captain until the last of his men had returned, then he holstered his revolver, took hold of a grappling line and clambered, hand over hand, to his ship. As the crane began to lower the women to the battleship's deck the grappling lines were cast off. Petroff jumped from the rail, ran to his bridge and disappeared. A moment later the ironclad's engines began to turn and its big guns moved to menace the passenger vessel. 'Oh, goodness,' breathlessly murmured a young American girl as the liner receded. Shouldering their weapons, the crew gathered round the platform to inspect their prizes.

Petroff reappeared above. 'Mrs Persson,' he called in English. 'Would you join me, yes?'

Leaving her luggage on the platform Una stepped off, pushing through the hot bodies to climb up to the bridge. Petroff awaited her. He was pleased with himself. 'Do you really intend to rape us?' she asked.

He smiled, enjoying the idea for a moment. 'Certainly not. The women may pick anyone they choose to be their husband. I shall marry them myself. We think in the long-term, you see. It is the children we want. Good stock, wouldn't you agree? Some of the finest blood from the Old and New World.'

'And who am I to marry?'

'The choice is yours. You are free to decide. We are democrats, of course.' He offered her a cheroot which she accepted.

As he lit the cheroot for her she said: 'I was just

congratulating myself that I'd avoided one suitor with minimum embarrassment to both parties.' The cheroot began to smoulder. He blew out the match. 'Still,' she continued, 'I suppose this is a much healthier situation, though I'd be happier if there was less talk of freedom of choice, comrade.'

Petroff was amused. 'I take your point. But you are right. We are running a very healthy revolution, as I told "Brown".'

'How much time are you giving me to decide?' Through her thin dress the morning sun had begun to warm her skin.

'As long as you like. In the meantime, I invite you to join us. I can have a uniform modified for you.'

'You're disappointing me. Now I'm being offered a job.'

'An enjoyable job. Look how happy we all are! You would also receive a big pistol, like mine.'

'I have my own weapons, in my luggage.'

He folded his arms on the rail, sighing with pleasure, looking to starboard where the SS *Queen Victoria* could still be seen, her four funnels smoking, on the horizon. 'The sooner we return to Havana the better. They will repair their wireless shortly and the American war-fleet will be chasing us. I hope you'll consider me, by the way, Una. We would have beautiful children.' He tilted his cap to shade his eyes.

'I'm not sure it's possible for me to have children,' she said speculatively. 'It might cause all sorts of trouble. "Browns" are very,' she smiled to herself, ' "unstable".'

'That would be a shame.' He had only taken note of the first remark.

'Yes,' she said. She watched as the women, in their expensive négligées, were taken to their quarters. The men were excessively, if sardonically, polite. She envied the women the simplicity of their situation. 'It's odd, isn't it? There are so many ways of losing a revolution.'

EIGHT

In which Catherine Cornelius takes part in a union of two nations

'They're gonna fink yore th' bleedin' delivery boy!' Mrs Cornelius floundered up from the dip in the iron bed, casting off some half-a-dozen blankets and an emerald-green quilt. The bed shook and creaked. Catherine felt the vibrations on the floor beneath her feet as she stood at the door. ' 'And me me 'arscoat, love.'

Catherine crossed quickly to the chair on which her mother's many garments were piled. She selected the stained and faded man's woollen dressing-gown and the Savage Club tie and passed them over. Mrs Cornelius, in musty liberty bodice and drawers, began to pull the dressing-gown around her, securing it with the tie. 'You 'ad such lovely 'air, an' all.'

Catherine stroked the back of her naked neck. 'Don't make me feel embarrassed, Mum. There's lots of girls have Eton crops now. Lots of society people, and actresses and that.'

'Yeah ...' said Mrs Cornelius darkly. With only the remains of yesterday's make-up her face had a pale, pitted look, a dignity not normally distinguishable. She began to sip the cup of lukewarm tea Catherine had left on the littered bamboo table beside the bed. 'Well, there's 'ores wearin' more than yore wearin'. It don't mean everyone's gotta start 'angin' abaht Piccadilly, does it?' She cast a cold eye over the beige rayon frock, copied by Catherine from an original Molyneaux she had seen in last month's *Vogue*. 'Yer show it all, gel, and there's nuffink left ter offer 'em.'

'What,' said Catherine mockingly, 'the customers at the flower shop?'

'And where *is* th' flah shop?' Her mother matched her tone, bettered it. 'Eh? In Shepherd's bleedin' Market! When I arsked Edna ter give yer the job I also bloody arsked 'er ter keep a bloody eye on yer, an' all! Y'should 'ear the stories she's told *me*!'

'I have, Mum. Don't worry. I'm not the only girl in the world wearing short frocks these days.'

Mrs Cornelius began her morning cough. 'Yaaaah! Kar! Kar! Yaaaaah! Kar, kar, kar!' Catherine called good-bye and ran down the stairs, out on to the damp, bright pavements of Blenheim Crescent. She pulled on her coat as she walked to the corner, turning up Kensington Park Road, past Sammy's pie shop (not yet open), keeping pace with two totter's carts which had emerged from the mews running behind the Cornelius flat, where all the rag-and-bone merchants had their stables. Catherine was barely aware of the strong smell of mildew and manure the carts bore with them, for she had known the smell ever since her family had moved here at the end of the Great War. The carts turned off at Elgin Crescent, heading towards the richer parts of Bayswater, and she hurried on up the hill to Notting Hill Gate, to catch the tram which would take her to Mayfair.

Although her Auntie Edna (not a blood relation) was already opening the shop when Catherine arrived no mention was made of her lateness. Monday mornings were normally fairly slow and gave the staff a chance to assess and arrange the stock, ordered that morning by Edna Bowman and delivered from Covent Garden. All along the paved court of the Market other shopkeepers were opening up. 'Lovely day, dear, isn't it? Spring's 'ere, at last.' Auntie Edna was a tiny, cheerful woman, rather heavily made up, who had known her mother since the early days in Whitechapel. Edna had done quite a bit better for herself than had Mrs Cornelius; she had received the capital for her shop from an admirer, long-since dead, of whom she had been particularly fond. As Catherine went to the back of the shop to hang up her coat, Edna called: 'You're the first to arrive. Nellie 'asn't turned up. Get Ted to 'elp you with them boxes. Like your 'air-do.'

'Glad someone does.' Catherine put her coat on the only hanger. 'Mum thought someone would take me for Ted.'

Edna shouted with laughter. Ted himself appeared, wheeling his big black delivery bike through the court. He wore a fresh apron, a striped blazer and moleskin knickerbockers. Although only fourteen, he was nearly five foot ten, fat and ruddy, with a faint black moustache and a permanently morose expression belying a sharp sense of humour.

'Morning, Ted,' said Auntie Edna, still laughing.

'Morning, Mrs Bowman.' His large eyes regarded her with considerable gravity. 'You really shouldn't start before they open, you know. It's bad for the liver.'

'Cheeky blighter,' said Auntie Edna affectionately. 'Give Cath an 'and with the big boxes will yer. Nellie's not 'ere yet.'

'Probably married 'Is Lordship over the week-end,' suggested Ted, letting down the bike's iron stand with a clang. It was a familiar joke. Mr Stopes, the dignified butler from the Cannings' house in South Audley Street and popularly known in the Market as His Lordship, was sweet on Nellie, who thought a butler beneath her. Nellie was not merely an assistant in the shop. She was, she said, a Floral Artiste. Sometimes she would go to customers' houses and arrange their flowers for them. As a result she had seen how the other half lived and had set her sights on having nothing less than the best for herself.

Catherine and Ted began to carry the cardboard boxes of irises into the shop. Outside, Auntie Edna passed the time of day with the owner of the ironmonger's next door. They were talking about a man who had assassinated somebody in Germany and who was now on trial for murder. The ironmonger, apparently, had known the murderer when he had been a prisoner of war in England. ' 'E was a meek little blighter, too.'

When all the boxes were empty and the flowers transferred to pots and vases Catherine, now in a green overall, began to arrange them. Auntie Edna finished her conversation and came in. 'You've got a knack for it, Cath – better than Nellie, really. That's a very tasteful arrangement.' She moved a daffodil, thought better of it, replaced it where Catherine had originally put it. 'Where could that silly girl 'ave got to?' A customer entered. It was the old lady who looked after the Member of Parliament whose flat was in Curzon Street. 'Good morning, Mrs Clarke.' Auntie Edna raised her voice a fraction. 'Lovely, isn't it?'

'He's coming up from his constituency today, you see.' Mrs Clarke frowned, staring hard at Catherine as if trying to determine her sex. Catherine snapped a stalk too short and sighed. 'So I thought I'd get him a bunch or two of nice spring flowers. What have you done to your hair, dear?'

'It's the Eton crop,' said Auntie Edna, 'isn't it, Cath? The latest fashion.'

Catherine became conscious of a slight flush on the back of her freshly-shaved neck. She continued to arrange the flowers.

'Well I never,' said Mrs Clarke. 'How much are the daffs?'

'Sixpence a bunch this morning I'm afraid.' Auntie Edna shook them in their vase and removed a few to show her.

'Give us two, love,' said Mrs Clarke.

As Mrs Clarke left and Auntie Edna put the shilling in the till Catherine glanced through the shop's window and saw someone looking in, his face partially obscured by the broad leaves of the aspidistra and the feathery foliage of the ferns used for display. She knew, by the way he began to study the tulips, that he had been looking at her. She started to move towards the back of the shop, wondering if Mrs Clarke was outside soliciting opinions about recent hair fashions. The man remained at the window. Then he was gone. He stood in the entrance to the shop, the light behind him. He was good-looking, middle-aged, dark. He was dressed in formal but slightly old-fashioned clothes: grey frock-coat and trousers, grey waistcoat, grey homburg. He had a wing-collar and a yellow cravat with an amber pin in the shape of a moth. He carried a black, silver-headed stick and, as he entered the shop, she saw that he wore light tan shoes with spats. He had the air of a foreigner who had spent some years in England. Catherine had never seen him before but Auntie Edna recognized him with pleasure. 'Oh, good morning, Mr K! Just back in London, are you?'

'From my island retreat, yes. I returned recently.' He had a deep, soft voice, with an accent. 'You have no orchids today?'

'I'm afraid not. I could order you some for tomorrow.'

'If you would, Mrs Bowman.'

Because he did not look in her direction Catherine became convinced that he was probably aware of her attention. She turned her back and began to clip the ends off some irises. 'There's not a very big selection at this time of the year, really,' Auntie Edna was saying. 'They had some roses in the market, but I didn't fancy them. Forced flowers never last, do they?'

'No, indeed. Then let us have a great many beautiful English spring flowers, Mrs Bowman. Give me three bunches of everything. I shall turn my apartment into a celebration of the season.'

'Your flat'll be more like Kew Gardens, Mr K!' Auntie Edna giggled. 'When shall I have them sent round?'

'This afternoon. About three o'clock. And I will need somebody to arrange them for me.'

'Oh dear. Well, Nellie's off today. She might be in later, but . . .' Auntie Edna called: 'Miss Cornelius!'

Catherine was forced to face her aunt and the foreigner. 'Yes, Mrs Bowman.' They were always formal in front of this kind of customer.

'D'you think you're up to arranging some flowers for Mr K?'

'Well, if Nellie can't do it . . .'

'She's got a lovely touch,' said Auntie Edna to Mr K. 'I

think you'll be satisfied. Can you go round with Ted at three, love?'

'Of course, Mrs Bowman.' She continued to be embarrassed. She made herself lift her chin, to look back at him, but luckily he was already turning, smiling at Auntie Edna.

'Thank you.' He raised his hat as he left, causing Auntie Edna to stare fondly after him. 'He's very gentlemanly, that Mr K. Ever so polite, Cath. And one of our best customers.'

'What does he do?'

'He's Greek. Owns a lot of ships and stuff. He's got flats all over the world, but he prefers to live in London most of the time. It's his favourite city, he reckons. They say he's a millionaire. You'll do well this afternoon. Nellie once got a quid for arranging his flowers for him. He loves flowers. Has fresh ones every day he's in London. I could keep going on his custom alone when he's here, but, of course, he has to travel a lot. I think he's got a wife in Paris, but he never brings her with him. Maybe they're divorced. He took a fancy to you, you could tell. Kept looking at you while you were arranging them irises. He might tip you more than a quid, who knows?'

'He seemed very nice.' She thought she flushed again, though Auntie Edna didn't seem to notice. The back of her head felt so vulnerable since she had had her hair cut.

'You'd better do his flowers as soon as you've had your lunch, Cath. Three bunches of everything.'

'All right, Auntie Edna.' She wished that Nellie were here, to do the arranging. Nellie had a brashness, a self-assurance which could carry her through a situation. Besides, Nellie relished intense stares from dark-eyed millionaires: her hopes for the future depended on them. Mr K did not seem a bad sort and she was sure he had no real interest in her – he had probably also been trying to guess if she were a girl or a boy in her short hair and overall – but she was afraid that she would be awkward if he was there when she was arranging the flowers, that she might let Auntie Edna down. She tried to stop worrying; after all, the odds were that he wouldn't want to hang around while she was working. He probably had too much to do.

By lunch-time she felt better, was even amused by her own nervousness, but when she and Ted set off for Hertford Street she was abstracted and hardly heard what Ted was telling her about his dad's having gone for a job as a baker only to find, when he got there, that the bakery was kosher. Ted was balancing the flower boxes on his bike and she was carrying four big cellophane-wrapped bunches in her arms, wishing that she had remembered to wear her overall, or at least her coat, for she could feel water running down her right knee.

Ted stopped outside a house with a black door. The paint looked fresh. There was a brass plate on the wall beside the door: *Koutrouboussis and Son*. 'Is that Mr K?' she asked. 'Kou-trou-bou-ssis.'

'Bit of a mouthful, eh?' said Ted. 'I think the old man's dead or gone back to Greece. This is his son.'

A maid opened the door at Ted's ring. 'Ah, the flowers.' She was small and Chinese. Catherine thought she had never seen a more beautiful girl. She was dressed conventionally, in a black and white uniform. 'We go upstairs, please.' Catherine and Ted followed the maid up a fairly narrow staircase. Judging from the look of the doors on the ground floor, Mr Koutrouboussis's business was conducted there. The maid came to a door at the top of the stairs. She opened it and led them into a wide hall. The hall was furnished opulently with slightly unfashionable chinoiserie, although the preponderance of lacquered wood and black-framed mirrors was not overpowering and, against this setting, the maid no longer seemed incongruous.

'Isn't it lovely,' whispered Catherine.

It was not to Ted's taste. He said nothing as he wiped his boots on the mat. They followed the maid into a large sitting-room, also furnished in a mixture of oriental styles and *art nouveau*, again giving an impression of lightness. Catherine thought it was probably more like a Japanese room than a Chinese one, though she could not have defined the difference. It was odd to see, through the large french windows which opened on to a balcony, the familiar Mayfair street.

The maid handed something to Ted as soon as he had set his boxes down. 'This is for you, thank you.'

'Thanks very much, love,' said Ted. He lumbered from the room. 'See you in a little while, Cath.'

'Yes. Cheerio, Ted.' Her voice sounded feeble in her own ears. She looked helplessly at the maid. 'Where do you want me to begin? In here? Are there some vases?'

With Ted gone the maid's manner seemed to change. She was no longer brisk. Her voice became at once more intimate and virtually inaudible. 'I will fetch pots, Miss.'

Alone in the sitting-room, Catherine bent and removed the lid from the nearest box. It was full of daffodils. She began to look for suitable surfaces on which to place the vases, wishing that she had some idea of Mr Koutrouboussis's preferences. The door opposite opened. He was smiling, wearing a dark brown quilted smoking jacket over the waistcoat and trousers he had worn when he had come to the shop. He was smoking a cigarette in a holder. 'Ah, the little girl from Mrs Bowman's. What shall I call you, my dear?'

'My name's Catherine Cornelius, sir.' She suppressed a strong satirical urge to lisp and curtsy and wondered almost with horror where such a notion could have come from, particularly since she felt so nervous. For his part he bowed, with an air of light mockery. 'I am honoured to make your acquaintance, Miss Cornelius. Your beauty outshines the beauty of the flowers you bring me.' His tone had the effect of relaxing her almost too much. She smiled in return as he held out his hand for hers. His soft lips, his moustache, touched her knuckles. She became gay. 'Where would you like me to start, Mr Koutrouboussis?'

He was evidently pleased that she had pronounced his full name. 'There is a large vase which the maid will bring. I think a selection of all the flowers could go in that, on top of that cabinet there, where they will catch the light. What do you think? Women have a better sense of these things.'

'I think it would look very well there,' she said. She was flattered. The maid came in, carrying the large fan-shaped vase. 'Thank you,' said Mr Koutrouboussis. 'Put it on the cabinet, please.' As the maid left to fetch another vase he said, 'You think it unusual, a Chinese girl for a maid?'

'Unusual in these parts, sir.'

'I brought her with me from Hong Kong. I love feminine things, you see. And Chinese women are the quintessence of femininity. I celebrate femininity where most men, particularly men of business, try to banish it. We are born of women. I refuse to deny my mother's blood.'

For a moment Catherine wondered if he were trying to tell her that he was a pansy, so that she should not be afraid of being in the room alone with him, but he continued:

'These days everyone is trying to stop women being women. It was the war, I suppose. Or perhaps it is fear of emancipation. If women are to have the vote, they say, then let us force them to become masculine – then we shall not be afraid of them.'

Catherine was now certain that he disapproved of her hair. She became confused again. 'I'm not at all sure, Mr Koutrouboussis.' His laughter calmed her. 'Oh, I am sorry, Miss Cornelius. I am not referring to your delicious hairstyle. It is lovely. It displays an exquisite neck, draws attention to a perfect face, a delightful figure. Your femininity, I assure you, is emphasized. Your presence gladdens my heart. You must come to arrange my flowers every day.' The scent of the anemones she had been holding now seemed very heady and she wondered if the room itself were perfumed. Perhaps, being foreign, he was wearing perfume himself. A thought came to her, that it was his praise which made her feel so dizzy, but she decided it was, after all, the anemones. 'Thank you,' she said.

The maid returned with two tall vases on a tray. At her master's instructions she placed the vases on a small table standing before the french windows. She seemed to be smiling, although her eyes remained directed downwards. 'I will fetch more pots,' she said.

'I'd better be getting on with my job, sir,' said Catherine easily. 'Mrs Bowman's a bit short-handed today.'

'Of course.' He waved her towards the large vase. 'Will it embarrass you if I watch? I admire skill, particularly those skills at which women excel.'

She smiled. 'I'll probably make a terrible job of it now. It's my first time, you see. In a house, I mean. I've only done the arrangements in the shop up to now.'

'If it seems to me that I am making you shy I will leave, I promise you.'

She drew a deep breath and nodded. 'All right, sir. It's a bargain.'

He seated himself in an armchair with a padded oval back. He drew a small table with an ashtray on it towards him.

Although she felt self-conscious, his flattery had given her confidence. She felt rather like a dancer who knows she has an appreciative audience, and the ambience in the apartment, cool, comfortable and slightly erotic, also helped to put her at her ease. As she worked she was hardly aware of his presence. The arrangement came easily and was finished quickly. 'There. Will that do?'

'You are an artist, Miss Cornelius.' He rose to admire the display. 'You have studied this sort of thing?'

'Studied?'

'Flower-arranging. In Japan . . .'

'Oh, no. I like doing it. It's what I enjoy most about working for Mrs Bowman.'

'And what do you do, other than working for Mrs Bowman?'

She selected some more flowers and approached the first of the tall vases. The maid entered, carrying a round, pewter vase, decorated with semi-naked ladies wearing flowing drapery which, with the stylized lilies and water-lilies, made up the main design. 'Well, nothing really,' she replied.

'You do not paint?'

Catherine was amused. 'I never thought of it. I haven't any talent.'

'Oh, I think you have talent. You should go to art school.'

She smiled, saying nothing. She snipped some of the longer stems of the tulips. The maid left the room again. He walked to the window and looked out. 'What a beautiful day it is. Will you dine with me tonight, Miss Cornelius?' She was taken aback and yet at the same time the question came as an inevitable one so she answered 'Yes' without thinking, then she hesitated, the scissors in one hand, the tulips in the other. 'I'm not sure. I mean . . .'

'I suppose it is the springtime,' he said gently. 'But I would be honoured.' He turned to regard her. 'Not a question one should ask a respectable young English lady, really. But I do not regret the impulse. And you said "Yes" before you began to change your mind. Why not follow your first impulse?'

'Well, there's my mother,' said Catherine lamely.

'She has warned you about rich men who would rob you of your virtue and leave you with nothing.' He made a quiet joke of it. 'I promise you, Miss Cornelius, that I value your virtue quite as highly as your mother would.'

'And I've nothing to wear,' she added.

'You look exquisite in what you are wearing now. The frock is absolutely *à la mode*. Wear that. We shall dine in my apartment.'

'I couldn't . . .'

'The maid will remain here.'

'Oh dear.'

'I can see that you want to accept. Are you afraid of me?'

She wet her lower lip with her tongue. 'It would probably be better if I were, Mr Koutrouboussis.'

'Please accept.'

She told herself that she did not wish to anger him. Indeed, she very much wanted to win his approval. She had to think of Auntie Edna's business. Mr K was her best customer. It would, however, mean lying to her mother. It would not be the first time, of course, 'When shall I come?'

'About seven. I like to dine fairly early.'

She knew that he intended to seduce her and she began to feel a heady excitement. He bowed. 'I will see you at seven.' He touched her shoulder. He inclined his head; his eyes were serious. He left the room.

She worked automatically, filling vase after vase with flowers. Some of the vases were removed by the little Chinese girl and taken to other rooms. As soon as he had gone she had begun trying to consider how she might release herself from the agreement she had made, but she could think of nothing. If she left without giving him a good excuse as to why she could not come back that evening there would be no way of escaping without angering him. She imagined that he would be very angry if she let him down – not heated, but cold, possibly vengeful. And yet, even out of loyalty to her mother's friend, could she commit herself to the bargain? She had to consider it: he could ruin her. Unless, of course, Mr Koutrouboussis were to marry her. It was possible that he might have fallen in love with her when he had seen her in the flower shop. No, he was already married. She sensed, however, that he would be loyal, whatever happened. She knew a moment's humour – perhaps he would set her up in a flower shop.

After she had left the flat, and during the rest of her day at the shop, on the tram home, she continued to debate with herself not about the wisdom of seeing him that night (she knew that she had reached that decision the moment he had asked her) but whether he would look after her if she did get into trouble. He seemed a sentimental man and he had demonstrated his kindness. He was also very attractive, the sort of man who had always attracted her. Sophisticated, free, original – a modern bandit-king, in a way. And certainly she had never felt more feminine than when she had been at his flat. As the tram approached Notting Hill Gate she glanced at the clock over the watchmaker's shop. It was already a quarter past six. She would be late.

She ran all the way home and was so out of breath when she reached the front door of the house that she had to pause for a moment before going upstairs and letting herself into the flat. 'Mum?' To her relief her mother was out, probably still working at Sammy's pie shop where she helped part-time. Sammy himself had been Mrs Cornelius's boyfriend of some years' standing. Catherine wrote a note saying that she was going to a dance with Nellie and might stay at Nellie's overnight. She knew that her mother would be suspicious but it was better to invent a simple and conventional excuse than a complicated one which her mother would resent as insulting both her intelligence and her sense of decorum. She put on a little make-up, took her best coat from the cupboard, pulled her new cloche over her head, filled her tiny evening bag with a few necessities, all the while hoping desperately that her mother would not arrive back before she could leave, and then she fled down the stairs again, out into the darkening street, past the pie shop, retracing her steps to the tram-stop, seeing from the watchmaker's clock that it was ten to seven. She would only be about five minutes late, with luck.

When she returned to Hertford Street she realized that she did not know the number of the house. Almost all the doors looked alike to her, but eventually she found the one with the brass plate. She rang the bell. The Chinese maid opened the door. This time the girl's smile was direct and friendly and her eyes were appraising. 'Good evening, Miss . . .'

'Good evening. Mr Koutrouboussis is . . .'

'He said to show you up, Miss.' For a second time that day the maid led Catherine to the apartment, took her coat in the hall (now filled with flowers) and showed her in to the sitting-room. She was surprised at how fine her arrangements had been; they were certainly the best she had ever done. As before, the other door opened and Mr Koutrouboussis emerged. He wore a different smoking jacket, dark green, with dark red lapels. It was longer than the one he had worn that afternoon, almost a dressing-gown. 'My dear.' He seemed innocently delighted. 'You see, I, too, am informally dressed. You do not mind?' She shook her head. He crossed to a cabinet of decanters and glasses. 'What would you like to drink?'

'Dry sherry?'

'I think you will like this one. It is very light.'

'I'm sorry if I'm a bit late,' she said. 'I had to go home and tell my mum.'

'That you were coming here?' He handed her the sherry and indicated a place for her on the lacquered ottoman with the woven-cane back. She sat down. She decided not to answer his question directly.

'I left her a note,' she said. She sipped the sherry. He had the art of making her feel at once sophisticated and vulnerable. She enjoyed the sensation, but now that she knew that she was to be seduced she no longer had the same reservations about offending him. 'This is lovely sherry. What's it called?' He told her a name in Spanish. She decided to look at the bottle later, then she glanced across and remembered that he had poured the sherry from a decanter. He had drawn the heavy curtains over the french windows and the room had a luxurious, tranquil atmosphere; she felt safe in it.

The maid came in. 'The soup,' she said.

Catherine had finished her sherry. He took the glass from her and helped her rise. 'You are such a graceful creature. You are like a faun.'

She had not been listening. 'Fun?'

'That is how you would pronounce it?' He was politely interested as he led her across the hall and into the dining-room with its electric flambeaux on the walls which were papered with a raised flock pattern showing Chinese horses and soldiers. This room, although in the same style as the others, had a much more masculine air to it. The dining-table and the chairs were heavier. Even the tableware was of heavy porcelain and silver. She had felt completely at ease in the sitting-room but here she felt like an interloper; like a child taking its first meal with its parents. After a moment's bafflement she selected a large soup spoon from the array of cutlery. She ate in silence, for he made no attempt at conversation. The soup was delicious, light and faintly fishy, with more than a hint of the sherry she had been drinking earlier. The maid cleared away the bowls and brought the main course, some sort of cutlet in breadcrumbs. 'I hope you will forgive a very simple meal, my dear.' With the cutlet were thin fried potatoes, spinach and some kind of vegetable she had never tasted before and which she didn't like very much; similar to sliced, cooked cucumber. Expecting a great deal from the meal she ate slowly, savouring it, sipping the wine he poured for her. The whole effect on her was to make her feel more alive to sensation than at any time since her first experience of puberty. It seemed to her that her skin tingled at the lightest touch – her napkin against her wrist, her arm against a glass – and a sense of well-being filled her so that, when the maid brought flaming crêpes suzette she could do little more than taste a morsel, enjoying for the first time that exquisite combination of bitterness and sweetness. Finally the Chinese girl came in with the cheese, and Catherine sampled something pungent, foreign and soft. Then at last there was a tiny glass of port, which warmed her through.

'We shall have coffee in the sitting-room,' he told the maid, and he had touched Catherine's arm as he helped her from the chair. She was a little dizzy, but not unpleasantly so. He escorted her back to the sitting-room, back to the ottoman. The room was full of floral scent, but she was not sure if it came from the flowers themselves. A small table had been placed near the ottoman. There were a pot of coffee, some brown sugar, a jug of cream, two small porcelain cups. The tray, *art nouveau* silver like the big vase she had filled that afternoon, matched the coffee things. 'I suppose all this looks a little old-fashioned to you,' he said.

'Oh, no! I've always liked it. I liked it before it came back.'

'Came back?'

Something unwanted was emerging in her mind. She dismissed it successfully. He was stroking her neck. 'You are very young. Are you afraid of me?'

'I could be.'

'Yes. How old are you, Catherine?'

'Twenty-nine?'

He smiled. 'If I knocked about thirteen years away would I be closer?'

'To what?'

'To your age.'

'Maybe.' She might have shrugged.

'You are very delicate.' He stroked the line of her jaw. It was wonderful. 'Utterly feminine. You are everything a young girl should be and so rarely is. You know that I intend to possess you.' She nodded as his dark eyes came towards her own and she felt first his moustache touch her upper lip, then his lips touch both of hers at first softly and then aggressively until his tongue was pushing through, parting her teeth, to touch her tongue, and she had closed her eyes as his body pressed against her soft breasts and her thigh and his arms grasped her about her shoulders and her waist, and then he had gently bitten her lip and she was sure that she tasted her own blood, but it was not pain she felt; it was an electric sensation that passed through her entire body and it was followed by another of possibly greater intensity as his thumbnail seemed to make a tiny incision in the back of her neck. She had probably gasped, for he withdrew his tongue, leaned back from her and with his other hand gently touched first one breast and then the other. 'Will you come with me?'

'Yes.'

He led her through the door by which he had first entered the room. His bed was the largest, the most opulent she had seen. The sheets were of dark blue silk, the cover was of a lighter blue embroidered with a single Chinese motif. There were candles burning in a candelabra and it was these which gave off the floral scent, heavier and more erotic here. 'Undress,' he said. 'I will join you in a moment.' He went through another door, presumably into his dressing-room.

She took off her frock, her underclothes, her stockings, putting them neatly on a nearby chair. She drew back the sheets and climbed into the softness of the bed; it became the universe. She had never felt more naked. She turned her head at a sound and he was standing beside the bed. The hair on his chest was almost grey, his belly was slightly rounded, seeming to shade his genitals as he moved in the candlelight. After he had got into the bed he did not immediately touch her but lay for a moment looking at her. Then his hand stroked her face. She kissed it. He stroked her neck and her shoulders, her waist, her stomach and he touched her pubic hair only for a moment before he withdrew and stroked her breasts. And then his hand was firm on her waist and he had rolled towards her so that his body touched hers and she thought she could feel his soft penis against her thigh while he kissed her forehead and her ears and her neck and her shoulders, then her breasts and her waist and her thigh, his right hand still firmly holding her waist. She wanted his whole body against hers. She moved towards him but he held her back and with his sharp-nailed thumb stroked her pelvis. She tried to move her vagina towards the thumb, but again he held her, his thumb stroking more gently. He moved his hand quite suddenly so that she rolled hard against him and his nails slid down her back and were like tiny knives moving across the flesh of her bottom, her inner thighs and the backs of her legs, behind her knees so that she forgot her immediate sexual needs, giving herself up to his cruel and gentle fingers, lying now on her stomach as he continued to caress her.

Gradually, perceptibly, the touch of his finger-tips, scarcely felt, profoundly sensed, was replaced by the lightest pressure of his fingernails on her shoulders, neck and back so that she anticipated and welcomed the pain when it began to come, when he drew her on to her back, stroking and scratching her waist, breasts, stomach and groin until her sexuality was completely sublimated and she wished only for greater pain, for catharsis by means of his subtle and relentless cruelty, and she moaned very faintly, unable either to speak or to cry out, even as she became aware of another presence in the room, of his parting from her, of a soft body moving into the bed beside her, kissing her delicately upon her cheeks and her lips and her breasts, caressing her waist and her pelvis, touching the lips of her vagina, her clitoris, so that she lay completely still while the Chinese girl murmured to her, pressing her small, rounded breasts to her own, taking her hand and placing it against a vagina that was, to her surprise, completely hairless, like a child's, parting her legs a little, kissing her chin and her stomach and, finally, her vagina, her tongue firm and controlled as it licked her clitoris. Then Catherine's hands found the Chinese girl's head and grasped it as she tried to bring the girl up to her so that she might kiss her in turn, but at first the girl resisted, only gradually acquiescing, kissing her navel and her breasts again until at last her lips were on Catherine's and her tongue was in Catherine's mouth and her hairless pubis was hard against Catherine's vagina, moving with a rhythm that was at once gentle and demanding, and to which Catherine responded, shuddering as she felt the beginnings of orgasm. She felt him move, felt a quick hand on her body, on the girl's, an awkward movement, a break in the rhythm which she could not tolerate, then it was gone and the girl was kissing her again, one leg across Catherine's leg, and Catherine could no longer tell if the moans were her own or the girl's, for she identified the girl almost completely with herself. Without altering her rhythm, the Chinese girl moved her hand and it held something that was cold, smooth and hard. Catherine was afraid. Still on top of her the Chinese girl put the thing to the lips of Catherine's vagina and began slowly to move it inside. Now the cathartic pain and the orgasm were coming simultaneously. Catherine screamed as she was ripped; it was as if her entire body had been torn in two; from feet to head a cold fire ran through her again and again and she was sobbing, sinking, only partly aware that the girl had moved to join the man and, in turn, was crying as he took her.

By the time Mr Koutrouboussis had begun to push his flesh into her dry, painful vagina, she was wholly abstracted, noting the areas of his body where he was hard or where age betrayed itself in softness, listening with a kind of distant affection to his grunts as he rapidly reached orgasm and flung himself away from her. She felt liquid cooling between her legs and took a corner of the sheet to wipe it from her, peering through the candlelit darkness for the Chinese girl. The girl smiled at her from the doorway, blowing her a shy kiss before she vanished. Mr Koutrouboussis seemed already asleep. In a moment, Catherine slept, too. She was awakened by the Chinese girl, wearing a silk robe, bringing her a cup of tea. Mr Koutrouboussis was not in the bedroom. 'Gone out,' said the Chinese girl. 'Business.' She bent and kissed Catherine on the forehead. 'Feel good today?'

Catherine winced as she moved. 'I never felt better.'

The Chinese girl drew back the sheet and stroked Catherine's body. 'Shall I bring more tea? We drink together?'

'Oh, yes.' She began to sit up, arranging the many pillows for herself and the girl. She took the cup from the table and sipped the scented tea. She could not tell what the time was, for the room was still dark. The Chinese girl came back with her own tea-cup and got into bed with a sigh of pleasure. She had her hair-brush with her and, after a moment, began to brush her long, straight black hair. Wordlessly, Catherine took the brush from her and combed it through her hair, arranging it almost as, yesterday, she had arranged the flowers in the sitting-room. 'Thank you,' said the girl. 'You are beautiful.'

'You're beautiful.' Catherine parted the girl's gown and stroked her pubis. This morning it did not seem quite so smooth; it was faintly bristly. 'Do you shave there?'

'He likes it.' The girl giggled. 'I like it, too. But it itch, you know. Have to do every day.'

'Will he want me to do that?'

'Oh, yes. Later I do.'

'Does it hurt?'

'Little bit.' The Chinese girl turned on her side so that she was facing Catherine.

'What's the time?' asked Catherine.

Again the girl giggled. 'No time here.'

'I've got to go to work.'

'Work?'

'To the flower shop.'

'Oh, yes.'

'Does he want me to come back? Tonight?'

'You want to come?'

'To see you.'

'Nice. Yes.'

'Then I'll have to send a postcard to my mum so that she'll get it this evening.' Catherine looked for her clothes. They were no longer on the chair. 'My frock?'

'Look. He said to wear that.' She indicated a silk kimono, similar to her own. Catherine laughed. 'I can't go to work in that.' She got up. Her legs were a little stiff and she had a pain under her ribs on the left, and in her back, like the beginnings of a period. She groaned and straightened. 'Goodness, I do feel well. I shouldn't. Should I?'

'Always feel good next day.' The Chinese girl moved like a cat in the bed. She watched Catherine with affectionate amusement.

'It doesn't seem wrong,' said Catherine. 'I feel guilty about not feeling guilty. Do you know what I mean?' She opened a cabinet and found her clothes neatly folded on one of the shelves. The cabinet was full of women's clothes, including underwear that had not been in vogue for thirty years. She closed the doors. There was a hand-basin in one corner of the room. It was of black marble. The taps were jade green. She began to wash. 'Are you sure you don't know what the time is?'

'Early. You not stay with me today?'

'I'd love to, but if I don't go into work the lady at the shop will get in touch with my mum.'

The Chinese girl understood. 'You have large family?'

'No. There's just my mum and two brothers. I don't see my brothers much at the moment.'

'No sisters?'

'No.' Catherine got into her underclothes, pulled up her stockings and secured them. 'Can I borrow your brush?'

'Here.' The girl came across and with a few quick movements brushed out Catherine's crop.

'Will he be angry that I've gone?'

'Mr Koutrouboussis probably be out all day. I am sad. You stay.'

Catherine guessed that the girl was capable of better English but knew that her simplified syntax was attractive. She kissed the girl. 'Can you meet me for lunch? I only get half an hour.'

The girl shook her head. 'I must stay.'

'I'll nip round, then, to see you.'

The girl smiled. 'Nice.' She became grave as she took Catherine's face in her hands and kissed her on the lips. 'You promise.'

Catherine laughed. She was full of well-being. Her body felt lighter, more her own. She felt beautiful. 'I promise. If Mr Koutrouboussis comes back before I do, tell him I'm sorry. Tell him why I had to go.' She left the flat. The street was warm and sunny. Her body ached but there was a spring in her step. She had never been more aware of her body, nor more pleased with it. She turned the corner, entering Shepherd's Market. To her surprise it was earlier than she had guessed. Auntie Edna hadn't arrived yet. She would have to get a watch.

'Well,' said Edna Bowman, turning up five minutes later to unlock the shop, 'you're looking lovelier than ever, my girl. What is it? A touch of spring? You in love?'

Catherine grinned at her, wishing she could tell her what had happened. 'Maybe.'

'Nice young feller, is he?'

'Oh, Auntie Edna . . .' She averted her eyes.

Auntie Edna chuckled. 'Sorry, girl. You keep smiling like that and we'll double our profits. It's amazing how good a smile is for trade.'

At lunchtime Catherine ran round to Hertford Street. The girl answered the door. She was in her uniform again. She took her by the hand. 'He back,' she whispered, 'but not for long.'

'Does he want to see me?' She had hoped not to meet him. She had come to see her new friend.

'He going out.' They entered the sitting-room. He was standing with his back to them, looking at her flower arrangement. It was only with an effort that she could believe that she had known the flat for less than twenty-four hours. As the Chinese girl closed the door Catherine immediately relaxed, became euphoric with a sense of safety. He turned, reached out for her and took her by the back of the neck. 'You are happy, I can see. Tell me, have the orchids arrived at the shop?'

'This afternoon.'

'Bring them on your way home – as it were. Tell your aunt I saw you in the street and asked you to come at five. That means you will be able to leave early. I will be back at seven. It will give you some time alone together.' He smiled fondly at both of them. 'My two little girls. I want you to think of us as the father and the sister you do not have.'

He was dressed in black, for business. He took a gold hunter from his waistcoat. 'I waited to see you, but now I must go. You wish to be with me tonight again?'

She lowered her eyes and nodded.

'Good. It is a shame that I must work in the world.' He looked about the room. 'But it makes this private world so much sweeter.'

'Your business is shipping, isn't it?' said Catherine on impulse, thinking she should respond. 'I love ships.' She hated them. She was always sea-sick.

'Oh, ships are involved.' He laughed as if he guessed that she had lied. 'I am an import–export specialist, you know. Well, that is the conventional term in my trade.' He placed his hat on his head and stroked her hair. 'I am, my dear, an old-fashioned war-profiteer. An exploiter of conflicts.' He ran his thumbnail down her spine.

NINE

*In which Miss Una Persson returns to Europe
in her efforts to discover the exact Nature of
the Catastrophe and the Role of Women in
the Revolution*

In the Via Veneto the crowds were still marching, having tried to set fire to several buildings, including the American Embassy and Thomas Cook's. The noise was not much louder than that which could normally be heard at this hour, from taxi-drivers, drunks and harlots. Una was grateful that the water was still hot as she turned the heavy chrome taps of the great white tub and used the shower attachment to rinse her short chestnut hair. She was alone in a vast bathroom, full of mirrors and Egyptianate metal, in her suite at the Albergo Ambasciatori, still in her opinion the best hotel in Rome and a fitting headquarters for the Provisional Government. When the phone rang from the other room she was already wrapping heavy white towels around her head and body; she walked without haste from the bathroom, sat down on the double bed and picked up the receiver.

'Did I wake you, Una?'

'Who's that?'

'Petroff. I just got in.' He was excited, unashamed. 'They said you might be asleep.'

'But you rang anyway.' It was typical of him.

'The phone never wakes you when you're really asleep, Una. Nothing does. Too much gunfire, eh?' He was in a friendly mood. She had absolutely no desire for a sentimental reunion, particularly after his wretched compromising of the San Francisco situation which lost them their foothold on mainland USA and resulted in a complete if temporary victory for the Philadelphians.

'What are you doing in Rome?' She was cool.

'Aren't you pleased to hear from me? I came in my official capacity – for the discussions. And to join in the celebrations, of course. (Have you a beau, currently?) You have won. Aren't you pleased?'

She rarely relished victory. 'There's a lot of work to do, yet. There have been repercussions, you know, over that Vatican business.'

He was plainly making an effort to sound sober. 'Yes. My people were not happy to hear about it. It was unnecessary brutality. Unfortunate.'

'Well, I might see you later. I'm going to sleep now.'

'You won't be at dinner, tonight?'

'Perhaps.'

'It's your duty to be there, surely?'

'I'm notorious for my moods. But I'll probably see you in the bar, just before dinner.' She immediately regretted relenting, but Petroff's charm had already had its usual effect. She would have to avoid him. She began to dress, furious with him for putting her in this position. She had intended to go out, to visit Lobkowitz who had arrived yesterday. He was too late to be given accommodation in the Ambasciatori and was staying two blocks up, in the St James, a flashy, recently erected place where most of the Balkan delegates had been quartered. Now, unless she wanted to risk bumping into Petroff downstairs, she would have to ring and invite Lobkowitz to her suite when she would have preferred to have met her old friend on neutral ground, in the bar or in a restaurant. She was not sure of his attitude towards her: he might misinterpret her invitation on both political and personal grounds. Already her life was getting far too complicated. One action produced a dozen permutations. The previous day, making her speech in the Coliseum, she was sure that she had seen Jerry Cornelius, Catherine's brother, moving through the audience holding a scrawny stray black and white cat, and she knew that he would not be here without a good reason. There were far too many ambiguities in Rome on this particular May day. In her view they were prematurely celebrating their settlement with the Neapolitans over the Vatican issue.

By the time she had dressed in her Chanel pleated skirt and matching grey pullover she felt much better. Before putting through the call to Lobkowitz she decided to have another look at her notes. She sat down beside her desk, unlocked the drawer and withdrew a fat folder. The notes were even more confused than she remembered; some of them she could not understand at all; some of them referred to events which, she was sure, had not happened anywhere and could not possibly happen in the future. She dismissed, for instance, the whole idea of the Neapolitan royalists taking either Rome or Genoa under their idiot king Alfredo, and it seemed unlikely that they would raise money by selling Capri and Ischia to the Germans and, as a result, receive tacit German military support in their campaign.

The Vatican business was unfortunate, yet she could sympathize with Costagliola's impulse to eradicate the problem at a stroke, even if it had meant an awful lot of Michelangelo and Leonardo going down the drain. It certainly showed that Costagliola meant business and had created a good deal of useful confusion in Naples, as well as Venice, Florence and Turin (whose governments were relatively sympathetic to Rome) and throughout the whole Catholic world. Costagliola had also received a considerable amount of secret support since then; some from quite unlikely sources and, as he had calculated, there were now between ten and fifteen self-elected Popes in Italy alone. She had heard there were at least three in France, one in Ireland, two in America and two in Spain. Greece had a couple of contenders in the field, as did Ethiopia. As yet, there was no news either from Constantinople or Avignon. Already fighting had broken out in Brindisi and Cozenza between supporters of rival Popes. There was, incidentally, a thriving trade in art fakes which the dealers alleged had been salvaged from the ruins of St Peter's.

Perhaps, after all, the Roman situation was sufficiently stable for her to consider moving on. She certainly wanted to convince herself that it was stable: she had had enough of Italy for the moment, though it remained her favourite European country, and it looked as if something interesting was happening in Dalmatia, which was why she particularly wanted to see Lobkowitz, whose election to the Central Committee as Chairman in a free poll throughout Bohemia in the previous year had been one of the most surprising events in an astonishing (and heartening, she thought) pattern. Lobkowitz was probably the only aristocrat holding any authority in Central Europe and had calmly continued to use his title. At one point there had been a movement to ban him from the Conference but Una and many others had been vociferous in demanding that he came. If the main Salzburg–Rome line had not been blown up he would have been here two days earlier.

She decided to phone his hotel.

Picking up the receiver she had to wait for several minutes before someone answered, took the number and told her that there would be a delay for perhaps a quarter of an hour before a line would be free. Patiently, she replaced the phone and returned to her notes. Petroff's arrival had affected her nerves. That and the glimpse of Cornelius had succeeded in confusing her more than it should have done. Both men were unpredictable, both could possibly make claims on her, as ex-lovers. Cornelius might even be trying to alter the balance of power, working some crazy scheme of his own. She wanted to give all her attention to Lobkowitz and then leave Italy as quickly as possible. It was an effort to maintain her resolve. As it was, she had already allowed Petroff to affect her plans.

The phone rang almost immediately. She picked it up quickly and then regretted her action – it could be Petroff or even Cornelius on the line. But they were calling Lobkowitz's hotel. She asked for him, heard a click, thought she had been cut off, and then it was his voice: 'Prinz Lobkowitz.'

'Good evening, Your Highness,' she said.

'Ah, Una! I called earlier, but you were asleep. Can we meet?' He was eager.

'I wonder if you would mind coming here, to my rooms. Someone has arrived and I don't want to see them yet. You have a pass?'

'They gave me one a few minutes ago.'

'You'll come?'

'You're alone? Myself, I'm in no mood for general conversation.'

'I'm alone. It's on the second floor. Use the back staircase if you can. The lifts aren't working too well. Number 220.'

'I'll come now, yes?'

'That would be excellent. Again, I'm sorry . . .'

'Of course.' He rang off.

As she rose to go to her bedroom there was a tap on the door. 'Who is it?'

'Message, madam.'

Reluctantly she opened the door. It was one of the young waiters from the restaurant. He held a large envelope out to her. He had probably been tipped to bring it, so she gave him nothing, particularly since she disapproved of the necessity. She thanked him and closed the door, opening the envelope to find a fresh red rose inside. As she removed it, one of the thorns pricked her finger. How on earth had Petroff found such a thing in Rome at this time? Or had Petroff sent it? There was no message. She sighed and dropped the rose on top of her folder of notes, continuing into the bedroom to tidy her hair and dab a little eau-de-cologne on her neck and forehead. She took a deep breath and felt more relaxed. Another knock. She was more cautious as she opened the door.

Lobkowitz looked older. His hair was completely grey. His familiar quiet smile gladdened her. He was tall, stooped, gentle. He had not changed.

'Oh, how lovely to see you.' She admitted him. She kissed him lightly on the cheek. 'You're looking so well. Your journey doesn't seem to have tired you at all.'

'I enjoyed it. I have a superstition about train trips. If the ride is trouble-free then something awful will happen when one arrives. You know the sort of thing. You, too, are looking extraordinarily well, Una. What's your secret of eternal youth?'

'You'd never believe me.'

He removed his soft felt hat and unbuttoned his ulster. 'It's raining. It's hot in Rome now! Have you been downstairs lately? So many people! So many old comrades!' He gave her his hat and coat and she hung it in her wardrobe. 'What a lovely room.'

'I gather yours is not very good.'

'I anticipated worse. And we have no right to demand luxury, have we?'

'I suspect it's the last we'll have in Rome. I'm making the most of it. Would you like some whisky?' She took the bottle from the drawer in her desk.

'A little one. Thank you.'

'How are things in Bohemia?' She poured some whisky into glasses. 'I'm sorry there's no mineral water. You'll have to drink it as it comes.'

'We seem to be coping.' He sipped the drink. 'I don't know what will happen after the honeymoon.' He shrugged. 'I don't expect to last more than one term.'

'You have popular support.' Una was surprised by his pessimism. 'They wouldn't dare get rid of you!'

'I shan't stay if the rest of the Committee is dissatisfied. It would be pointless.'

'Yes. I see what you mean.'

'I suppose you do, Una.' A small smile. 'I was surprised at you, in Albania, refusing the presidency after all your good work.'

She rubbed her forehead, amused. 'I'm an international troublemaker, not a national one. I like to move on.'

'You've accepted no position here in Rome?'

'Nothing permanent. It's one of the reasons I wanted to see you alone. I was wondering what you thought about Dalmatia.'

He wrinkled his nose. 'You're going there next?'

'Probably. If they can use me.'

'There are very few people wouldn't give you a job, Una. Your experience is legendary.' He unbuttoned his military jacket, pulled up his trousers and sat on the edge of the bed. From the street the sound of the crowds had dissipated so that it was possible to hear the noise from the hotel's ground floor: laughter, shouts, sudden bursts of clapping. 'But you won't accept leadership, will you? Is that the feminine part of you?'

She considered this. 'I know many men who feel as I feel. I gave up Albania for the same reasons that I gave up the stage when I became successful. It doesn't suit me to be on the winning side, I suppose. I'm embarrassed by lack of criticism. Could that be it?'

'You haven't thought of it before?'

'I've reached no conclusions. Besides, I felt sorry for Zog.'

'You see!' He was not wholly serious. 'You are a woman! You could argue, couldn't you, that femininity is the essence of radicalism? You must be in opposition or you are not happy. You must feel that the force to which you are opposed is more powerful than you.'

'Are you talking about women in general?'

'Yes.' He frowned, smiling to himself. 'Well, perhaps I'm not talking about Queen Victoria. Unless her petulance was the direct result of her resenting the responsibility she was told she had. Don't all successful revolutionaries similarly resent the power they are given? Is that why they will often invent new enemies, when their original enemy is defeated? Why they never realize that they have ceased to become the least powerful force and have come to be the most powerful one?'

Una lit a cigarette and immediately felt a pain in her chest. She put the cigarette down but did not extinguish it. 'What about Dalmatia?'

'I'm sorry if I seemed condescending, Una.'

'It's not that. Frankly, the discussion bores me. I've had it so often, you see.'

'Yes. Forgive me, anyway.'

'Do you think they have a good chance in Dalmatia?'

'It depends on the Turks. If they give support to the existing régime then any revolution will be difficult. You could help there, of course. You know the Turkish mind.'

'Hardly. I've known a Turk or two, that's all.'

'Well, it would help. Could I have a little more whisky?'

She poured it into the glass he held out. She was glad that his hand was steady. She had seen too many shaking hands in the past few days. 'So you'd think I'd be useful?'

'Of course.'

'And they wouldn't resent me?'

'Certainly not.'

'Then I'll go. Another couple of days. As soon as the conference is over.'

'It's a relief to know you'll attend the conference at any rate.'

'Are you laughing at me, Prinz Lobkowitz?' She was not annoyed.

'Oh, I don't think so. If you detect anything hidden then it's my admiration.'

'You'll make me self-conscious.'

'Indeed? You should be beyond such feelings now, surely? Perhaps you identify this shyness with your idealism. You are still afraid, I suppose, of becoming cynical.'

'But I am a cynic. I'm trying to change the world. I'm altering history, or think I am.'

'Is that cynicism? If so, it isn't what I meant.'

'You think it would do me good to accept responsibility?'

'Well . . .' He gestured.

'I'm too immature.'

'Ah, yes, we are all that.'

'I haven't enough faith in my own convictions. I can't retain a conviction, not in detail. I'm exactly the same as I was as a child. I believe in love and justice. Free will, free speech, enlightenment, kindness. It's as general and as simplistic as that. One act of inhumanity shocks me. It still shocks me, Prinz Lobkowitz. I have killed people myself. I have inadvertently caused the deaths of many innocents. Perhaps I feel too guilty to accept power.'

He scratched his head. 'Perhaps you are too innocent to be offered it.'

'Now you are certainly condescending.'

'I apologize again. I can think of no one nobler than you, Una. That nobility could destroy you. It has destroyed others like you.'

'Is this flattery?' She rounded on him, smiling, but she felt very awkward. 'I assure you I'm not always in this mood. Seeing you has plunged me into it. It's your own nobility you're discussing, not mine.'

He laughed. 'Oh, yes, perhaps. I'm a very noble person. I am aware of it sometimes. And it disgusts me. I am not flattering you, Una.'

'That's something.' She finished her drink. The smell of the whisky was offensive to her. 'I'm very bewildered today. The man I wanted to avoid is Petroff. You remember him? From the Spanish Main? The Barbary Coast? I wasn't expecting him.'

'I thought he was completely *persona non grata* here.'

'Apparently not. And I think I saw Cornelius yesterday.'

'Frank?'

'No, the other one.'

'Is that surprising?'

'He's my personal omen of disaster. I think he was nicknamed the Raven once. Like Sam Houston. Well, he's my raven.'

'And what disaster do you fear?'

'I don't know. Do you want another drink?'

'Thank you.'

Again she poured the whisky into his offered glass. 'I said personal, and it is personal. Perhaps I feel my identity threatened.'

'And that's why you're so nervous tonight?'

She had not known that he had been aware of it. 'Yes.'

He got up and walked across the room. 'Is this the bathroom?'

She nodded. He went inside and locked the door. She heard him pissing, then listened as he pulled the chain and washed his hands. 'At least you have a toilet which works,' he said as he came out. 'Perhaps the news about Mr "Brown" has disturbed you?'

'What's "Brown" doing?'

'Oh.' Lobkowitz looked at his hands. He said softly: 'He died.'

'Was he killed?' She had expected it.

'Suicide.'

'The fool.' She sat down heavily in her chair by the desk. 'The bloody fool. He was married, wasn't he?'

'With a couple of children. But they were living apart, I gather. It was in New York. He left a note – a very confused note. The authorities had limited his movements a great deal, you know, in the past year. He had nothing to do. He was writing rubbish. He had no close friends left. So he killed himself.'

Her sense of guilt was suddenly so intense she had to force herself to be rational: the effort produced in her a coldness, something very close to a clinical state of shock. 'What a waste,' she said.

Seating himself on the arm of the chair Lobkowitz gripped her shoulder. 'It happened over a month ago,' he said. 'Were you still fond of him?'

She nodded, wishing that she would cry, wondering at her own callousness when she found that she could not. 'Of course. I haven't seen any newspapers – only the one we produced towards the end of the fighting. He was my first lover, you know.'

'Oh, Una, how thoughtless of me. I am sorry.' The words were so conventional that they succeeded in comforting her. She began, at last, to cry, conscious of the hand which still held her shoulder. And as she cried it seemed that all the tension of the past two days washed out of her so that she wondered if Lobkowitz had deliberately given her the news of 'Brown's' suicide at that moment, knowing that this was how she would respond. She tried to apologize. He murmured to her. He helped her from the chair and made her lie down on the couch. She kissed the hand that stroked her face.

'Poor "Brown",' she said, 'poor bloody "Brown".' She sniffed. He gave her his large white handkerchief. She blew her nose. 'I'm sorry.'

He sighed. 'Don't try to pull yourself together yet, Una. Not yet.'

'I hate losing my self-control. You must be tired. It's a burden . . .'

'On the contrary, I find your response very satisfying.'

'What?'

'I feel much better when I see you reacting naturally. You were very tense when I came in. I have never seen you so bad. Perhaps you should go back to England for a while? It is very orderly over there. Or Sweden? Even better. You need to rest, to be away from violence and politics.'

'I can't rest very often. It's not in my nature. I feel so guilty, even about going to sleep, unless I am completely exhausted. What did the papers say about him?'

'Most of them were kind. I saw the obituary in the London *Times*. They said he was a brilliant political theorist but a confused practical politician.'

'Yes. He killed all the wrong people!' She tried to laugh but began to sob again and now the sobs seemed to come from the deepest parts of her body. She could scarcely breathe. 'Why couldn't they leave him alone? He was doing no harm!'

'Words seem to mean more to an American than to most Europeans, Una. It is the large peasant population. They have a greater faith in the magic of language. Perhaps they had more reason, therefore, to be afraid of him.'

'Oh, what bastards they are!'

'He chose to live there.'

'He always picked the wrong countries. Germany. England. America. Those horrible Teutons.'

Lobkowitz chuckled. 'Like you and me, Una?'

'Exactly,' she said. Her throat and chest were very painful

now and her nose felt sore. 'I think I've got a cold. Oh, shit!' She blew her nose on his handkerchief. 'Why must it always happen when I've got a speech to make? My Italian's bad enough as it is.' She began to cough.

'I think you'd better go to bed,' he said. 'Can you get food served in your room?'

'Usually, though it takes them ages to bring it.'

'Shall we dine here, together?'

'That would be lovely. I won't bother to go down tonight. But haven't you any appointments?'

'Nothing important.'

'There's a menu on that little table,' she said. 'They don't give you a very wide choice and the chances are that there's only one main course available. I'll have the soup to start. This is very good of you.'

He reached for the menu. 'I am acting entirely from self-interest, I assure you.' He looked at the card. 'What do you want? Minestrone or stracciatella?'

'Stracciatella, please. It won't be very hot.'

'Do you care what you have?'

'Something light. Veal, if possible. Or chicken.'

He picked up the telephone, waited, then spoke softly, in English. 'We should like to order a meal in our room. Madame is sick. Just a cold. Thank you. Yes, we will have stracciatella for two. Veal cutlets ... Roast chicken? Fine. Oh, yes, cheese and so on. And coffee. Of course. Thank you.' He replaced the receiver and turned back to her. 'There! They were very concerned. You are as popular here as you are everywhere.'

'Not quite everywhere.' She began to weep again. 'This is stupid. It's self-pity. Nothing to do with "Brown".'

The phone rang. She tried to answer it, but he blocked her, answering it himself. 'Prinz Lobkowitz. I am afraid that Miss Persson is indisposed at present.'

Una giggled through her tears.

'She has a touch of influenza, that is all. Yes. I don't know.' He put his hand over the mouthpiece. 'Did you receive a gift, Una, just recently?'

'No.' She glanced at the desk. 'He means the rose.' She hesitated. 'Say, no.'

'I am sorry,' he said, 'she says . . .'

Una thought of the bribed waiter. Petroff could be vengeful in small matters. 'Say I received a flower.'

'She received a flower. Yes. I will tell her. Good-bye.'

'What a splendid protector you are, Prinz Lobkowitz.' She blew her nose again. 'You are corrupting me, you know, with your terrible avuncularity. Is it what you want to do?'

'Oh, secretly, I suppose.'

'What did he say?'

'On the phone? Just that he was passing through and might see you in Madrid.'

'Madrid?'

'He's going there tonight, he says, if he can make a connection in Milan.'

'Why is he going to Milan?'

'He didn't say.'

'He only arrived an hour or two ago.'

'It wasn't Petroff,' said Prinz Lobkowitz as he removed his jacket, 'it was Cornelius.'

She looked across at the rose and began to laugh, careless of her own hysteria. 'That gives an entirely different complexion to the message. Put the rose in some water, would you, my dear?' She stretched her arms wide on her cushions. 'Good old Cornelius. Gone. On the way to Madrid. Splendid! I feel a new woman already.' She got up and began to march round the room, singing in Spanish. *'Comrades, to the barricades, for honour and justice are ours!'*

Prinz Lobkowitz watched her expressionlessly for a few minutes, then he stepped quickly towards her and seized her by her arm.

Una screamed. His mouth was hot on her streaming eyes.

TEN

In which Catherine Cornelius continues to explore the promises of Eastern wisdom

'Lovely here, isn't it?' Ahmed leaned on the pole and the punt surged forward on the current. Catherine's heart sank.

'Mm,' she said. She was dressed all in white. Her frock was an original Hartnell, very simple, with the natural waistline. She wore two strings of pearls. Her strapover shoes were white. Her Gainsborough hat was white, with a white ribbon; even her little bag was white. Her gloves and her stockings were white. As Ahmed had helped her into the punt he had said how virginal she looked. He had, as she had hoped, been much impressed. He had met her from the station in the taxi which took them directly to the river where his punt was waiting. When he had invited her to Oxford she told him that she had always wanted to go in a punt on the Isis. And here she was. Unless, she thought, it was the Cherwell.

'Is it as nice as you expected?' He smiled down at her. He was looking very nifty himself in his striped blazer, straw hat, creamy Oxford bags and soft off-white shoes. He had eager, handsome features.

'Oh, yes, it's lovely.'

He gave the pole a further shove. 'You're not disappointed?'

'Not at all.' She looked dutifully at the willows, the shrubs and the lawns. Sunlight rippled on the water. Another punt went by, filled with cackling youths; they were sweating.

'This is my favourite stretch,' said Ahmed. 'For punting, at least.'

'Mm.'

'You look so perfect.' His dark eyes were fond. 'Like an old-fashioned picture. You're beautiful, Catherine.'

She smiled.

'Is anything wrong?' he said.

'Oh, no.' She had known her period had started when she got into the taxi, but she had not had the presence of mind to ask him to stop before they reached the river.

'You're tired,' he was saying. 'Perhaps we should have had a cup of tea first. Never mind. You relax there. I'll do all the work.'

'You look very handsome,' she said. She had been looking forward to this for three weeks, ever since she had met him at the party in London. She was a sucker for dark foreigners, particularly Greeks or Indians. It had seemed such a stroke of good luck, meeting him two days after Mrs Goldmann had caught her and Mr Goldmann in his private office out at the studios (he had got her a job as a trainee script-girl) and had made Mr Goldmann fire her on the spot. She had enough money saved for at least six months if she lived at home, and could think of no nicer way of spending her holiday than with Ahmed, who had a rented house in North Oxford where, he had said, she could stay whenever she liked. She had promised him that she would come down for today, to go on the river and look round his college (the vacation had begun so there was little danger in bumping into the two old boyfriends who were also at his college).

'You're flattering me.' It was evident, though, that he agreed with her.

She tried to be amused by her situation, knowing that her nervousness was exaggerating the sensation of seepage. She had tried to spread her dress so that she would not be sitting on it. She could not help glancing down, expecting to feel the dampness at any moment. She stretched the material of the dress away from her as best she could. There was so much of it.

'How is London?' He guided the punt away from the bank. 'You've given up working for that film producer? You told me.'

'Yes.'

'My father was thinking of investing some money in talkies. Not here, though. In America. Someone's starting a new company in Hollywood. Maybe I could use my influence to get you a job.'

'That would be nice.' Carefully, she shifted her position on the padded seat. Her sanitary gear was in her bag. She wondered how she could get him to stop the punt.

'I *am* thirsty,' she said. 'It would be nice to have a cup of tea. Is there somewhere you know, by the river?'

'Oh, yes. But let's go a bit further first.'

'All right.'

She leaned back, closing her eyes, pretending to doze.

'Look,' he said, 'you can see my college from here.'

She opened her eyes. Beyond the trees were some Gothic buildings.

'The dreaming spires.' She became inane.

'Yes.'

They went under a bridge.

As they passed back into sunlight he withdrew the pole letting the punt drift, and climbed over the central seats to reach her. 'I have to kiss you now,' he said romantically. He pushed his face forward and the punt rocked. He kissed her cheeks. She did her best to smile at him. 'I've embarrassed you,' he said.

'Oh, no. I'm sorry.'

He stroked a lock of her hair. 'Why "sorry"? You think I'm forward, don't you?'

'It's not that,' she said. She couldn't tell him the truth. 'I'm just a bit self-conscious. There are so many people about.'

'Of course.' He returned to his end of the punt and retrieved the pole. He seemed angry.

'Don't be cross,' she said.

'No, no.' He plunged the pole into the water and almost overbalanced. It seemed that he swore in his own language. The punt jerked and she had to grip the sides to keep her position. Desperation dominated all other considerations. 'I really would like to stop soon.'

'You're not well?' He was brusque.

'Um . . .'

'Another ten minutes or so and there's a marvellous little place where we can have some tea.' He looked at his watch. 'And there's somewhere I'd like to take you for lunch. It *is* almost lunch-time. If you could wait . . .'

'No, just a cup of tea. I . . .'

'Very well.'

She was fed up. She had anticipated an idyllic day and now she was spoiling it. She tried to explain. 'I'm feeling a bit faint, you see.'

'Quite.' He poled in silence. He scowled. She realized that he thought he had made a fool of himself.

She tried to laugh. 'I'm really not playing hard to get, Ahmed.'

'No, no. It was my fault. Bad manners.'

'Your manners are perfect!' To herself it sounded as if she protested too much. 'Perfect.'

'You're very kind.'

Her tension increased. Harry Goldmann had at least been easy-going. She had forgotten how touchy young men could be. An older man might have guessed what the matter was.

'I've been so looking forward to seeing you.' She tried to start afresh.

'Yes.' He, too, made an effort. 'It seems such a long time ago, doesn't it? Only nineteen days since that awful party. You know Jamie well, don't you?'

'I know Yvette. She's an old friend. You weren't at the wedding.'

'No. I had to go home for a couple of months. My mother was ill.'

'I'm sorry.'

'She's better now. Incidentally, I told my father that we would meet him. He rang this morning to say that he was coming down. He's in London at the moment. Some business. I couldn't make it another day and it was too late to get in touch with you.'

'I'd like to meet him,' she said courageously. She was actually curious about Ahmed's father. Yvette had told her that he was one of the richest men in the Near East. Apparently he also held some sort of religious title.

'I wanted to make this our day.' He was almost accusatory.

Absently, she said: 'I'm sure I'll feel better later.'

'Oh, I didn't mean that.' It seemed that he had.

She became depressed and began to look forward to getting the train home. She had been vague about the train she planned to take back to London, preferring to leave her options open, but now it was obvious that there was no point in her staying. All she could hope to do was keep him interested until she could see him again.

'Here,' he said. She turned. There was a small building ahead. A few tables were scattered on the lawn beside the river. She tried to see if there was a lavatory. All the tables were unoccupied. Ahmed pushed the punt towards the little wooden jetty, jumped out with the line and tied up. Carefully she rose, swaying. She could feel no dampness against her legs. He helped her disembark. They walked along the gravel path to the tea shop. A man in shirt-sleeves was sitting outside; he was adding figures in a small black notebook. He glanced at them as they approached, then pointedly looked down at his book.

'Good morning.' Ahmed was polite. 'Are you open?'

'Open again at three.' The man wrote something in the notebook. 'Sorry.'

Ahmed became ingratiating. 'You couldn't get this lady a cup of tea, I suppose? She's not feeling very well.'

'Sorry. The wife's off.' He continued to write. He seemed deliberately rude.

Ahmed controlled his temper. 'It wouldn't take a moment, surely, to make a cup of tea? That's what you sell, don't you?'

'The wife's off.'

Ahmed's voice became a falsetto. 'If you were a gentleman, sir, you would . . .'

'Well, I ain't.' The man sounded as if he was glad of it.

'Oh, come on,' whispered Catherine. This was unbearable. 'Let's try somewhere else.' She couldn't see a lavatory and could not, now, ask.

'So you won't serve us,' said Ahmed grimly.

'Nothing to serve you *with*,' the man told him. He indicated the 'Closed' notice on the door. 'The wife's got the key. I couldn't get in if I wanted to.'

'You're not a very good representative of your country,' said Ahmed contentiously.

'Never said I was.' The man yawned, frowning at Catherine as if to ask her what she was doing with this black man, anyway. He got up from the bench and put his notebook in his back pocket. He began to walk around the building.

'I should punch his nose for him,' said Ahmed. She was tugging at his arm.

'Let's go, Ahmed.'

'And you know what you'd get if you tried.' The man calmly watched them return to the punt. 'Don't you?'

'I'll never come here again!' Ahmed helped Catherine embark and untied the line.

'Just as well,' the man called happily. 'Good riddance.'

'You know why he was so rude, don't you?' Ahmed's voice was still shrill a few minutes later as they continued down-river. 'He didn't like a white girl and an Asian together. You know that?'

'Oh, he's probably rude to everybody.'

'No. You learn to recognize it.' He scowled again.

At least, thought Catherine with relief, he was no longer furious with her, or, if he was, he was turning all his anger against the man at the tea shop. 'My father could buy and sell the whole of Oxford.' Ahmed glared at the trees and the fields. 'If he knew who I was, he wouldn't have dared to be so insolent.'

'There's lots of people in England just like that,' she said. 'And they're all running tea shops. They want your money but they hate serving you. They resent you.'

'How I loathe this country sometimes.'

'I know what you mean.' She was glad that she was able

to support him. 'English people can be so bloody bogus.'

'A nation of damned hypocrites.' He echoed her swearing.

'Absolutely.'

'What a rotten thing to happen, though. I wanted to give you the loveliest day you've ever had.' He sighed.

'Don't think about it. The river's wonderful. I'm enjoying myself.'

'You don't feel ill any more?' Concern.

She was desperate enough, at this point, to hurl herself willy-nilly into the water. 'Well, I would like to stop, actually. When we get the chance.' She was sure she heard him groan. She looked about her. On the other side of the river was a spinney. If she could somehow get a moment to herself, she might be able to fix it. 'What a pretty wood. Perhaps we could lie in the shade for a while. Would you mind?'

He seemed pleased. 'Not at all.' With a couple of brisk shoves he got the punt across, took hold of an overhanging branch and drew them in to the bank. 'Can you get out by yourself?'

'Oh, easily.' She clambered ashore. The smell of the leaves and the earth was delicious. The wood was dark and thick. She had her opportunity. 'This is lovely.' Pretending to be entranced, she ran into the trees. 'Wait there for me, Ahmed. Wait on the bank. I shan't be long.'

He was laughing. 'Can't I come?'

'No.'

Carefully, lifting her dress, she stepped over the roots and fallen branches until she reached a large oak whose trunk was big enough to hide her. As quickly as she could she took the apparatus from her bag, unwrapped it, pulled up her skirt, pulled her pants to her knees and began adjusting the napkin, fumbling with and almost dropping the pins.

'Catherine!' He was coming through the wood.

'Just a minute!'

He laughed. 'What a mysterious young dryad you are!'

Her pants snagged and in her haste to get them up she almost broke the elastic, but at last it was done and she was able to smooth her dress down, snap her handbag shut with an enormous sigh of relief, and cry: 'Come and find me, Ahmed!'

He must have been close; he reached her almost at once. 'You look radiant,' he said. He was puzzled. 'A moment ago you were so pale. Perhaps the motion of the water doesn't agree with you.'

'Maybe. I've always been a bit prone to sea-sickness. That's why I can't bear the idea of going abroad.' She smiled and held out her arms. 'Hello, Ahmed.'

Bewildered, he approached. 'You are as whimsical as the English climate.' He embraced her, kissing her gently on the lips. 'You're so beautiful. I think I love you, Catherine.'

Her laughter was forced. 'This is a bit sudden!'

'No more sudden than your change of mood.' He released her. He was almost wistful.

She kissed him back. 'Ahmed, I promise I won't be difficult from now on.'

He nodded slowly. 'You must have heard many people proclaim their love for you.'

'Not very many.' She stroked his dark head. 'Let's sit down for a minute. Have you got a gasper?'

From the inside pocket of his blazer he took a gold case, from his trousers he took an automatic lighter, displaying them. 'You'll get your dress dirty,' he said. 'Wait. I'll fetch the cushion things from the boat.' He had become cheerful and eager again. She was glad her risk had been worthwhile.

He came running back from the punt with the corduroy cushions in his arms. He spread them under the tree. 'That's thoughtful of you, Ahmed.' She seated herself demurely. He sat down beside her, leaning on his elbow, one leg crooked, offering her the open case. She selected a Turkish cigarette, thought better of it, but it was too late: he had snapped the case shut, replacing it in his pocket. He clicked the lighter and she accepted the flame. Immediately she inhaled she felt sick. She coughed. 'Oh, it's a bit strong.'

'You'd rather have a Virginia?'

'I think so. It's silly of me.'

'Not at all. I prefer Virginia myself.' Again he proffered the open case.

She let him light the next one as he had lit the first but the smell of the Turkish tobacco was still in her throat. She held the cigarette in the fingers of her left hand, unsmoked, taking a deep breath of the sweet air. 'Ah, alone at last!'

'Yes.' He picked a twig from her hair. 'I've been rushing you about rather, haven't I? You must think me an awful boor.'

'Don't be silly. I'm sorry that I spoiled it all. I really feel a hundred times better now.'

'It wasn't anything to do with me?'

'Of course not! I've been looking forward to coming ever since you asked.'

'You are a most beautiful girl!'

She was cheerful. 'And you're a most handsome man.'

'I'm serious, Catherine.' His voice was low. His black eyes studied her face. He stroked her arm. 'I love you.'

'You don't know me. I'm a terrible person.'

'I don't care if you have other boyfriends.'

'That's not actually what I meant.' She was tender. 'As it happens, there isn't anyone else.'

'Would you be mine? I mean, just mine?'

'I'm not really a flirt, Ahmed. If it works out, there won't be anyone else, honestly.' She wondered why she was giving him such assurances. It was not like her. 'But we don't know one another very well, do we? Look at the trouble I've caused you so far.'

'That wasn't your fault.'

'It might have been.'

'No!' He was emphatic.

'Well, it might have been . . .'

Again, without even attempting to draw her to him, he lunged awkwardly, clumsily kissing her on the cheek. It had not occurred to her before that he might not be very experienced. Now she put her arms round him and kissed him firmly on the lips. He moaned. She released him, conscious of the cigarette in her left hand. She took a puff.

His eyes were anxious. 'I'm going too fast for you . . .'

'Why don't we just lie here and relax for a moment?'

He was upset again. 'All right.' Resting his back against the tree he lit a cigarette for himself. There were always more cigarettes than embraces in these situations, Catherine thought with some amusement. She was beginning to feel hungry.

'I fell in love with you the moment I saw you come into that awful room,' he was saying. 'I wrote some poetry.'

'Have you got it with you?'

'No. It's at the house. I was afraid of losing it.'

'Will you let me read it later?'

'Oh, I want you to.' He turned towards her.

'I'm looking forward to it.' She did her best to put as much warmth as possible into her voice. Actually, the reaction had just come and she would have been glad now to be lying in the relative comfort of the punt, able to enjoy the day. 'What year are you in, then, at your college?'

'Third starts after the vac.'

'And what do you want to be, when you've finished?'

'Well, I'm reading English, you know. I had some thought of becoming a writer, but I'm not sure. My father is keen to take me into the business.'

'But you'd rather write?'

'Oh, I could probably do both. There are public responsibilities, you see, being my father's eldest son, as well as private ones. A man is expected to live and behave in a certain way, in my own country.'

'Quite.' She had only a vague idea of his meaning but, as usual, she found herself attracted to the idea of a man with slightly mysterious responsibilities. They were probably religious duties, she thought romantically. She extinguished her cigarette in the moss. 'Well, perhaps we'd better be moving along, eh?'

'Oh, no. It's lovely here.' He also put out his cigarette, stroking her hair again. She decided to make the best of it and reached to take him by the back of the neck, gathering him in. His body was firm against hers. She could feel his stiffening penis on her thigh. He was half on top of her.

'Oh, Catherine!' One of his hands was trapped behind her. The other began to squeeze her left breast which, as usual, had become sore with the advent of her period. She ignored the pain, tried to get some pleasure from the sensation, kissed him as passionately as she could. His hand stopped squeezing her breast and moved inexpertly down to her groin. Careful not to startle him, she moved the hand back to her breast.

'Catherine, please...'

'Not here, Ahmed.'

'At my house? We could go there now.' His voice was muffled.

'Later. Honestly. I'll explain.'

He continued to slide his penis against her thigh. She moved her own body, hoping to make him come, hoping that that, at least, would satisfy him for the time being. His grip was painful on her swollen nipple. She tried to goad him to a faster rhythm. 'Oh, darling,' she murmured. 'Oh, Ahmed.'

'C-c...'

His grip tightened. He jerked. She could hear his teeth scraping. He hissed. She kissed him.

His eyes were glazed as he looked down at her. He seemed about to ask a question. She hoped that she seemed receptive. 'Would you like another cigarette?' he asked.

'Yes please.'

He fumbled his case and lighter from his pockets, put two Virginia cigarettes between his lips and lit them, handing her one.

'Thanks.'

He was staring through the trees at the river. Suddenly he got to his feet. 'Oh, good God, I'm sorry.'

She was surprised. 'Sorry?'

'You must be disgusted with me.'

'Don't be silly. I'm only sorry I couldn't...'

'Please! It's me! It's me!'

'Ahmed...'

'I love you, Catherine. Really.'

She struggled up, brushing leaves and bracken from her frock. 'Look, this is stupid. I wanted you to – well, you know...'

With an expression of agony he began to pick up the cushions. He seemed about to cry.

'Ahmed, dear.' She approached him. He avoided her, stumbling towards the river. He dropped a cushion. He swore and picked it up again. 'I've made a fool of myself. You can't have any respect for me, Catherine. I behaved like a complete outsider.'

She began to run after him. He reached the punt and flung the cushions into it. He would not look at her. 'Ahmed. It's all right. I'm trying to explain!'

'Why should you have to? I thought you wanted ... I couldn't ...'

'Ahmed. Let's forget about it.' She sat down heavily. The punt rocked and he almost overbalanced into the water. 'We'll have some lunch. You'll feel better, then.'

'If you still want to spend the day with me ...'

'Of course I do.'

He seemed more at ease, but he handled the pole with far less assurance than previously, turning the boat against the current.

'We'll lunch at The Mitre,' he said.

By the time they were eating she had lost her appetite and was regretting that she had ordered such heavy food. She left most of her whitebait and spent the main course trying to make her game pie as small as possible. She drank nearly a bottle of wine and it improved her spirits, though she began to feel sick. When he asked her whether she had to go home that day she said that she had to be home fairly early because her mother was alone and unwell. He received the news with a kind of sinister resignation which made her feel that she should have remained and let him find out about her period for himself. There was every chance, of course, that he wouldn't know, even when confronted with the bulky evidence. He was making her feel inexplicably guilty and at the same time kept behaving as if his few spasms in the wood had filled him with an ineradicable sense of shame. She was reconciled. It was not the first time she had expected to be swept off her feet by a remorseless despot only to find herself saddled with a confused, miserable and self-punishing tyro. Petulantly, she recognized the re-emergence of her maternal instincts as she did her best to cheer him up with promises of pleasure to come.

There was a tense and depressing walk through the almost deserted streets of Oxford until they passed through an enormous, ancient arch and entered the quadrangle of his college. He had his hands in his pockets and was taking an interest in the gravel. 'You can be very cruel,' he was saying. He had said similar familiar things during lunch. 'Don't you realize what you're doing to me? I'm only human. I hate ambiguity, you know. Why can't women be more direct?'

'I am being direct,' she said, but she had no taste for the ritual. 'If I was more direct, Ahmed, I'd shock you.'

'Is it because of my race, the fact that I'm an Asian? Is it because I'm different?'

She laughed. 'Different?'

'You ought to admit it, you know. To yourself, if not to me.' They were climbing some steps. 'This is the oldest part of the building.'

She pushed her lower lip out, to show interest. She found one old stone building much like another and she had made the college trek before, in Cambridge. There didn't seem a lot to choose between the two establishments. 'I'd rather go out with an Asian boy any day,' she said. She felt ridiculous. His accusations were making her say silly defensive things.

'Oh, you're too kind!'

She had anticipated that response. 'I find you sexually attractive, Ahmed.'

He looked nervously up and down the passage. They walked on.

'You see,' she said as they struck some cloisters, 'I've shocked you. You'll think me forward now.'

'No. I think girls should speak their minds. It makes things easier for everyone. But there's such a thing as a time and place, isn't there?'

'I see.' She controlled her impulse to tickle him or to kick his shins or to grab his balls from behind. 'I'm having a period. That's why I've been a bit strange.'

'I've heard that one before,' he said bitterly.

'It has been a bit abused,' she admitted, 'as a face-saver. Well, I've said it. You'll have to take it for what it's worth.' She knew that she must still be drunk. Ahmed certainly was.

He stopped and inspected his watch. 'Try and pull yourself together before my father gets here. He's rather old-fashioned, you know.'

She tugged at his arm. 'Ahmed. Don't be boorish.'

'I am what I am.'

Her laughter was unforced. 'Ahmed! Let's calm down.'

'I am perfectly calm.'

She was sure that her hair and her dress needed attention and thought of asking him where she could go to prepare herself for meeting his father, but then she decided that she did not care.

'We'd better go this way,' said Ahmed. He guided her through another portico. 'This part was constructed in Henry the Eighth's reign, I believe.'

'Ho, ho,' she said. 'What for?' She winked at him. In this sort of situation she found that she could easily fall back into an imitation of her mother. She felt comfortable in the role. 'Did he keep all eight of 'em here?'

'He had six wives,' said Ahmed, 'at different times in his life.'

'Yes,' said Catherine. 'I forgot.'

They walked back through the quadrangle. As they reached the pavement of the street a red and yellow Rolls-Royce pulled up at the kerb. Ahmed smiled, forgetting all conflicts. 'It's the dad!' He became excited. 'He's a bit early. Oh, that's terrific!' He waved at the car. A shadow waved back. With his hand on her elbow, Ahmed drew her towards the limousine, opening the door. 'Hello, father! This is Catherine Cornelius, the girl I mentioned.'

His father was heavier than Ahmed. He had jowls, a thick-lipped, self-indulgent mouth, a prominent nose, an intelligent eye. He was wearing a white European suit and a Panama hat. There were a great many rings on his chubby fingers. Catherine fell for him immediately.

'I'm very pleased to meet you,' she said.

'How do you do, my dear.' He addressed his son. 'Shall we use the car to go somewhere?'

'Good idea,' said Ahmed. 'Hop in, Catherine.' She hopped, sitting beside the older man while Ahmed used one of the collapsible seats opposite.

'What a beautiful young woman you are,' said Ahmed's father. 'Ahmed is very lucky.'

'Thank you,' said Catherine.

Ahmed suggested that the car drive out of Oxford so that they could have tea beside the river. He winked at Catherine, but she did not catch the significance. Winding down the glass panel, he instructed the chauffeur where to go.

Ahmed's father, Catherine began to realize, was embarrassed by her presence. She had the impression that he had come to Oxford for a specific reason and wished to be away as soon as possible. The car drew up outside a fenced area. A number of people were seated in the open, enjoying their tea at tables set on a lawn which ran down to the river. Catherine didn't recognize the place at first. It was only when she saw a man, now in a white coat, serving a family near the river that she understood Ahmed's wink. He had deliberately returned to the scene of their morning encounter. Ahmed instructed the driver to take the car right up to the gate, then he wound down the side window and called to the white-coated man as he walked towards the building. 'Hi! I say, have you a table free?'

The man turned, inspected his territory, pointed to a table that was evidently vacant, and continued to set out places for the customers he was serving. He had not recognized

Ahmed, neither had he been impressed by the large motorcar, but Ahmed was undismayed. He stepped from the Rolls-Royce, helping first Catherine and then his father to the ground. He led them through the gate to the table. They all sat awkwardly on the benches. Ahmed's father had the amused expression of one who was joining in a children's party. He beamed at everyone. 'This *is* jolly,' he said.

The man arrived to take their order and it was then that he remembered Ahmed. He stared Ahmed directly in the eye. 'And what can I do for you?' he asked blandly. 'Set tea for three suit you?'

'Have you strawberries and cream?' said Ahmed staring back.

'Strawberries and cream for three?' The man made a note on his pad. 'And the set tea?'

'That would be lovely,' Catherine said anxiously.

'Cornelius.' Ahmed's father spoke suddenly. 'Any relation to the Barber of Baghdad Cornelius?'

'Barber?'

'The comic opera, you know. German. Last century. A great favourite of mine when I was a student.'

'I'm afraid my family's very ordinary,' she said.

He patted her hand. 'People always say that about their families. They always think it's true, I suppose. Are you of Dutch or of German origin?'

'English,' Catherine told him apologetically. She had the feeling she was being pumped. Perhaps Ahmed's father wondered if her intentions towards his son were honourable.

'I didn't know Cornelius was also an English name.' He seemed disappointed, perhaps with himself, for displaying ignorance.

Ahmed was still glaring after the man who had taken their order. 'He is being deliberately rude,' he muttered.

'I think it's natural to him.' She tried to lighten the atmosphere. 'Ahmed says you're thinking of investing some money in a talkie company.'

'Oh, I'd thought of it. My advisers keep telling me that one should invest in restaurants, couturiers and mass entertainment during times of economic decline. Bread *and* circuses, in fact. Possibly they are right.'

'Oh, I think so. I was working for a film company until recently...'

'Aha! You are an actress!' This seemed to relieve and enlighten him.

'No,' she said, 'just a lowly script-girl, I'm afraid. I worked behind the scenes.'

'Forgive me.' He spoke as if he had insulted her. She seemed to be able to make both father and son feel guilty at the drop of a hat. However, she was getting the picture. Ahmed's father was probably already working out how much she was to cost him when it came to a pay-off.

'That's all right,' she said. 'I'm not a gold-digger from Broadway – or Shepherd's Bush.' She spoke casually, as if she had not interpreted the implications of his questions. 'Anyway, as I was saying, the film company couldn't *help* making money, no matter how bad the films were, as long as they were talkies, of course.'

Evidently he had not seriously considered investing in films. She had not held his attention, although he pretended to be listening. She began to feel self-conscious, wondering if she were still drunk. He took a watch from his fob pocket. 'I hope they will bring the tea soon,' he said. 'I don't want to use any more of your time than necessary.' He stared hard at Ahmed and then seemed to reach a decision, taking an envelope from his jacket. 'This is what I told you about, my boy. I have spoken to Samiyah's father. It is all arranged for next year, when you return.'

Catherine pretended to be interested in the river.

'Oh, thanks,' murmured Ahmed. He put the envelope in his own pocket.

They ate their tea and chatted about how green the English countryside was. When they departed Ahmed left an enormous tip on the table and waved, in a lordly way, to the waiter who watched them go, pocketing the money casually as if it was no more than his due. They all got back into the car.

'Well, I must be returning to London,' said Ahmed's father. 'Where can I drop you?'

'What's the time?' asked Catherine.

'Catherine's going back to London, too,' Ahmed told him.

'Oh, perhaps...' He made the offer reluctantly.

'I'm going on the train,' she said. 'I've a return ticket. I think there's a fast train at five past five.'

Again he withdrew his watch. 'It's almost that now. Are you sure I can't—?'

'Yes thanks.' She would have liked nothing better than to be driven back to London in a comfortable Rolls, but she wanted at least a few moments alone with Ahmed, to try to save something from the situation. Moreover she was conscious of having come between them and she felt sorry for the older man. Doubtless he had wished to see his son alone. On the other hand she had the impression that Ahmed himself was glad of her presence, that he had wished to avoid a heart-to-heart with his father.

'You'd better drop us at the station.' Ahmed sounded miserable. He said something to his father in his native language. His father replied. The name Samiyah was used several times. Ahmed scowled and his father laughed and patted his knee. The car entered the station forecourt.

'Forgive me,' said Ahmed's father. 'It is the worst possible bad manners, to babble away in one's own language like that.'

'Not at all,' said Catherine. She wanted very much to make a good impression on him, though she did not know why. 'It is a beautiful language. It was like listening to music.'

'Oh! Ha, ha!' He clapped his hands together. 'Very fine. Ahmed is extremely lucky! Well, good-bye, Miss Cornelius. I hope we shall meet again.'

'I hope so, too.'

As the Rolls drove away from the station Catherine waved. Ahmed saluted. 'I'm dreadfully sorry about that. It really put the finish on a perfect bloody day, eh?'

She shrugged. 'Not to worry. I expect there'll be other days.'

'I can phone you?'

'We're not on the phone at home. But write. Drop me a postcard.'

'Yes. I'll copy out those poems.'

They walked into the station and looked at the timetable. There was a train to Paddington in three minutes' time. 'That's lucky,' she said.

They found the platform and sat down together on a bench.

'I'm afraid I made the most awful ass of myself,' he said.

'Don't be silly.'

'You're probably used to more sophisticated men, eh?'

'Both you and your father seem to have me firmly placed as a *femme fatale*!' She took hold of his hand, smiling. 'You should see where I live!'

'Oh, no!' He was eager. 'Oh, certainly not. Father might have made that mistake, but he didn't get the impression from me. Honestly, Catherine. I told you. I love you.'

'Oh, all right.'

'I'll send you those poems.'

'That would be lovely.' She kissed his cheek. The train was coming. She got up. 'Well . . .'

'You'll write back?'

'Of course I shall. And I'll see you again, very soon.'

'I hope so,' he said.

'By the way.' The train had drawn into the station. A few people got out. She headed for a second-class carriage. 'Who is Samiyah? Your sister?'

He became evasive. He opened the compartment door for her. Catherine began to laugh and a huge sense of relief swept through her. She knew. 'She's the girl you're going to marry! Your father's just finished the negotiations!'

His expression of alarm made her laugh still harder. She sat down in a corner seat.

'It's nothing to do with me,' he said. 'Really, Catherine.

It's something my father arranged with Samiyah's father years ago. In my country . . .'

'It's all right.' She closed the door and opened the window, leaning out so that she could kiss him on his worried forehead. 'I'll see you soon, Ahmed. Send me those poems!'

'Yes.' He was doubtful. 'You're not upset?'

'Oh, a little.' She thought she had better say that in order to save his feelings. She waved her hand to him as the train trembled and pulled away from the platform. She had quite enjoyed herself, now she reviewed the day. The lady in the opposite corner stared at her in dismay as Catherine began to sing:

> 'There was I, waitin' at the church,
>   Waitin' at the church, waitin' at the church,
> When I guessed he'd left me in the lurch,
>   Lor, 'ow it did upset me!
> Then all at once he sent me round a note,
>   'Ere's the very note, this is what he wrote,
> Can't get away to marry you today –
>   My wife won't let me.'

'You can't beat the old ones, can you dear?' warily remarked the lady in the opposite corner.

ELEVEN

In which Miss Persson attends a meeting of veterans

A fly, one of the last survivors of the season, buzzed wearily about her face. Down below, in the thickly wooded valley, a wounded airship sank towards the waters of the Rhine. She heard the distant echo of a roar, primeval: she might at that moment have fancied herself some Parsifal, her quest Arthurian. It was the autumn of 1933. Although the afternoon sunlight was misty, each detail of the landscape was sharply defined in greens, browns and golds, with the sky a sharp blue-grey above.

She had arrived too late to witness the battle, bound to be decisive, between the tanks and the airships, but now, as she stepped deliberately into the middle of a wide unpaved forest track of churned orange mud, she came upon a camouflaged tank. There was every indication that the machine had been abandoned; its cannon pointed towards the tops of the pines, its engines were silent, a beam of dusty sunshine illuminated a section of its tracks like a delicate searchlight. The tank bore no markings, but seemed to be of a familiar Bavarian type; it was probably, therefore, part of the victorious fleet, unless it had been requisitioned by an enemy.

From within the tank there was a creak of metal. The hatch of the turret began to open. Una Persson cocked her Lee-Enfield and raised it to her shoulder, sighting on the hatch.

As if squeezed from a blackhead a yellow face slid into view. A frightened, bloodshot eye regarded her weapon.

'Oh.' Una lowered the rifle a trifle. 'It's you, you little wanker.'

Jerry Cornelius offered her a weak wink and then, as his confidence increased, raised his shoulders above the level of the hatch. Again, he hesitated. 'Um . . .' He was wondering if she were friend or foe.

'How did you manage to get out of this one?' she asked severely. To have reached his present position he would have to have left the battle early. The odds were that he had not even taken part in the fighting. 'Another breakdown?'

'Oh, come on!' He was getting cocky now. 'I survive, Una.' He pulled his mean body into the soft daylight and began to slide down the dented armour of his tank until his feet touched the thick pile of pine needles raised by his vehicle's tracks. He glanced at his flashy watch. 'Have you seen Frank?'

'It was probably him I shot,' she said. 'I thought it was you. He ran away.' She pointed towards the barbed wire, visible through the trees, the remains of some earlier and forgotten battle. 'He must have left a good deal of himself behind. I've never seen anyone go through wire so fast.'

'You're on foot?'

'My motor-bike ran out of petrol about three kilometres back.'

'So you missed it?'

'Yes. Frank wasn't on our side, was he?'

She could tell by the way that he leaned his back against his tank, with folded arms and crossed legs, that she had frightened him. She knew very well that Frank was with the North Germans and she had not for a moment doubted his identity: Jerry had an entirely different way of panicking. She uncocked her rifle and slung it over her shoulder, approaching him. He was still nervous, but passive.

'Cheer up, Jerry,' she said. 'The war's almost over.'

'It's never fucking over,' he declared moodily. 'I'm getting tired of it, what with one thing and another. I deserve a rest.'

'It must be your monumental self-concern which makes you so charming.' She licked her handkerchief and began to dab at the dirt on his face. 'When you go to pieces, Jerry, you really go to pieces.'

'It's shell-shock,' he said defensively, but his spirits were already improving. 'Did you see our attack? It was a classic.'

'Actually,' she told him. 'I was looking for Petroff. Isn't he with you?'

'If he is, we're really scraping the bottom of the barrel.'

She was offended. She put her handkerchief away. 'You don't like him? I thought you had a lot in common.'

'Bloody hell! Anyway, he's calling himself "Craven" these days, for obvious reasons. You haven't got any time for him either, have you?'

She resisted the urge to defend Petroff, contenting herself with, 'He seems okay to me. Now.'

'Poncing about. He only joined for the uniform.' Jerry began to dust at his own leather combat jacket.

'You've got a scrawny little spirit, Jerry.' Her remark was somewhat hypocritical since she had had exactly the same thought about Petroff. 'Has Petroff stolen your glory, then?'

Jerry yawned and shook his head. 'I don't think so. It's about all he hasn't pinched. In return, I got his crabs.' Reminiscently he scratched his crotch. Una experienced a sympathetic twinge (at least, she hoped it was only sympathetic). She became depressed.

'So you haven't seen Petroff?'

'Didn't expect to. You'll find him at headquarters, if anywhere. Sucking up to any general who happens to be available. He's lost his style, has Petroff.'

'No,' she said to the first part of his remark, 'I radioed.'

'Then he's gone over to the Prussians. Temperamentally, he should have been with them all along. Christ!' He became enthusiastic. 'You didn't see any of them go up, I suppose? We were using incendiary shells as a matter of policy, but we didn't expect them to be using hydrogen. Boom! Boom!'

She sniffed and lit a cigarette. 'You sound like that horrible little friend of yours, Collier. He's not with you today?'

Jerry frowned, consulting his dodgy memory. 'He got left behind during the Shift, didn't he? It's a shame. This is just the sort of fighting he likes best. Better than shooting HTA stuff. Those airships take ages to come down, even when the whole gasbag's burning. What a shame it can't last.'

'So you were actually in the battle?'

'I broke ranks, chasing one of the last of the ships. Her engines had conked out and she was drifting on the wind. I thought I'd be able to pot her, but I only got one shot in before I lost her behind the trees.'

'She's down,' said Una. 'If it's the one I saw a few minutes ago. She was making for the river. Hadn't you better rejoin your squadron?'

He scratched his ear. 'Was there anyone with Frank?'

'Not that I saw.'

'A little bloke, looks a bit like Charlie Chaplin. Toothbrush moustache? Used to be on the Bavarian side?'

'Come off it, Jerry!'

'I'm serious,' he said. 'Frank's trying one of his lone-hand stunts again.'

'There's no possible way he could . . .'

'Frank's an optimist.'

She rubbed her lip. 'So was Petroff. I wonder if they're working together.'

'No. Petroff would have been too frightened. His nerve has gone completely.'

'I wish you'd stop crediting Petroff with your own cowardice.'

'Why shouldn't I? He was my replacement, wasn't he? After Prague?'

'So that's what it's about,' she said. 'I'll never believe the heights of egotism men can rise to.'

'Speak for yourself,' he said. 'After all, Frank's only trying to put things back the way he remembers. It's you who's changing the rules, Una.'

'There aren't any rules,' she told him.

'That's women for you.' He grinned his cheap triumph.

She became impatient. 'Do you think Frank will . . . ?'

'We'll know soon enough, if he has any success. You prefer little wars, don't you? Civil wars.'

'I suppose I do. It keeps things tidier. World wars change things too much, too quickly. They're hard for me to identify with.'

'Personally,' he said, 'I'd like to see one big one get it all over with for good. It's all right for you, you always take the glamorous jobs.'

'Nonsense.' She knocked a piece of dried mud off one of the tracks. 'You're frighteningly simple-minded sometimes, Jerry.'

'*Aquila non capit muscas.*' He shrugged. He was back on form and twice as aggravating. 'Come on. I'll give you a lift.' He helped her climb up the side of the tank and down into the stuffy interior. It stank of disinfectant and after-shave. 'I was sick,' he apologized. 'It's the vibrations. All that bouncing about.'

'I think I'd better drive.' She handed him her Lee-Enfield and seated herself at the controls, squinting into the periscope. 'Is this reverse?'

TWELVE

In which Catherine Cornelius is confronted by the Horrors of War

'When the 'ell you gonna get married, Caff,' said Mrs Cornelius absently as Catherine pulled on the jacket of her suit, buttoned it up and tugged it into place over her hips.

'There's no one *to* marry, is there, Mum?'

Mrs Cornelius folded the wet newspaper around the crumbs and vegetable scraps and hesitated before she took the lid off the waste-bin and threw the bundle in. 'Ask Sammy if 'e got that bit of pork for me, will yer, Caff? On yer way ter work'll do.'

'All right, Mum.'

It was impossible to tell how Mrs Cornelius leapt from one association to another. 'Still, ya always come 'ome in the end, doncher?'

'Yes, Mum.' She was trying on the turban she had just bought with the last of her coupons.

'More'n ya c'n say for them two.' She meant Catherine's brothers. 'But Frank's doin' well, I 'ear, these days.'

'In the army?'

Mrs Cornelius guffawed. 'Wot d'*you* fink?'

'I thought he was called up.'

'Well, yeah, but 'e left, didn't 'e? I suppose that's why 'e didn't come 'ome. There was some chaps from the army come rahnd. You know, arskin' after 'im.'

'When was this?'

'Baht a monf ago.' Mrs Cornelius chewed at a piece of pastry. 'When did you git back?'

'Week before last.'

'That's it, then. A monf.'

'And Jerry?'

'Come off it!' Mrs Cornelius spluttered with mirth. 'Prob'ly workin' for the bloody Germans.' There was a certain pride in her tone. 'I *told* yer all this, Caff.'

Catherine's memory had become very hazy of late. 'Oh, yes. I remember.'

Mrs Cornelius gave the suit her appraisal. 'Not bad. *Very* up-to-date. We don't age much in our family, do we?'

'I suppose we don't.' It was hard to see anything in the long frameless fly-specked mirror. She shook out her perm and patted at it. 'That's better.'

Mrs Cornelius was rooting about in the junk on her mantelpiece. 'There was a postcard from Jerry. From France.'

'What, recently?'

'Nah! Two years ago! 'E'll turn up, jest like you. When the war's over. Wiv nowhere ter stay but 'ere.' Mrs Cornelius abandoned the search. 'It was a nice pee-see, though.' She sighed and waddled to her chair. 'Cor! It takes it aht o' yer, dunnit?'

'What?' Catherine carefully turned her lipstick a fraction of an inch above the case and began to apply it.

Mrs Cornelius shrugged. 'Life.' She began to leaf through a copy of *Lilliput*, looking at the pictures. 'Blimey! It's disgustin'. Feel like puttin' the kettle on fer a cuppa, Caff?'

'Yes, all right.'

Catherine finished making up and went to fill the kettle. Through the dusty window she could see all the way across to the ruins on the corner of Ladbroke Grove and Elgin Crescent, where the bomb had landed. 'What's disgusting?'

'These nude pitchers.' Mrs Cornelius dropped the magazine to the pile beside the chair. She yawned. ' 'Ow's it goin', then? Up at the pub?'

'Not bad.'

'Must see a lot of fellers in there, eh?'

'They're mostly old, Mum. There's a war on, you know.' Catherine lit the gas and put the kettle on the ring.

'Soljers on leave, though.'

'Some. I don't fancy soldiers.'

'You're not like me there. I never could resist the buggers.'
Mrs Cornelius fidgeted in the chair.

'They go off and get killed, don't they?'

'Well, some of 'em do, yeah.'

'So there's no point in marrying one, is there?'

'Didn't say there was.'

'Oh, I thought that was what it was all about.'

'You ought ter fink abaht it, though, Caff.' Mrs Cornelius was serious. 'I was first married at sixteen.'

'And deserted by the time you were eighteen. With three kids.'

Her mother smiled reminiscently.

Catherine looked at her wrist-watch. It was half past ten. She was due at the pub just before eleven. She preferred the lunch-time hours. It was often busier, but much less confused. Sammy had got her the job last week. The pub was just across the road from his pie shop. Over the years Sammy had found employment for all the Cornelius family in the district, but none of the jobs had ever lasted long and some of them had turned out to be decidedly dodgy. But he had given Frank his first real start, selling imperfect clockwork toys off a stall in the Portobello market. From that Frank had gone on to cut-price frocks and invested his profits in stolen booze to re-label and sell to the posh pubs around South Ken. The army must have interrupted a steady upward movement in his career. He would be in the black market by now. A spiv. It was funny that someone as doggedly honest as Sammy had so many contacts in what you might call the benter side of the wholesale–retail trade. Poor old Sammy, she thought. She heating the teapot over the steam from the kettle, warming the leaves that were still in there. Tea was short. Her mother rarely benefited from Frank's business ventures. She half-filled the pot and stirred the brew round. She put the lid on the pot.

'There you are, Mum. I'll let it stand a bit, shall I?'

'Better.' Mrs Cornelius was leaning over the arm of her grease-spotted chair, searching amongst her magazines for one that was not completely read through. She extracted a yellowed copy of *Red Letter* and began to look at the first story, rubbing at a flea bite on her neck as she concentrated.

'I don't know how you can tell those stories apart,' said her daughter. 'The plots are all the same.'

Mrs Cornelius grunted, turned two pages rapidly and set the *Red Letter* aside. 'I've read it,' she said. 'Wot?'

'Shall I get you another on my way home?'

'Book?'

'What d'you want?'

'*Peg's Paper*'ll do.'

'They're not printing it any more.'

'Bloody war.' Many of Mrs Cornelius's favourite weeklies had disappeared because of the paper shortage. 'Well, get me wot you can, Caff.' She considered this. 'Don't get me nuffink like *Picture Post*, though. I've 'ad enough o' the war. All they seem ter do . . .'

'I'm with you there,' said Catherine. 'You want to forget about it, don't you? While you can.'

'We could all go up tomorrer.' Mrs Cornelius spoke with some satisfaction. 'I might drop in for 'alf a pint, if I go aht. If I do, I'll get me own book.'

'Okay.'

'But arsk Sammy abaht that pork.'

'If you come in, I'll go straight on from work,' said Catherine.

'Where ya goin'?'

'West End. Pictures.'

'You be careful. Wot's on?'

'Some comedy. With Cary Grant.'

'Good, is 'e?'

'He's all right.'

'Goin' on yer own?'

'No.' She was deliberately mysterious.

'So you '*ave* got a feller!'

'No!'

'Oo yer goin' wiv, then?'

'Girl friend.'

'Oh. Do I know 'er?'

'No.'

'Where d'ya know 'er from?'

'I met her up the labour exchange. You know – just after I got back.'

'So she's local.'

'Portland Road.'

'Wot's 'er name?'

'Rebecca.'

'Rebecca wot?'

'You're not really interested, Mum.'

'I am. Honest.'

'Her name's Rebecca Ash.'

'Maybe she's got a boyfriend – oo's got a friend.'

'Her boyfriend was killed. He was in the RAF. Battle of Britain.'

'Oh. Poor fing.'

'So you can see why I don't want anything to do with anyone who's in the war.'

'Were they engaged?'

'Due to get married. He was shot down a week before the wedding.'

'Oh, dear!' Mrs Cornelius was fascinated. Her eyes gleamed. It seemed to Catherine (and perhaps it was unfair of her) that this story was a good substitute for *Peg's Paper*. Maybe that was why so many fiction magazines died during a war. There was plenty of drama going on in real life.

'Were they young?'

'That's enough, Mum. I don't like to talk about it. Neither does Rebecca. She's had a lot of tragedies. She's got relatives in Germany. In the concentration camps.' Catherine wished she hadn't offered this information. It was whetting her mother's appetite.

'She Jewish, then?'

'Her mother was. Her father was Polish. He got wounded in the Spanish Civil War.' Catherine was proud of her new friend's romantic ancestry and she continued in spite of her better judgment. 'He was in Russia during the revolution, but he escaped.'

'An aristocrat?'

'They had a castle and land in Poland. They lost everything. Her real name's something like Aserinski, but they changed it when they settled in England.'

Mrs Cornelius had come to life. 'You ought to bring 'er rahnd, Caff. Poor kid. What 'appened to 'er mother?'

'She died of TB.'

'Tut-tut,' said Mrs Cornelius sympathetically, avidly. 'And 'er dad?'

'He started getting these dizzy spells. He was run over by a bus.'

'Poor *fing*.'

Catherine adjusted her turban on her head and ran her tongue round her red lips. 'Must go, Mum. Shall I pour you a cup?'

'There's a love ...'

Catherine took one of the new Woolworth's cups she had bought and measured milk and sugar into it before she poured the tea on top. 'There you are.'

'Fanks, Caff.' Her mother stirred the tea. 'Probably murdered, eh?'

'Who?'

'Yore friend's dad.'

'Why?'

'Russians. They never let anyone go.'

Catherine shook her head. 'Likely. Or maybe it was the bus company found out he hadn't paid his fare from Shepherd's Bush.'

'Don't joke about it, Caff. Ya never know.' Mrs Cornelius relaxed with her tea, her mind full of fantasy. ' 'Ow terrible, though ...'

Catherine Cornelius left her mother with her dreams. She had now made it completely impossible for Rebecca Ash ever to meet her mother. It would be altogether too embarrassing.

When she got to the corner of Blenheim Crescent and Kensington Park Road she saw that Sammy's shutters were still up and there were no fresh smells of cooking, though the stale ones lingered. She banged on the door. 'Sam!' She still had plenty of time to get to work for the pub was a couple of seconds away, on the opposite corner. The Blenheim Arms. The day was cool and grey. She wished that she had brought her mac. She heard a sound from the back of the shop.

'Sammy!'

Carpet slippers shuffled on the tiles of the floor. The blind was raised. Sammy stood behind the glass. He was wearing his apron already, over a roll-neck-pullover and corduroy trousers. He smiled at her. ' 'Ullo, young Cathy.' He unbolted the door at top and bottom, turned the key. 'Wot can I do fer you?'

'Morning, Sammy. Mum wondered about the pork.'

He tapped the side of his nose. 'Don't worry. 'Nuff said, eh? I'll drop it round. Or shall I pop it across to you at the pub?' He wiped a fat, greasy forehead which had been tanned by years of exposure to his pans and his gas-jets. 'An' I'll bring you over a fresh pork pie, eh?'

'Well,' she said, 'I might not be going home after I leave work.'

'Fair enough. I'll get the lad to take it down. 'Ow you keepin', Cathy? The job okay?'

'Fine thanks, Sam.'

'You ought to be doin' better, though,' he said, as if he had failed her. 'Receptionist or secretary or somethin'. What'd they say up the Labour?'

'It's war work mostly. Factory jobs.'

'Oh, you're too good for that.'

'I'd do it if I had to,' said Catherine, 'but the job at the pub gives me free afternoons. That's something.' She glanced across the street. 'Well, they're opening up. See you, Sammy.'

'Take it easy, Cath.' He shut his door and drew down the blind.

Mrs Hawkins was already behind the bar. 'Cold enough for you?' she said as Catherine came in.

'Not half,' said Catherine. 'Where do you want me today?'

'Better stay in the private bar, love. I'm sorry about last night.'

'He was drunk,' said Catherine. 'He didn't mean any harm.'

'The way he grabbed you! Filthy old devil.'

Catherine grinned. 'He wasn't really up to much else, was he?'

Mrs Hawkins folded her thin arms under her breasts and roared. She was a pleasant, sensitive woman. Mr Hawkins was inclined to be as drunk as his best customers by the end of an evening and she was used to helping him to bed, often before the pub shut. He was a sweet-natured man and Mrs Hawkins didn't seem to resent his habits. 'Want a little something to warm you up, love?'

'I'd better not,' said Catherine. 'It never does me much good during the day.'

'I know what you mean.' Mrs Hawkins raised the hinged section of the bar to allow Catherine through. 'I don't think he'll show up for a day or two, though. Not after what you gave 'im!' She roared again. 'A real touch of the Knees Up Mother Browns, eh?'

Perhaps because of last night's trouble the pub was not as busy as it normally was and Catherine spent most of her time polishing glasses and, when her mum came in at about half past one, chatting.

' 'Ad ter get a *Woman's Weekly* in the end,' said Mrs Cornelius, settling herself on a stool at the corner of the private bar and sipping her half of bitter. 'There's only a few stories in that. Mostly it's 'ints.'

'How to make a pie out of two bits of gristle and some mouldy turnips,' said Mrs Hawkins, coming through to get some bottles of light ale for the public bar. 'It makes you laugh, doesn't it, Mrs C?'

'Not 'alf.' Mrs Cornelius drained her mug. 'Or 'ow ter get the caviar stains out o' yer mink stole!'

They all enjoyed this joke.

'All right!' called Mrs Hawkins, detecting a murmur of impatience from the public bar, 'just coming.' She winked at Catherine and her mother and left with an armful of light.

'Give us anuvver, Caff,' said Mrs Cornelius holding out her glass mug.

As Catherine pulled the handle of the beer pump, her mother said: 'I saw Sammy. 'E reckons we can both go rahnd to 'im fer Chris'mas. Watcher fink?'

'Nice.' She put the half pint on the bar. 'Only I might not be home over the whole of Christmas.'

'Wot? Workin' 'ere?'

'No. I sort of partly promised Rebecca that I'd spend Christmas with her. At her flat.'

'Oh.'

'She'll be on her own, you see.'

'Yeah.' Mrs Cornelius reached for her drink. 'So will I be, won't I?'

'Not if you're with Sammy.'

'Well, Sammy's not family, is 'e? Not really.'

'Maybe Frank'll turn up. Or Jerry?'

'Some 'opes. Ah, well.' Mrs Cornelius was genuinely trying to hide her disappointment with the result that Catherine, in turn, felt genuinely guilty.

'The only family she's got is probably in Germany, you see, Mum. In a concentration camp. They might not be alive at all. So . . .'

'Oh, yeah. I can see that. Well, that's the time for charity, innit? Chris'mas. So you won't be arahnd fer Chris'mas dinner, even?'

'Well, I'll try to get over.'

'Wish y'd told me a bit earlier.'

'It's not December yet, Mum.'

'No, but there's all the arrangements. Y'know 'ow it creeps up on yer.'

'There is time to change the arrangements.'

'Yeah.' Her mother finished the beer and began to slide her

bulk from the stool. She buttoned up her moulting fur collar. 'Okay, then, Caff. See yer later. Cheerio.'

'Cheerio, Mum.'

Catherine felt depressed after her mother had left. She would have been glad of a few more customers to serve, to take her mind off her guilt. Instead Mrs Hawkins came back at a quarter past two.

'You might as well get off now, Cath, if you like. Still going to the pictures?'

'Yes.'

' 'Ope it's a good 'un.'

'Cary Grant,' said Catherine.

'Is 'e the one with the moustache? *Gone With The Wind*? Or the other one?'

'The other one,' said Catherine. 'Thanks, Mrs Hawkins.' She would go straight to Rebecca's, even though it had begun to drizzle outside. She couldn't face going home to pick up her coat. She got her bag from where she kept it under the bar and swung the strap over her shoulder. 'Well, bye-bye, then. See you this evening.'

'Bye-bye, love.' Mrs Hawkins winked at her. She probably thought Catherine was going to meet a boyfriend.

Catherine walked hurriedly down Blenheim Crescent, crossed Ladbroke Grove, went down the rest of Blenheim Crescent, the posher bit with its big trees and front gardens, into Clarendon Road and then round into Portland Road. Rebecca actually owned the little terraced house and had done it up beautifully, with the number in brass figures, 189, on an apple-green door. The area railings were also painted apple-green and the window frames were a sort of peach colour. Rebecca lived on the ground floor and basement and rented the rest to a couple, both musicians with the Royal Philharmonic Orchestra, who had two children. Rebecca had inherited the house from her parents.

Catherine rang Rebecca's bell.

'You're a bit early.' Rebecca opened the door. She was wearing a long pink quilted housecoat. 'Come in.' She had thick black curly hair and large black eyes. Her eyebrows were high and plucked thin. She had a long face, with full lips and a large, broad nose. She often described her features as horsey, but Catherine insisted that she had the classical beauty of an ancient Greek goddess. She looked a little bleary, as if she had just woken up. She had been, until recently, a cellist in a string quartet, until the two male members had been conscripted for war work in the pits. Now she sometimes filled in for another cellist who lived in the country and couldn't always get to London.

Rebecca led the way down to the basement. Originally it had been two separate rooms, but now about a third of it was a kitchen and the other two thirds were a sort of bed-sitter. She scarcely ever used the two rooms upstairs, unless she was practising.

A record was playing softly on the big cabinet electric gramophone. It was piano music. Catherine thought it was probably Mozart, who was her favourite composer. She sat down on the wide divan opposite the gramophone. 'That's beautiful. Is it Mozart?' She felt diffident about music in Rebecca's company.

Rebecca nodded. 'Coffee? It's fresh.'

'Thanks.'

Rebecca took the aluminium coffee-maker off the stove and placed two large breakfast cups on the table. The flat was as neat as usual. Even the divan, which was also her bed, had been made up. 'I had a job last night,' said Rebecca. 'Filling in for Stephen, as usual. So I was late getting in.' She yawned, as if to emphasize her remark. 'How are you, dear?'

Catherine found that she was also yawning. 'I was all right up to about an hour ago. Then my mum came into the pub.'

Rebecca was sympathetic. She brought the coffee over and sat down with Catherine. 'That's the new suit, is it? It's smart.' She fingered the material of the skirt. 'Oh, it's lovely.' She kissed Catherine on the cheek, adding softly, 'Nice to see you, love.'

Catherine squeezed her arm. 'I've missed you. It's been two days.'

'Seems a lot longer.' Rebecca stretched and put her coffee on the Indian rug at her feet. 'What was the row about? With your mum.'

'Oh, nothing. It wasn't really a row . . .'

'Didn't she want you to go out?'

'No. It's all right.' Catherine didn't want to make Rebecca feel as guilty as she had felt. 'If you still want to go to the pictures I thought that Cary Grant would be nice.'

'Well, let's think about it,' said Rebecca. She seemed distracted.

'Are you okay, Rebecca? There's nothing wrong?'

'No!' Rebecca patted her knee. 'No, I've just woken up, that's all.'

'D'you want to try the suit on, before you get dressed? You said you wanted to, remember?'

'That's a good idea.' The record finished. Rebecca went to the gramophone and removed the big twelve-inch disc. 'Is there anything you'd like to hear?'

'Whatever you want.'

'I won't put anything else on for the moment.'

'Right-ho.' Catherine reached out to take Rebecca's hand. 'Come here and give me a proper kiss. Oh, I've missed you such a lot!' Rebecca fell on to the bed beside her and Catherine hugged her, kissing her on the mouth. 'Oh, Rebecca.' They had become lovers almost as soon as they had met. Catherine had seduced Rebecca here after they had got drunk one night at a club, when two airmen had tried to pick them up. As Rebecca had said, a little self-consciously, the following morning, at least you could be fairly certain that if you fell in love with a girl you weren't likely to worry about her being called up.

'I love you very much,' Rebecca said. 'I always will, Catherine.' Her big eyes were full of tears. Her face was intensely serious. They kissed again. 'It's wonderful. It never for a moment felt strange. It happened so naturally.' Catherine smiled and stroked her friend's cheek. The words were familiar but she always relished hearing them. 'Shall we just stay in, then, this afternoon?' she suggested.

'I'd like to go to bed,' said Rebecca, 'and have a cosy day together.'

'I'd like that, too.' Catherine lay back on the divan and pushed her shoes off her feet. 'That's better!'

'The marvellous thing is,' said Rebecca, 'that we'll always be friends, no matter what happens to us.'

'Yes,' agreed Catherine. She unbuttoned her jacket and began to fiddle with the hooks and eyes of her skirt. She clambered out of the suit. 'That's better.' In underclothes, stockings and suspenders, she padded across the floor to put the suit on a chair. 'There you are, when you want to try it.' She undid her suspenders and carefully rolled her stockings down her legs. It was hard enough getting any kind of stockings, these days. She took off her girdle. 'Phew! I'm putting on weight, I think.'

'I like you a little bit dumpy,' said Rebecca. 'It makes me feel better. That lovely pink skin. I'm jealous. We're like Snow White and Rose Red, one as dark as dark can be and the other the fairest of the fair!'

Wearing her slip, Catherine came back to the bed. She got into it with a sigh. 'This is the most comfortable bed I've ever slept in.'

Rebecca drew the heavy red curtains. 'It's foggy outside now. Was it foggy on your way here?'

'No. There's no point in going to the West End. We'd never get home.'

Rebecca took off her housecoat. She had large, pendulous breasts. They were the only thing about her that Catherine didn't like; she had always preferred small, rounded breasts, like her own. 'Move over,' said Rebecca. 'You're on my side.'

Catherine shifted towards the wall.

'You're not too cold, are you?' Rebecca asked. 'The radiators went off in the night.' She had a delicious, musty smell to her.

'Oh, no. Warm as toast. I'm just a bit tired. Tireder than I realized. To tell you the truth, I'm a bit nervy. It must have been Mum.'

'What did she say?'

Catherine did not want to mention Christmas. 'Just the usual stuff. She started off by telling me I ought to get married. I told her this wasn't exactly the right time to be thinking of the future, something like that. Then I said I was seeing you and she asked a lot of questions.'

'You think...?'

'Nothing like that. She just wanted to know what you did and who your parents were. She got very interested when I said you were half Jewish and half Polish.'

Rebecca was amused. 'Why? Is she anti-semitic?'

'No. There's more than a drop of Jewish blood in our family, anyway. Mum's not like that. But she hasn't much to occupy her mind, so she takes an interest in other people's business. You know the sort of thing.'

Rebecca nodded. 'And that was all?'

'Yes, really.'

'Why don't you turn over and let me massage your back for a bit. It'll help you relax.'

'Would you mind? I'd love that.'

'Turn over, then.'

Catherine pulled away her cushions and settled herself with her arms at the sides of her head. Rebecca began to stroke her body. 'Is that nice?'

'Perfect.'

Rebecca massaged her shoulder blades.

'Are you sure that job at the pub's right for you?'

'It's all there is, apart from helping with the war effort.'

'It's not so much the work as the people you have to deal with. That must be a strain.'

'It's not too bad. Last night there was a bit of trouble. An old bloke took a shine to me. I'd been ever so nice to him. I thought he was harmless. Just before closing time I was on the other side of the bar and he made a grab for me. Hands everywhere. You know. Without thinking I gave him one where it hurts most.'

Rebecca said: 'You poor thing. But that's what I meant, really.'

'That's the only time it's happened. Oh! Smashing! Ah!'

Her muscles seemed to be expanding under Rebecca's hands. Rebecca moved her body closer so that her vagina was resting gently against Catherine's hip. The massage continued.

'I wish there was something you wanted to do,' said Rebecca.

'I'm not trained for anything. I left school at fourteen.'

'You ought to go to art school, or apply for RADA or something. You've got plenty of talent for anything.'

'You're not the first to tell me that. Only I can't paint, I can't act, I can't write. My talent seems to be for making people think I've got talent. My brother Frank's got a talent for making money. My brother Jerry's got a talent for causing trouble...'

'Is Jerry the one you...'

'Yes.'

The pressure of Rebecca's vagina on her thigh became a touch harder. Catherine turned her head so that she could see her friend. 'That excites you, doesn't it? The idea of me and my brother.'

Rebecca nodded.

'It's only the idea that makes it any different,' said Catherine. 'Once you get used to it, it's no different at all. Like everything else. Except maybe more friendly.'

'Like us.'

Catherine didn't reply. 'As I was saying – all our family are thought to be talented, but we haven't a real success amongst us. No education for one thing, of course. No will to improve ourselves, I suppose. Frank's an artist when it comes to thinking up shady deals. Jerry's quite a good guitar player. Jazz and that, though. I don't know what we'd have been good at, if things had been a bit easier for mum.'

'Your dad went off?'

'My mum must be the most deserted woman in the world. *She's* got a talent for losing husbands!'

'That was Cornelius.'

'That's what he called himself. Apparently he used the name "Brown", too. Maybe that was why mum was so interested in you. My dad was supposed to be Russian, or half-Russian. I can't remember. She's got a lot of different stories – probably all from him! Oh, that feels so good.' She fell silent as Rebecca massaged her just below the ribs.

Rebecca began to kiss her head and ears.

'Just a minute,' said Catherine. 'I'll take my slip off.'

When she had removed the last of her clothes, she lay on her back while Rebecca kissed her body. The kisses were delicate, fluttering against her skin and arousing her only very slowly. She knew that Rebecca was already very much aroused and this also had the effect of increasing her desire, but she was enjoying the sense of anticipation and happily could have spent the best part of the afternoon in quiet loveplay if she had not been aware that she had to be back at work in just over two hours. She glanced at her watch. It was almost three o'clock. She decided to concentrate on helping Rebecca reach orgasm, stroking her, whispering to her, scratching her lightly, then reaching down past Rebecca's bottom and touching her at the base of her vagina. Rebecca began to push herself against Catherine's thigh, moving rapidly up and down and from side to side, gasping, her wet mouth against Catherine's ear and cheek, calling out as she came.

Rebecca's orgasm had aroused Catherine more than she had anticipated. Kissing her friend, she rolled again on to her stomach and began to masturbate. In a moment, Rebecca started to stroke her again. The orgasm was short and intense; it left her feeling edgy. She turned on her side and they embraced. 'That was terrific,' said Rebecca. 'Are you okay?'

'Oh, yes. Fine.'

'You're not, though, are you?'

'It can't work every time.'

'Is there anything . . .?'

'No. Maybe another massage if I don't relax. I'm sorry.'

'It wasn't anything I was doing wrong?'

'Don't be daft. My mum really got me worked up. I'm sure that's it.'

'Are you sure she doesn't think anything?'

'No. She was a bit disappointed when I told her I'd be spending Christmas here.'

'Oh.' Rebecca seemed startled.

'You asked me to. If . . .'

'I want to spend Christmas with you, Cathy. I couldn't want anything more. But there's a chance I won't be here now. So if it means a nasty scene with your mum . . .'

Catherine could not understand. 'You didn't say anything about going away.'

'I hadn't made up my mind, then.'

'You were so keen on us being together over Christmas.'

'I know. I still am.'

'What hadn't you made up your mind about?'

'I didn't tell you. I didn't want to be talked out of it. And you would have talked me out of it. I knew you would. It's silly. It's all mixed up with Robert and self-denial, and guilt about his being killed, but it seemed the right thing to do.'

'Do what?'

'I applied to join the WAAFs.' Rebecca began to cry. 'I got my letter yesterday. I've been accepted.'

'Oh, Christ!'

'So I don't know where I'll be at Christmas, you see. But if they let me come home, of course, I want to be with you.'

'Oh, fuck!'

'If it wasn't for the war . . .'

At this rate, thought Catherine, just before depression engulfed her, people are going to start handing me white feathers.

It seemed that everybody she knew was marching off to war.

THIRTEEN

In which Captain Una Persson considers questions of comfort

It was not uncommon for Una Persson to experience the sensation of *déjà vu*; but here, in the ruins of Oxford, with a discoloured mist rising from the damp ground, it overwhelmed her; she felt it as another might feel vertigo. She became dizzy, her identity began to fall away from her; she panicked. The ruins re-adjusted themselves, shifting their proportions: a building which had been almost whole now vanished, another was partially resurrected. Then they were stable again. Una thought she felt her clothes writhing on her body as they, too, were re-arranged.

'Some sod's up to something.' She spoke aloud. The sound of her voice brought her back to sanity. 'But then,' she added, 'some sod's always up to something.' She took deep, regular breaths to slow down her heart-rate. She leaned heavily against the balustrade of the broken bridge where she had been standing studying the river. The river had scarcely altered: thick green weed grew in it. There was slime; a strong stench of stagnation.

The bomb which had taken out Magdalen College had also destroyed a fair amount of the bridge's superstructure, but it still functioned. Una looked at one of her watches, wondering if she had actually agreed to meet someone here. She could not remember making the arrangement or with whom she had made it. She turned up the collar of her black trench coat and put her bare, cold-reddened hands into her pockets which were filled with pieces of paper, rags and unspent cartridges. From curiosity she removed one of the pieces of paper. It was folded several times, was grey with dirt and tattered. She opened it. The letter was written in Cyrillic and at first she assumed it was from a Russian, then she realized that the letter was in Greek. It was headed Hydra, Monday, and referred to recent disastrous events in Athens. Substantially it was a love-letter but the signature had been on a subsequent page. She searched through her pockets for the missing page without success. A creased visiting card from Naomi Jacobsen, 77 Blvde St-Michel, Paris, rang a bell. She turned the card over. Something had been written on it in pencil and was now almost completely obscured save for the words 'Cornelius' and 'relationship'. She pushed the stuff back into her pocket.

She began to wonder about the date. The ruins were not new; they could be up to a hundred years old. She considered the possibility of an overshoot, which would also explain the sensation she had first felt upon arrival. She decided to wait no more than five minutes longer. She strode to the other side of the bridge, noticing how silent everything was, how still, as if all life had ceased to exist in the area.

It had begun to rain. The drizzle either stank as forcefully as the river or it brought out more of the existing smell. She wished that she had a hat. She heard a footfall. A man came out of some trees by the river bank and climbed carefully towards the bridge, slipping in the wet moss and grass. He reached the bridge, tested a piece of stone before using it to lever himself up and stand coughing into a large white handkerchief. He wore grey flannels, a tweed jacket with leather patches at the elbows; a dark green polo-neck sweater, a woollen scarf. His hair was turning grey. He also wore horn-rimmed glasses. Una suspected the outfit. It was too typical of a don, she thought, to be anything other than a disguise. He stopped coughing. 'Miss Persson, of course?' His voice was without vibrancy: English middle-class. 'Or should I say Captain?' He seemed friendly. 'I'm Chapman. We have met, actually, but you probably don't remember.'

'Munich?'

He laughed. 'Hardly! It was just after the last war. In Geneva.'

Una did not remember. She was not sure, at that point, where Geneva was. She nodded, offering her hand.

He hesitated, now, before taking it, but more from surprise, she guessed, than reluctance. The shake was hearty, unspontaneous, like an Englishman trying the flamenco. She began to dislike him.

'Well, Mr Chapman.' She rubbed her hands together. 'Where to now?'

'The child's in my rooms, of course. I left her there for safety. Did you bring any transport of your own?'

'None.'

'Wise, really. But it will take a little while to arrange from our end. You'll stay to lunch, I hope.'

'Thank you.'

'Good. You were dropped in, yes?'

She ignored the question. 'What sort of transport can you offer?'

'We've still got a couple of autogyros that are airworthy. One of those should get you to London.'

'Fine.' She now knew her destination, but was still unclear about her mission. Chapman seemed to sense this.

'They did brief you all right?'

'There wasn't much time. If you could outline the basic stuff again I'd be grateful.'

'Of course. We go this way.' He pointed through the dark, unhealthy trees in the direction from which he had come. 'You'd better let me be first. We can't afford to do anything about improving the roads. Oxford is supposed to be completely deserted, so we're a bit nervous of advertising.'

They slid down the slimy bank. He led her along a squelching path through the trees and bushes. 'We're lucky that the School's still operating in any way. Makes you value learning a bit more, eh? When I look back! Nothing more ludicrous, is there, than a middle-class Marxist English don.' He chuckled. 'Still, by and large we manage to keep ourselves pretty comfortable here. And there are a few traditions worth preserving.'

'I never knew one,' murmured Una.

'What? Aha! Yes, of course.' He seemed nervous of her, anxious for her good opinion. What sort of authority was she representing?

A bramble snagged the skirt of her coat. She stopped to pull free. He waited for her, his breath steaming, his eyes shifting. His insecurity seemed to increase whenever they were in the open. He led her across a marshy lawn. The drizzle had almost stopped and in the distance she could see that two wings of a college were still intact, though surrounded by ruins. She thought she detected a dim light in one of the grease-papered windows. It was even more overcast than it had been when she arrived. She wondered if it were, after all, twilight. Then she remembered that Chapman had mentioned lunch.

'The cloud's very low,' she said.

'Yes,' he replied in some relief. 'Yes.' Blocks of rubble began to appear in the soft ground. They reached a plateau of broken brick; they climbed over fractured granite until they could look down at a door. Some of the wreckage had been cleared, enough to make it convenient to enter and leave the door. He slid down and knocked on the iron-bound oak. 'This was blown straight off its hinges,' he said with pride, 'but was otherwise completely unharmed. Good wood, eh? It stood up to Cromwell, too.'

The door was opened by a middle-aged woman holding a candle. She had pleasant, frightened features. She darted a smile at Una before she had gone back into the shadows. Una wondered what sort of enemies induced such behaviour. She became melancholic.

'This is Miss Moon,' said Chapman, closing the door behind them. 'Ah! Safe and sound again, Eunice.'

'Would you like a cup of tea?' asked Eunice Moon. She wore a crumpled tweed skirt, a grey cardigan and a darned maroon sweater. The strength of her features was obscured by folds of coarse skin as if she had been at one time much fatter. There were pronounced bags under her mild grey eyes.

'I'd love one,' said Una, anxious to respond as comfortingly as possible, at least until she had worked out what she was supposed to be doing here.

Eunice Moon held the candle above her head, leading the way up stone steps covered with threadbare coconut matting. They reached a gallery. She held the candle over the carved balustrade. 'That was the hall,' she said. 'We don't use it now. It's impossible to heat, for one thing.' Una thought she heard the movement of rats in the darkness below. They ascended another stairway. The flagstones of the next passage were also covered with worn carpeting. Eunice Moon stopped at the third door on her right and opened it. 'Here we are.'

The room had a small fire in it, burning some sort of smokeless fuel. The fireplace was surrounded by a large fender which had brass and leather seats at either end. The woodwork was dark and highly polished. There were photographs on the walls and mantelpiece, books on the shelves set into alcoves on both sides of the fireplace. The room seemed to Una to be a self-conscious reproduction of a late-Victorian study. There were a couple of pieces of blue china on a sideboard opposite the fire. There were leather, high-backed armchairs. The room was lit by oil-lamps. There was a kettle on a stand over the fire. She could see neither fork, toast nor crumpets. Chapman took her coat and, in her long divided skirt, riding boots, leather shirt, she sat down in the chair he indicated, leaning forward to warm her hands. The kettle began to boil.

Eunice Moon removed the kettle and made tea in a large earthenware pot. 'It's Earl Grey, I'm afraid. It's all we have.'

'My favourite,' said Una. It was not, but she had always thought her preference for ordinary Indian popular brands of tea to be a bit vulgar.

Eunice Moon poured the tea and handed her the cup, which was pink willow-pattern. 'There's no sugar or milk at the moment. And, of course, no lemon.'

'I don't take them.' Another lie. 'This is just what I need.'

She smiled at Miss Moon. The woman's voice was tragic; it seemed to contain the fragments of a different voice, one that had been animated.

'And nothing to offer you to eat, until lunch-time,' Chapman said, standing to one side of the fire and accepting his own cup. 'Thanks, Eunice.'

'Actually,' said Eunice Moon very shyly, as she pulled her cardigan about her, 'we were told that they might send some supplies down with you.'

'They said nothing to me. I'm sorry.'

'Oh, we can manage.' Chapman was cheerful. Unlike the woman he seemed to enjoy the actual inconveniences of the life they were leading. 'Normally there's fresh bread, you know. I go to Aylesbury, where there's a baker. I should have gone today. And we had some rich tea biscuits up until yesterday. I must remember to ask for some. I don't know where Mr Whiting gets them from, do you, Eunice? He's a wonder.'

She nodded at him, pouring her own tea.

'Actually, we take a bit of a risk,' Chapman continued. 'If it wasn't for the people's good will we'd be scotched, of course. But we give a good service in exchange for the little luxuries. They send their children to us for whatever education we can give them. There isn't a school in Aylesbury now. In a round about way that's how we came across the girl – through one of her friends saying something to Eunice.'

'How did you get her here?' asked Una, for want of anything else to say.

'Well, of course, that's why I sent to London for the gold. Not for myself. You hadn't heard?'

'Gold? You're bribing her?'

Even Eunice Moon smiled at this and Chapman laughed aloud. 'Not her, Miss Persson. You must be unfamiliar with what's going on in these parts. I thought the same state of affairs existed in London – and Birmingham's notorious – or was. No, no. We bought the girl. It was the only way to get her. The farmer who had her wouldn't let her go. We couldn't make an enemy of him or bang would go our cover and our heads would be bound to roll.'

'She was working for the farmer? A slave?'

'In a manner of speaking.'

Una wondered why the child had been purchased. Her dislike for Chapman had increased.

'Wait till you see her,' chuckled Chapman, 'and you'll see why she was so expensive. I must say...' Eunice Moon caught his eye and he became embarrassed. 'Sorry, Eunice.'

'Of course,' began Miss Moon, 'she'll hardly...'

'You'll have to think up some sort of story in London,' Chapman said. His cup clacked against his saucer. 'To cover what's been going on. Luckily, the farmer didn't know who she was.'

'I can't think how she ever turned up in this part of the world.' Miss Moon shook her head. 'I'd heard that she had been killed with the other child, near Salisbury, wasn't it?'

'Salisbury,' confirmed Chapman. 'There were certainly two children in the photographs, though badly burned. They were buried in the Cathedral, when the FKA were pushed back for a while. Then, of course, the Cathedral got a direct hit when the FKA recovered, so...'

'So there was no real proof, apart from those photographs,' said Eunice Moon. 'Anyway, I don't think there'll be much doubt about her identity. She was very reticent before she learned we were friends. After that, everything she said confirmed who she was. Physically, there's no question.'

'She's nervous, naturally,' continued Chapman, placing his cup and saucer on the mantelpiece beside a photograph of himself in a black gown and mortar-board. 'But she knows she'll be safe as soon as you get her to London.'

'And she's heard of you, which helps,' added Eunice Moon. She sighed and collected up the cups, putting them on a brass Chinese tray.

The woman left with the tea things. Chapman sat down in the other chair. 'It's been a very nerve-racking time for her,' he explained. 'You can imagine.'

'Quite,' said Una.

'We didn't leave Oxford with everyone else and we managed, as it happened, to live quite well. It's isolated. Nobody takes an interest in the place. We get along. Eunice didn't want to be involved in this business and it seemed odd that I, with my political convictions, should be the one to discover the girl and decide to tell London. But there you are.' He sat back in the chair. 'I thought it was for the good of the country. Anything's better than this sort of anarchy, isn't it? And your people should be able to control her.'

'Oh, certainly.' Una was beginning to recover her memory. There were images, now, of the group in London, but they were unspecific.

'We'll be glad to have her off our hands.' Chapman grinned. His pale features seemed to stretch in abnormal lines. He waved his hands, his fingers spread. 'Still, a bit of excitement stops you getting stale, as I told Eunice.'

'Yes,' said Una. She hoped that when she finally met the girl her amnesia would lift. It was the worst attack she had had for a long while, she thought. Carefully, she suppressed that particular line of contemplation.

'There's some hope now, at any rate, of order being restored throughout the country, of Oxford being rebuilt, of proper university life beginning again. I suppose that's what I'm chiefly hoping for, to be frank. Call it self-interest.'

Una could not resist a random and vicious question. 'You're not worried, then, about knowing the child's secret?'

Chapman frowned. 'What do you mean?'

'Well, I'm sure it isn't worth considering, but if you and Miss Moon are the only ones to know what was going on. With the farmer...'

He was still puzzled. Perhaps she had misjudged the importance of what he had told her.

'You don't think,' she continued, 'that there'll be an attempt to silence you both?'

'Kill us, you mean?'

'Or keep you locked up. There are, after all, medieval precedents. And we do seem to have returned to the conditions of the middle ages.'

'Not in our *thinking*, surely?' He stroked his upper lip where once, she was sure, a moustache had grown. 'Not in our judgements?'

She pretended to shrug off the problems she had herself raised. 'Some believe we've never really left the middle ages.' As she spoke, she received an inkling of the girl's identity or, at least, her political importance.

He took out his handkerchief and blew his nose. 'Well, I hope you inform London that it's certainly not in our interest to say anything.'

'I will.' She affected a comforting tone. 'Of course I shall. They'll see that.'

'It would be most unfair if . . .'

'Don't worry, Mr Chapman. Justice will triumph.'

'All I want to see is Oxford restored. And the other great universities, too, of course. Cambridge, at any rate.'

'If the population merits it,' she said.

'Get the country running properly again and we'll soon have the population.' He seemed glad to return to what were obviously familiar opinions. 'A constitutional monarchy is better than the kind of fascism, whether it's from left or right, that we've been experiencing. England could do worse than to start from scratch. Back to 1660. A genuine Restoration, in more senses than one.'

Una's mirth was spontaneous. 'And you a Marxist!'

'There's nothing really strange about it, if you accept that societies must experience certain stages in their development towards a state of true Socialism. You see, England's trouble is that she was the first nation to begin the experiment, just as she was the first nation to experience the industrial revolution – there are obvious disadvantages to being the first. You create a structure containing too many of the old factors and as a result you get far worse confusion than, say, in France or America – and they were confused enough.'

'You're confusing me!' Una spoke good-naturedly. 'Don't bother to explain, Mr Chapman. It's hard enough for any of us, these days, to rationalize our instincts with our politics.

Miltonian ideals are probably more suitable than Marxist ones, at this time.'

'I'm perfectly serious,' he said.

'I respect your opinions.'

'Can't you see what I'm getting at, though? We've got a fresh start, a new chance. Everything's broken down. We can rebuild it properly.'

'If there are enough optimists of your persuasion we might.'

'You think I'm foolish. You could be right. But being in London can also make you cynical, you know.'

'I know.' She began to warm to him a little more. 'So can hiding in Oxford make you cynical. You could argue that. In more fundamental ways. You would have dismissed your own statements as being thoroughly reactionary a few years ago, wouldn't you?'

'I'd argue now that we have to go back a bit before we can press on forward. It's a respectable argument.'

'And a conservative one.'

He shrugged. 'Circumstances shape one's political opinions. The circumstances are a bit different today from those of even two years ago. I welcomed the FKA at first. They had some good men, but most of those were killed in the early fighting, and the brutes that followed them were nothing less than bandits.'

'Bandits often make the most successful revolutionaries. Certainly they are very good at preparing the way. Robin Hood, Pancho Villa, Makhno.'

'Makhno was hardly a bandit.'

' "Trotsky" thought he was.'

'He was simply naïve. A martyr.'

'You've made my point.'

He accepted this with a stiff, ironical smile. 'All right. But you'd put Cornelius in the same category, would you?'

She sighed.

'Well?'

'Cornelius?' She had been taken off-guard. 'The leader of the FKA?' A guess.

'In actuality, for all he calls himself an advisor. Does he see himself as a responsible revolutionary, do you think?'

'He's very complex.'

'You knew him, didn't you?'

'I've had some dealings with him, yes.'

'I didn't mean to suggest...'

'No, no. That's all right. I'd call him something of an *agent provocateur*, with few discernible goals – a renegade, if you like. That is, the goals are probably private, half-conscious. And yet his heart's often in the right place and certainly he's been known to support some unlikely and unfashionable causes for apparently excellent reasons.'

'Well, as far as I'm concerned, he's a bandit – an assassin – and all you've done is describe a bandit, Miss Persson. Or would you prefer to dignify him with a more romantic title – soldier of fortune, perhaps?' He was becoming aggressive. Una brightened. 'God! Women will always fall for these flashy buccaneer-types!'

'I wouldn't call him that...'

'He works for himself,' Chapman went on, 'and not for any cause. That's a bandit.'

'All right.' She had discussed the Cornelius brothers' motives too often for the subject to hold any interest, but she liked Chapman better when he rose to her baiting, so she continued: 'He's done a lot of good for a great many of the poor devils abandoned by their previous leaders.' She had no idea what this would mean to Chapman.

'Really? You'd admit that he was entirely responsible for the Sack of Birmingham, wouldn't you?'

'He never liked Birmingham.'

'And Leicester? And Rugby? And Lincoln? Another cathedral...'

'He wasn't very fond of the Midlands at all.'

'Eunice's mother died when they levelled Wolverhampton. There's no sanity in killing innocent old women or kids. You're not serious, Miss Persson?'

Una wondered why Jerry always did take it out on Birmingham. It had to be personal.

'I didn't say he was sane,' she said.

'Just a disenchanted idealist?' Again the constipated grin. His irony.

'Aren't we all that?'

'Not me, Miss Persson. Not you, either, or you wouldn't be here.'

'I suppose not. Sometimes I think, however, that Jerry Cornelius is the only one who isn't disenchanted. He manages to enjoy life, in a desperate sort of way.'

'You could say the same for me,' said Chapman. 'And I've nobody's blood on my hands. Of course, I'm not exactly Douglas Fairbanks, either ...'

'It was you who made the remark about circumstances.' She was still being deliberately contentious.

'Well,' said Chapman with satisfaction, 'it'll certainly put his nose out of joint when you get back to London with your charge.'

Una was probably even more pleased by the thought than Chapman, but she said: 'He could win her over, perhaps, to his side.'

'Or go over to hers, more likely.'

'You wouldn't like that?'

'It would make my efforts meaningless.'

'Yes. I'm sorry, Mr Chapman.' She felt that she had probably gone too far. 'It is a factor, however, they'll have to consider in London. Little girls always liked Cornelius.'

'I think this particular little girl has had enough of men, however charming.'

'Exactly.' She had become alarmed by Chapman's change of colour. There were red, puffy blotches under his eyes.

'I know you were only joking, Miss Persson. I'm a bit on edge. It's been a strain. And I was trying to do my duty.'

'You've done it marvellously, Mr Chapman. Oxford will soon be a thriving university again. And I shouldn't be surprised if they don't make you Chancellor or something.'

'Oh, all I want is the old life back.' The prospect attracted him, although he did not seem willing to admit it to himself. He looked at the clock on the mantelpiece. It was half past twelve. 'Time for lunch. Would you like a glass of Madeira? We've run out of sherry, I'm afraid.'

'Madeira would be excellent.'

'You don't mind if she – the girl – lunches with us?'

'It would be a good idea to have a chat with her, to reassure her before I take her back to London.'

'Quite.' He poured three glasses of madeira, draining the bottle. 'Ah, well, that's that. Another link with civilization broken.' He brought her the drink, sipping his own. 'Enjoy it while you can, eh?'

'Shouldn't we toast the future?' Half-mockingly Una raised her glass.

'Or the Queen,' he said, joining in the joke. 'The future's been pretty thoroughly toasted, wouldn't you say?'

She took his meaning.

Eunice Moon entered. She had brought the girl. She was nine or ten years old, with a creamy skin, blonde hair to her shoulders, and wide blue eyes. Una could see why she had cost London so much gold. Una wondered if the farmer or Chapman had dressed her up in the green silk Alice in Wonderland dress with the white ankle socks and the patent leather shoes. Una began to rise. Chapman was already bowing, the glass still in his hand so that a little of the contents spilled. 'Your Majesty,' he said.

Una could see that already the child was no stranger to power.

FOURTEEN

*Innocents at home: in which the Cornelius
family celebrates a reunion*

'Oo-er, look at 'er face!' Mrs Cornelius shrieked with excitement. 'Covered in pimples. *And* she's got a case o' dandrufft!' She fell back on to the off-white plastic upholstery of her new settee. 'Oh, Gawd!' Her cheeks glowed under their rouge; tears fell into her powder, like rain on the desert.

'Well,' said Sammy patiently, 'is that good enough for ya?'

'It'll do, honestly, Sammy,' said Catherine over her shoulder. She was arranging mixed nuts in two glass bowls on the tawny sideboard. The sideboard was also relatively new, in the 'contemporary' style of the other furniture. Only her mother's armchair remained. Mrs Cornelius had refused to have it removed or recovered. Frank had brought her the furniture from the warehouse he was running. He was in the HP business. Everything was of light wood and imitation brass, white plastic; distemper dashes in three colours on the walls, jazzy red, brown, blue and yellow carpet. The spirit of the Festival of Britain recaptured in Blenheim Crescent. And here was Sammy with the TV he had hired for the week so they could watch the Coronation. The problem was that the portable aerial didn't give a very good picture, so he had added a length of cable and hung the whole thing out of the window. The picture was moderately better.

'I'll 'ave to go up on the roof,' said Sammy. He plucked at his shirt, where it stuck under his arms. 'I'll need an 'and, Jerry.'

Jerry was trying to crack a nut with his teeth. He sat in

his mum's old chair; there was a half-finished glass of pale ale on the arm beside his left hand. He wore a grey two-piece suit with narrow velvet-trimmed lapels and drainpipe trousers. His yellow paisley waistcoat was of satin. He had thick crêpe-soled shoes on his feet; they were brown suède. When questioned about his appearance he would argue that he was ahead of his time.

'What can I do?' Jerry remained seated.

'I'll lower the cable down from the roof. All you 'ave to do is plug it in an' then tell me when the picture looks right. Okay?'

'Okay.' Jerry abandoned the nut and jumped to his feet. Sammy disappeared through the door on to the landing and began to climb the ladder which went through the loft and up to the roof. Jerry opened the window and stuck his well-greased head out. 'Ready when you are, Sammo!'

Catherine heard a catcall or two from the street, as if in response to her brother's shout.

'Why's it gone off?' said Mrs Cornelius. She had only just realized that the picture had vanished altogether. The screen hissed, and agitated black and white dots fluttered all over it.

'They're fixing the aerial, Mum.'

'We didn't 'ave this trouble with the wireless.'

'You need a more powerful one for a telly, Mum.'

' 'Ardly seems worf it.' Mrs Cornelius reached behind her for a nut, her eyes still on the screen. 'It 'asn't broken dahn, 'as it, Caff?'

'No, Mum.' Her brother was holding on to the window frame and sitting on the sill, looking up at Sammy. 'You be careful, Jerry.'

'Oh, I'm all right,' said her brother. 'Down she comes, Sam. Ow! Watch it!' He slid back into the room, rubbing his eyes, holding the cable. He began carefully to dust grime off his sleeve.

Sammy's distant voice came from above. 'Plugged in?'

'Give us a minute.' Jerry found the socket behind the set and plugged it in. The sound came on, very loud – a posh, plummy voice talking about uniforms and horses.

'There they are!' cried Mrs Cornelius. Jerry came round to inspect the picture.

'Not bad,' said her son. 'That'll do, eh, Cath?'

'That's lovely.' Catherine stood behind the settee and watched the Horse Guards.

'Well!' Sammy was aggrieved. ' 'Ow is it?'

Jerry leaned out of the window again. Immediately there was another chorus of catcalls from the street. 'That's great, Sam. Leave it like that.'

'I'll do me best. It's stuck in the bloody chimney at the moment.'

Jerry gave his attention to the kids below. 'Ignorant little bleeders! Piss off!'

Catherine laughed. 'Don't pander to them, Jerry.'

Jerry seemed pleased with his sally. He swaggered over to the sideboard and selected a brazil-nut. 'When's the actual Coronation?'

'Should be on shortly.' Catherine winked at him. 'Did you only come over for that? Mum's been worrying.'

'I didn't know about it till I arrived,' he said. 'Did I?' He leaned on the sideboard, one hand in the slit pocket of his drainpipes.

'What you been doing?' she asked him. She liked his clothes. She liked to see him feeling confident. Most of his spots had cleared up and he looked, in his sullen, dark way, quite handsome.

'This an' that,' he said. He picked a tooth with a fingernail. 'You?'

'Much the same.'

For the first time, he looked her up and down. She was wearing her pink sweater and the full, blue ballerina skirt which reached down to just below her calves. 'You're looking your usual sexy self.' He grinned. He returned her wink.

'There she is!' Mrs Cornelius hugged herself, swaying on the settee, just as Sammy, covered in dust, returned from the roof. 'Oo! Look, Sammy! There's the coach!'

'That's not 'er,' said Sammy, 'is it?' He wiped his face and arms with a cloth from his pocket. 'Nah! That's not the State Coach!'

'Then why's she wavin'?'

Sammy's interest in the screen was technical. ' 'Orizontal 'old's a bit dodgy.' He moved to adjust it. 'There. Any better?'

The grey, poorly defined picture warped vividly for a moment and then was steady again.

'Didn't know it was snowing up West,' said Jerry in a deadpan voice.

Catherine dug him in the ribs. She enjoyed her brother's dry wit.

Sammy sat himself beside Mrs C. 'That's not *snow*,' he said. 'It's the screen.'

'Oh,' said Jerry.

She felt his hand on her bottom. He gave both cheeks a squeeze. With her long fingernails she pinched his leg.

'Stop fidgeting, you two,' said their mum. 'If Frank don't 'urry up, 'e'll miss it.'

Catherine trod on Jerry's foot. In retaliation he goosed her. She gasped.

'Sit *dahn*!' said Mrs Cornelius. 'Cor blimey! You're as bad as you ever was!' There were pictures, now, from inside Westminster Abbey. Mrs Cornelius moaned with joy. A choir was singing. Men and women in heavy, ermine-trimmed robes stood stoically about.

'They ought to start a roof fund,' said Jerry. 'It's snowing inside, too.'

'Bloody shut up!' said his mother.

Giving Catherine one last squeeze Jerry swaggered round the settee and slumped into the chair, picking up his glass of flat beer. 'You seen one coronation you seen 'em all,' he said. His knowing look disturbed Catherine. She followed him, sitting on the arm of the chair, leaning her hip against his padded shoulder. They watched in dutiful silence, touching one another from time to time, exchanging exaggerated expressions of lust. It was very hard for her not to giggle.

The ceremony over, Sammy turned down the sound on

the set. A woman, looking not unlike the Queen, replaced the picture of the Abbey. She wore long earrings.

'D'yer fink they're real diamonds,' said Mrs Cornelius.

'Not allowed to wear 'em on telly,' Sammy told her. 'They'd glitter too much. Well, wot about a drink?' He wiped sweat from his neck with the heel of his hand. 'Eh? To celebrate. The pub'll be open.'

Jerry held tight to her elbow. It was a familiar signal. She let him reply. 'I haven't seen Cathy for quite a while. Maybe we'll follow on later.'

'Yes,' she said, 'we'd like a bit of a chat.'

'You 'aven't seen yore mum for a good long time, either,' said Mrs Cornelius. 'Where's me bag?' She found it on the floor at her feet. 'Oh, okay. I could do with a Guinness after that. Come on, Sammy.'

'See you, then, Mum,' said Jerry.

'Yer'll be dahn, then?'

'Yeah. Soon, most likely.'

'Okay.' In her damp red and blue print dress she made painfully for the door. 'Cor! Me legs. Sittin' on that fing don't do 'em no good.' She resented Frank's reorganization of the premises. He was now threatening to move her to a ground floor flat – a basement. She guessed, as well as anybody, that he had designs on this place.

'See ya,' said Sammy, getting into the jacket of his best black suit. He was wearing a Union Jack in the button-hole. He waved at them. The door closed. Catherine listened as they went downstairs. Her brother stroked her knee.

'Shall we go into my room?' she suggested.

'Why not?' He stood up and walked ahead of her, opening the door on the left of the new sideboard. 'Well, it's nice to see you haven't changed your bit much.'

'I like to keep it familiar. I didn't half tear mum off a strip when she said she'd told Frank he could decorate in here.' She closed the door of her room, locking it behind her. He put his hands on her narrow waist, squeezing her as he looked her over. 'I'm so glad to see you, Jerry.' She kissed his nose.

The room had the old aspidistra in it. The dark green leaves obscured much of the light from the small window, but they helped to produce the atmosphere she liked. There were heavy, old-fashioned red velvet curtains, too, and she had covered her bed with a blue velvet canopy, and put red velvet on the top of her tallboy and dressing-table. There were big Turkish cushions on the bed and Afghan carpets on the floor, Japanese, Chinese and Indian prints on the dark walls. 'A proper little scene of oriental opulence.' Jerry let go of her waist. 'It never dates, though, does it?'

'It never will,' she said.

'I heard you were living with some bloke over in Hampstead. An actor or something. Well known.'

'That's over.'

He took a Japanese book from the shelf and began to flip through it. 'What happened there, then?'

'Oh, you know.' She stretched her body on the bed, her back supported by the big pillows. 'He had another girl-friend, as well as his wife. He couldn't keep it up, poor bugger, without something snapping. I got out before he turned on me.' She leaned to light a scented candle.

'Didn't he mind?' Jerry picked up two of her coloured bottles and held them to the candlelight. He was disappointed to find them empty.

'What do you think? Anyway, I don't care.' She was eager to tell him her more recent news. There was nobody else she was able to tell.

'Was he Greek?'

'The actor? As a matter of fact,' she admitted, 'he was. My fifth, I think. I'm running out of them.'

'What are you doing now, then?' Jerry finished his inspection and sat down beside her at last. He smiled affectionately. 'Eh?' He remained a little distant. Perhaps he was shy.

She fiddled with her wrist-watch. 'Something a bit naughty, I suppose.' The raspberry scent of the candle filled her nostrils.

Not unself-consciously Jerry hugged her. 'Let's hear it, Cath. You're dying to tell me.'

'It's embarrassing.' She wanted him to coax her.

'Now I'm really interested.' He licked her ear. 'Is it a bloke? Or a lady?'

'Well, a bloke, mainly.' Absently, she licked him back.

'Up to your three-card tricks, are you? Ho, ho...' He squeezed her nipple through her bra.

'Not exactly.' She stroked his neck. 'We could put a record on.' She indicated her new Dansette record-player.

'Who is he?' He squeezed her other nipple. 'Is he rich and famous, too?'

'He's a member of parliament.' She blushed. She was pleased with herself.

'Conservative?' His hand massaged her groin through her skirt.

'Absolutely.' She shifted her position.

'Ho, ho, ho,' said Jerry again. Carefully he removed his drape jacket, hanging it over the chair next to her bed. 'It's a change from Greeks, anyway.'

'His grandparents were Spanish.' She was almost defensive. 'Jewish probably.'

'Where did you meet him?'

'At his office. I was doing temporary typing for a while, when I last got home.'

'And he asked you round to his place to do some extra confidential work.'

'You are corny!' She kissed him. 'He's got this flat. You know, not his home. It's a *pied à terre*.'

'Or screwing gaff, as it's called in Frank's circles.' Jerry made himself more comfortable. 'Go on.'

'He's a right little creep, really,' she said, 'but I think that's part of the appeal. Know what I mean?'

'Not really. I'm a romantic.' He licked her wrist. 'Tasty.'

'I'm not going to tell you, if you make a joke of it.'

'Sorry.' He put his hand under her skirt and ran a finger over her nyloned knee. She moved closer to him.

'It's not a lot to do with sex,' she went on. 'At least, not for me. It might be for him. I can't tell.'

'What's he doing, then? Watching? Making you watch?'

'No . . .' She couldn't tell him. Instead she turned so that she was lying face down on the bed with one eye still on her brother. Her body felt heavy and her voice was slurred and muffled. 'Have a look for yourself.'

She felt him lift her skirt. He pulled down her panties. He said, 'Blimey,' as he touched the marks on her bottom. 'Are you like that all over?'

'Those are the most recent,' she said.

'And you enjoy it?'

'I love it. And it makes me feel great the next day. I've never felt better.'

'Blimey. Are those his initials?'

'Mm.'

'Bloody hell, Cathy. Are you sure you know what you're doing?'

'Not really. I don't care.'

'He could be a maniac.'

'No. I could easily handle him if I wanted to. That's what I mean about his appeal. He's not very strong.'

'Strong enough. What's he use? A razor?'

'He's got this special little gold knife. It doesn't hurt much.' She felt his lips on her bottom. 'It's all right, Jerry. I thought you'd – well, you know. I didn't mean to worry you.' She looked up. He was pale. 'You're a man of the world, aren't you? Done and seen everything?'

'It's a bit hard to take, Cath. You are my sister, after all.'

She couldn't stop the laughter. 'Oh, Jerry. You sound so pompous. You'll make me feel guilty. I thought you'd like it.'

'Like it? How d'you mean?'

'I thought you might like to have a go yourself.'

'Not a chance!' He pulled her skirt back.

'No, I don't mean with a knife, Jerry. Just the whip. I'm supposed to. He won't mind that. I bought one from that second-hand shop – you know, with the hunting gear in it –

up Pembridge Road. It's a riding crop. They're the best ones to use.'

He pushed the hair away from her ears and tickled her under the jaw. His initial shock had passed. His eyes were hot. 'You know me, I'm game for anything you want to do, Cathy.' He sucked his lower lip. 'So, if this is what you feel like, I don't mind having a – bash . . .' His voice tailed off. 'Hurting you, though . . .'

'It's lovely.' She put her hand on his heart. 'You're the only man I'll ever really trust, Jerry. I love you. Are you all right now?'

'Sure.' He glanced about him. 'Where's this whip, then?'

'Under the bed.' She wriggled over to the edge and felt for where she had lodged the riding crop between the mattress and the frame. 'Here it is.' She put it into his hands.

'You're corrupting me, young woman.' He swished the whip through the air.

'You don't have to.' She became confused. 'I'll understand. I don't want to spoil anything.'

'You couldn't. We're too close. We're almost the same person. I'll tell you what, though.' He grinned. 'Will you do it to me, after I've done it to you?' He always wanted to share her experiences, if he could.

'All right,' she said. 'You'll love it. I know you will.'

Jerry began to strip off his waistcoat. He unlaced his heavy crêpe-soled shoes. He drew off his bright orange ankle socks. Finally he removed his shirt and his narrow trousers and hung them with his jacket on the chair. He stood on the cream, red and green Afghan rug in his Y-fronts and his identity chain, his pale, skinny body tensed, the crop held uncertainly in his hand. 'D'you want to get undressed, too?'

'Okay.' She threw her clothes down on the floor.

'You have got a lovely body, Cath.' He fondled her. 'All right. Where do you want 'em and how many?'

'Just do three on my bum. Really, you shouldn't ask me – you should *tell* me. Warn me first, though.' She prepared herself for ecstasy.

174

His first stroke struck her at the base of the spine and she yelled. His second hit her just above the knees and she shouted 'Ouch' and began to turn over. But before she could stop him, he had sworn and struck again, this time landing squarely on her bottom.

'I was a bit off target,' he said. 'Was that all right?'

She did her best to sound pleased. 'Oh, yes. It was beautiful.'

'You need to practise,' he said. 'I didn't realize. That isn't half a horrible welt on your legs – and I think that's a bruise on your back. It is okay, then, is it?'

'Yes. Really.' She glanced up at him. He was scratching his balls with the end of the riding crop, scratching his head with his free hand.

'And that's it, then, is it?' He frowned. 'I could see how you could get into it.' He reached a decision. 'Right! Now you do it to me. Let's see what this is all about, shall we?'

Resignedly, she took the whip. She straightened her wounded back as he removed his pants and lay down on the bed. 'I'm ready,' he said encouragingly. His poor little white bottom wriggled as he made himself comfortable. 'Give it all you've got!'

'Are you sure you want me to?' She had never whipped anyone herself, not in earnest. Somehow it went against the grain; but she did want him to feel something of what she felt, and this was the only way.

'If you like it, Cath, I'll like it, won't I? You ought to know that by now.'

'Maybe we should leave it until later.'

'No. Come on.' His voice tried to reassure her. 'Beat me! Beat me!'

She lifted the riding crop high in the air but somehow, as it descended, it lost impetus and the stroke when it connected with his flesh was feeble. She followed that one with two more, equally feeble. She felt miserable. She dropped the whip.

'Well,' he said when she had finished, 'I suppose you have to be in the mood, really.' He sat up, rubbing his backside, fondling his cock. 'Yeah. I can see what it's all about. Yeah.'

'You didn't enjoy it, did you?' She was close to tears. 'I'm sorry. Maybe we're too close, you know. Too friendly.'

'We couldn't be much closer. Let's give it another try later.' He looked at her hesitantly.

'What?' she said.

His expression became appealing. His cock was erect. He seemed bashful. 'What about a quick wank to be going on with?' he suggested.

She winced as she knelt before him.

FIFTEEN

In which Una Persson confronts the final decay of capitalism

Frank Cornelius was changing when Una Persson left the vestry and entered the dressing-room, tracing him by means of the tinny tune issuing from his transistor. She watched him as he rapidly zipped his trousers.

'I enjoyed the sermon,' she said. 'You've found your vocation at last.'

'I didn't know you were about.' He did up his cuff-links. 'They said you were in some Poland or other. No wonder it's all breaking up.'

'It's the Conjunction of the Million Spheres,' she said.

He rubbed his blue chin. 'Don't be funny. There's a time and a place for mysticism.'

'Really I was looking for Jerry.'

'Do you think he came to listen to the sermon, too?'

'No, but my information was that you were working together.'

'Forget it!' He began, lovingly, to knot his tie, peering into the mirror of his locker. 'What are you after, Mrs Persson?'

'I'm a journalist. I'm on a job. I was supposed to cover the witchcraft stuff. You ought to know something about that. You performed the exorcism. Did you also take part in the rites?'

'Has Miss Brunner been talking to you?'

'Now she *is* a more likely candidate. Have you got her address?'

'It shouldn't take one witch long to find another.' He fingered the edges of his blazer.

'What about your sister?'

'Me and my sister don't get on. Anyway, she isn't about, these days. I don't think she exists any more. Jerry sent her to sleep, don't you remember?'

'No?' She was curious.

'Well, give the disc another spin. It might all come back to you.'

'Is this really all you do, nowadays?'

'Yeah. And I open bazaars, fêtes, sports days. I do weddings, christenings, funerals, exorcisms.'

'It's the exorcisms take up the most time, I suppose.'

'These days, yes. We live in a very superstitious age, Mrs Persson. Why try to swim against the tide?'

'You don't have to stay here, any more than I do.'

'Then why are you here, if you don't like it?'

'I'm trying to help.'

'So am I.' He smirked, smoothing back his hair. 'You're a bit short of charity, aren't you, Mrs Persson? I don't sit in judgement on people. That's the difference between us.'

'You can't afford to, can you?'

'You sound tired.' He rounded on her.

'So do you, Frank.'

'Do me a favour!' He put away his vestments. 'I've never been fitter.'

'Where do you think I might find Jerry?'

'Try the hospitals. Or the loony bins. He wouldn't let me treat him. I should think he's in one of his comas by now.'

'Copping out again.'

'See what I mean about judging people?'

'You could be right.' She drew her S&W from her pocket. 'I'll do a bit of self-analysis tonight. In the meantime, it won't stop me executing you, Frank.'

'You can't kill me. They can't kill any of us.'

'Effectively, I can kill you. I can take you out of all this. You might go somewhere nasty.'

'Jerry's staying at our mum's. Blenheim Crescent. Know where it is? He's resting.'

'In London.'

He contemplated her revolver. 'He knows I can't touch him there. It's a sort of sanctuary for us.'

'And Catherine?'

'Probably there with him. They always get together when they can.' He sounded petulant, resentful. 'What are you trying on, Mrs Persson? Still hoping to find a world you can change? You've no chance here. Or is it just the Truth you're after?'

'It hasn't occurred to you that all this was created by my manipulation of events?'

'Don't kid yourself!' He was amused. 'I shouldn't have thought it would suit you.'

'Things have to go through stages,' she said.

'And they never work out the way you expect.'

She put the gun away.

He cackled. He was enlightened. 'You're calling them all in, aren't you? You're worried. You think we *might* have fucked things up. Why?'

'Can you always remember everything you've done?'

'Of course not. But I don't feel guilty ... No – of course not ...'

'Can you remember now?'

'Yes.' He became alarmed.

'Work it out, then. I can remember, too. Almost everything. Clearly. Is that normal?'

He sniffed, playing with his tie. 'Jesus Christ!'

'I think there's time to get clear before the disintegration really hits,' she told him. 'You can have that information for nothing, though you deserve whatever happens to you. You've seen what *can* happen, haven't you? To people like you and me.'

'All right! That'll do.' He wiped his mouth.

She headed back through the arch. 'If I don't see you again ...'

'You're just trying to fuck things up for me here, aren't you?'

'I wouldn't do that. I'm not interested in individuals one

way or another. Maybe that's my trouble. You ought to know that, at least, by now.'

'Bloody puritanical bitch!'

She entered the cold air of the churchyard. She buttoned up her coat. The last of the congregation were getting into their cars. Those who had come on foot were plodding up the asphalted road towards the village. Una caught a whiff of charred flesh. She avoided a second sight of the stake and the corpse. The afternoon light was already fading. The sky was red behind the hill on which the village stood. A dog barked as its owner unlocked the door of his car. 'Good boy. Good boy.' An engine started. 'See you tomorrow, Harry.' Someone got on a bicycle, saluting a limousine. 'Bright and early, sir.'

Una could never get used to the alienating sights and sounds of the rural home counties. She controlled her fear, making for her helicopter. At least she had the information she was looking for. The sun sank. Getting into the chopper she looked back at the church. Candles were flickering in two of the windows. She thought she heard Frank chanting. She was pleased. At least he was more frightened than she was. The same could be said for the whole congregation. She strapped herself into her seat and started the rotors, lifting towards the first stars and the comfort of the darkness, of hatred divorced from its object. She flew over hard fields and stiff little towns, over mean rivers and petty hillocks and the pathetic remains of forests. All that was really left of the forest, she thought, was the stake and the black corpse hanging from it, for the inhabitants of this world seemed to have a profound will towards preserving only the worst aspects of their way of life and banishing the best. Was there any point at all to her trying to save them from their inhuman destiny?

She pulled herself together. Frank had been right. She was tired and, because of that, she was getting the usual delusions of grandeur. It was lack of sleep which destroyed many a promising revolution. She recalled the faces of all those many friends who had failed. She saw their redrimmed eyes, the lines: the intense stares of those denied the security of their dreams. And it was their efforts to find those dreams, to create them from the objective world, that brought doom to their endeavours and terror to millions. But was it possible, any longer, to distinguish between the dream and the reality? She had seen so many futures, so many ruins.

She yawned. The sooner she got to sleep herself, the better. She would not bother to visit Blenheim Crescent tonight but would leave it until the morning, when she could cope with the Cornelius family, particularly the mother, who would almost certainly deny that her children were at home.

It would not be the first time Mrs Cornelius would try, in her blind mistrust of reason, to stem the tide of history.

SIXTEEN

In which Miss Catherine Cornelius finds Fresh Romance

Jerry was laughing at his little mate Shaky Mo Collier. 'It's a complicated number, all right. Four bloody chords, Mo!' They leaned in the shadows of the alcove at the back of the stage, trying through a small practice amplifier at their feet, to get their guitars in tune. The alcove was of grimy, bare brick. Catherine thought the whole back of the club was more like a disused railway tunnel than anything else.

Catherine was confused and self-conscious, feeling like an interloper as, around her, young men in Italian suits humped electrical gear about, apparently at random, and exchanged mysterious jokes.

There were four groups playing tonight, Jerry had told her, and his group, The Blues Ensemble, was on third. They would go on stage at about midnight. It was now eight o'clock. Only Jerry and Mo had so far turned up. The drummer and the bass guitarist were coming together in the drummer's dad's van. Jerry was friends with The Moochers who were top of the bill and they had agreed to lend The Ensemble their amplifiers because they were going on last to play their second set which, if they were in good form, wouldn't finish until about four.

Two men, middle-aged and heavily built, also wearing Italian suits, came out of the darkness at the side of the stage. By their distinctive, menacing swaggers, Catherine guessed that they must be coppers. Her mouth went dry as she saw one of them put a hand on Jerry's shoulder and whisper in his ear. She was surprised that Jerry didn't go with them. Instead he stayed where he was and nodded seriously. Their mission finished, the two men sauntered back the way they had come.

'Who was that?' she said.

'Manager,' Jerry told her. 'They want us to do a longer set, to spin it out a bit. The Yellow Dogs can't make it.' He shrugged. 'There's an extra fiver in it.'

'That's not bad,' said Mo Collier. 'Over a quid each. That's about six quid for everybody. Blimey!' He was impressed.

'If we get paid,' said Jerry.

'They're all right here.' Mo was confident. 'They're straight. Johnny said so.' Johnny Gunn had fixed up the gig for them. He liked to call himself their manager and they paid him ten per cent of every gig he arranged. This was their first in Central London. Mo paused. 'Have we got enough material rehearsed?'

'We'll just jam the standards a bit longer,' Jerry said. 'Like everybody else.'

'Oh, good.' Mo preferred jamming. He began to play the chords of 'Bo Diddley.' He and Jerry were fanatical Chuck Berry and Bo Diddley fans.

Catherine felt cold and it seemed to her that grease was settling on her bare arms. She was wearing a cotton jumper and slacks. She wished that she had brought her chunky sweater.

'You bored, Cath?' Jerry asked.

'Oh, no. It's very interesting.'

'You could go through to the bar and get a coffee if you wanted to,' said Mo. 'They'll be open now.' Unplugging the lead of his guitar he walked to the side of the stage and pushed back the filthy curtain to look through into the hall. 'Yeah. It's open.'

'I think I will, then. Does anyone else want one?'

'No, thanks.' Jerry pulled a bottle from his pocket. It contained Coca Cola mixed with whisky (the club had no liquor licence). 'This'll do me. Did you manage to get the other stuff, Mo?'

'Naturally!' Mo drew a manilla envelope out of the top of his pullover. 'I got twenty.'

'Twenty what?' asked Catherine.

'Purple hearts. They're lovely.' Mo smacked his lips.

Catherine walked to the curtains, peering nervously through. There were about fifty people scattered about the hall. Nobody was dancing to the record playing through the loudspeakers. The sound was so distorted it was impossible to tell what the record was. As she went down the steps at the side of the stage everyone looked at her. She thought they must be wondering what she was doing here and she felt a bit shaky as she crossed to the far side of the hall to the little bar selling Espresso coffee, Walls' hot dogs, hamburgers and Coca Cola. The hall was painted a bright yellow all over. On the walls were pictures of various jazz musicians; until recently, this had been a modern jazz club.

'White coffee, please,' she said to the girl at the counter. The girl had dyed red hair and heavy, fantastic make-up. She looked worn out. She pulled the handle of her machine, holding the Pyrex cup under it. She put the cup in a Pyrex saucer. 'Shilling, love.'

'Cor!' said Catherine, taking the money from the purse in her left hand. 'And it's half foam!'

'Don't tell *me* about it.' The girl was friendly. 'You with one of the groups?'

'My brother's The Blues Ensemble.'

'Good, are they?'

'Not bad.'

'You heard The Moochers?'

'Not live. I saw them that time on TV.'

'They're really too much. Really groovy, you know. Fabulous!' The girl became confiding, leaning on the bar. It was the first time that Catherine had heard this sort of slang used naturally, without a hint of irony or embarrassment. 'Oh, good,' she said.

'D'you know any of them?' the girl wanted to know. 'D'you know Paul?'

'Is he the tall one?'

'Yeah! All the scrubbers hang around him.'

'I've met him once. I've only just come back to London, you see.'

'Where've you been?'

'Carlisle. Liverpool.'

'Liverpool! That's fantastic. The Cavern an' that?'

Catherine began to feel ashamed that she hadn't visited the Cavern, seen the Beatles or Billy J. Fury or Gerry and the Pacemakers. 'I was just working there,' she said. 'I didn't get out much in the evenings.' Gerard had been jealous of her going out on her own and he hated popular music. 'Oh, I've been there a few times.'

'That's my ambition,' the girl said, 'to go to Liverpool. But I suppose it's not the same now.'

'Not really,' agreed Catherine. That, at least, was bound to be true. 'Well...' She picked up her coffee cup and began the long walk back to the stage. 'See you, then.'

'See you.' There was admiration in the girl's voice. Catherine hadn't realized quite how much respect one got from being associated with beat groups. She grinned to herself, no longer bothered by the stares, as she pushed her way through the curtain.

Jerry and Mo had disappeared. She felt abandoned. A thickset young man went past. 'Looking for Jerry? 'E's in the dressing-room.' He pointed over his shoulder with his thumb. Jerry's group hadn't merited the dressing-room which was technically reserved for the main attraction. She approached the dark door in the wall and opened it. The lights were brighter in here. The room was roughly eight feet long by five feet wide. There were about ten people in it, including two girls in short plastic skirts and waistcoats, who were made up like the girls at the bar. Catherine couldn't help thinking how much like young prostitutes they looked. Were these 'scrubbers'? Jerry was leaning against a tiled fireplace. The dressing-room had long ago been lived in, it seemed. There were fragments of rotting carpet on the floor and two steel-framed chairs with torn plastic seats. As Catherine entered, one of the girls sat down, glancing curiously at her. Neither of the girls was speaking to anyone and yet they both seemed to take a keen interest in what the men were saying. Their language was as strange as the girl's at the bar.

'I dunno how he kept that riff going so long.'

'Put Black Diamonds on and see if they're any better.'

'Roy put them on his accoustic and pulled the whole bloody belly off!' They were laughing, enthusiastic, friendly with each other. Catherine thought she had never seen her brother looking more cheerful. This atmosphere seemed to bring out all that was best and most idealistic in him. 'Or it could be the pick-ups,' Jerry was saying. 'You could move them apart a bit more, couldn't you?'

'Not on my guitar, mate. What d'you think it is, a fucking Fender?'

Jerry passed his bottle round. With some dismay, she saw him put a couple of pinkish pills into his mouth. She hoped he knew what he was doing.

She thought that four of the boys must be from the same group. They all had pudding-basin haircuts, Brooks Brothers shirts with high, button-down collars and thin ties, cream-coloured jackets with thin green and blue stripes on them, and maroon trousers. Everyone wore scuffed black high-heeled winkle pickers. She noticed, in the corner, a very tall one wearing a short leather jacket and jeans. He looked more like a beatnik than the rest. His features while youthful were gaunt. He had his ear to his cherry-coloured guitar and kept plucking at the strings as if puzzled by something. He had a panatella sticking out of the corner of his mouth. Catherine thought he looked very romantic.

'Hello, Cath.' Jerry was merry. 'This is Brian – me old mate from school, remember? Ian. Bob. Pete.' She found it difficult to follow him, but she smiled at them all and they smiled at her. 'Nice to meet you,' she said.

'What a little darlin'!' said Brian appreciatively. He had a round, plump, cheeky face. 'How'd you fancy a big R & B star, Cathy?' Everyone laughed.

'The biggest he's ever been is two all-nighters in a row at

the Flamingo,' said one of the boys in a cream jacket. 'Anyway, you don't know what R &B is. All you're interested in is bloody Muddy Waters and Leadbelly.'

Brian grinned, to reveal a missing middle tooth. 'Well, I've gone commercial, 'aven't I?'

'If three quid a week's commercial,' said another, 'we're really in the big time now. I'm gonna get me a *monster* Cadillac car an' drive off down Route 66, goin' nowhere!' His attempt at an American accent seemed neither incongruous nor embarrassing, probably because of his enthusiasm.

'You'll be lucky.' Brian accepted the bottle. 'You told me you were behind with the payments on your Transit.'

Catherine began to enjoy the feeling of comradeship in the dressing-room. She was reminded of old films she had seen, of soldiers or airmen in the Mess, before they went on a mission. When Brian handed her the bottle, now almost empty, she took a swig. It was nice to be around people who were keen on what they were doing, who didn't seem to feel a need to justify it or rationalize it. She passed the bottle on and sat down next to the silent girl. 'Hello. Is your boyfriend in one of the groups?'

The girl seemed grateful for being spoken to. 'No. Me and Yvonne come from Haringey. We go to all the London gigs. We know Roy.'

'He's in The Moochers?'

'Yeah.'

'He's a friend of yours, is he?'

'Sort of, yeah.'

Somebody blundered past Catherine and fell against Yvonne. 'Sorry, darling.' He gave her breasts a squeeze. 'Coar!' He continued on his way, to speak to the gaunt guitarist in the corner. Catherine was surprised by the way Yvonne reacted. She looked at her friend as if she had scored a point, then turned. 'Do you mind?' she said.

'Not with you, darling. Any time,' said the boy absently, continuing to talk to the guitarist. 'What about it, then?'

'I wanted to start with "Mojo". You know, a good raver.'

'Yeah, but this way we build up to it.'

'I'd rather start with something easy.'

'Come off it, Paul. What's hard about "Memphis bloody Tennessee"?'

'Nothin'. But I like getting up on "Mojo". You know?'

'Okay, then.' As he stumbled back, he chucked Yvonne under the chin, 'See you later, darlin',' but he was looking speculatively at Catherine as he spoke.

The room had become very hot and the air was stale. Catherine could smell cigarette smoke, sweat and mould. She felt a bit dizzy. None the less she had begun to enjoy herself.

The heavily built manager looked into the room. His voice was aggressive, off-hand. 'Hurry it up, lads. You're on.' He spoke to no one in particular. It was evident that he didn't know one of the groups from another. Four of the boys separated themselves from the rest and picked up their instruments. 'See you,' said Brian to Jerry. He grinned at Catherine. 'See *you*, too, eh?'

Catherine grinned back at him.

Jerry came over. 'Want to hear them? They're not bad.'

'Do they do the same sort of stuff as you?'

'R & B? Sort of.' He took her hand. 'Come on.'

She was glad to be out of the dressing-room, into the comparatively fresh air. Peculiar whines and shrieks were coming from the stage. 'We can stand at the side,' said Jerry. They could see the stage now. The four young men were adjusting their instruments round their shoulders, kicking trailing leads clear of their feet, playing a few notes. The drummer kept thumping his bass drum and leaning down to adjust it. She saw one of them nod to the drummer who nodded back and immediately began a rapid roll around all the drums and cymbals in his kit. The noise was sudden and shook the floor as the guitars began to thump and scream out a fast eight-bar blues tune. She could clearly hear the words Brian was singing into the microphone. She craned her head to see the audience. Boys and girls were swaying on their feet, clapping inexpertly to the rhythm. The whole place was now packed, darkened.

> 'Come on baby, I'll show you how to dance,
> Let your hair down, baby, give me a chance,
> To show you the way to move.'

Brian began to play the mouth-organ into the microphone. Though the noise threatened to give her a headache (Jerry was apparently not affected at all) she found its vitality and attack more thrilling than anything she had ever heard before.

> 'That's right, baby, you're learning so fast,
> Gonna knock the future right back to the past.
> Now show me how to move!'

Brian yelled and almost fell backwards as he struck at his guitar, possessed by a madness she could never have guessed at when he had been the cheeky, friendly little lad back in the dressing-room. She felt as if she had witnessed some kind of religious transformation.

> 'That's right, baby, move it for me,
> You got such hips, you shake 'em just for me.
> Let's show 'em how to move.'

Brian was swinging his head from side to side so fast that it was a blur. 'Yeah! That's right!' he shouted. 'Oh, yeah! That's nice!'

The persistent beating of the bass, the high whining of the lead guitar, the swishing of the rhythm guitar, the rapping of the drums, produced in Catherine such a sense of joyful release that she wished now that she was in the audience, able to clap and sway with the others.

Without pausing, the group went into another number, a slower twelve-bar:

'I was driving down the highway minding my own mind,
Taking it easy and watchin' the signs,
'Cause I was goin' nowhere, I had plenty of time,
When I saw this little baby, she was jerkin' her thumb,
Hitchin' a ride, lookin' blue-eyed and dumb...'

Gradually her headache vanished. The music shuddered through her and every change was like a wave bearing her over a magical sea, and Brian's inexpert, wailing harmonica was like the cry of an exultant bird.

She stayed watching, even when Jerry returned to the dressing-room, still amazed by Brian's transformation from cocky youth to authoritative high-priest. It was as if she were privileged to perceive his whole being, all the secrets of a complex soul.

When they came off stage, Brian in front, they were sweating and their eyes were blank. Brian didn't even see her as he padded to the dressing-room. She had observed that particular kind of blankness only once before, in her own face, just after she had been beaten. She became alarmed.

'Aren't you going back in there for a drink?' The tall, gaunt guitarist was leaning over her. His face was as serious as ever. 'Terry's brought a bottle of rum.'

'Oh, I didn't see you there.' She smiled. 'You made me jump.'

'It's the sudden silence,' said Paul.

'Have you been watching them long?'

'No, just the last number. We do "Not Fade Away", too, but they do it better, I reckon.'

'You're the main act, aren't you?'

He nodded. 'Don't mean we're better, though, does it? We're just better known. We're beginning to get a reputation, as they say.' He sniffed and rubbed his long nose. 'It's your brother, isn't it, who's one of The Blues Ensemble?'

'That's right. Jerry.'

'Yeah. They're not bad, either.'

'I don't really know. I haven't heard them play. I saw

your group on telly that time. It didn't sound anything like this, though.'

'It wouldn't, would it? The BBC sound engineers are only happy if it's Gracie Fields or Alma Cogan. They don't know how to record an R & B group, so the sound always lacks power. They won't let you turn your amps right up in case it damages their equipment – and they balance out the bass until you can hardly hear it.'

'I didn't know that.'

'Yeah. If you want to hear any more, why don't you go out front and listen. It's better if you're in the middle. You get it all distorted from the side.' He smiled, tapping his ear. 'Like we do.'

'I enjoyed it, though.'

'Well, it's up to you.'

'When are you on?'

'First set's about half nine, I suppose. You gonna watch?' His mouth was thin and tight, but his eyes were steady, mildly insistent. 'Eh?'

'I'd like to.'

'Good.' He picked up his guitar. 'I'll be playing for you, then.'

'Thank you.'

'Don't mention it.' For the first time his smile was open. 'And I hope you like it.'

'I'm sure I will.'

'If you do, come and have a meal with me between the sets.'

'All right. If I do.'

'You will.' He hefted the cherry-coloured guitar like a broadsword. 'You'll like this.'

As she watched him stride back into the darkness Catherine knew why those girls were prepared to spend so many hours hanging about in the dressing-room. Before long, she thought, I'll be hanging about in there with them. But she knew better than to consider imitating their style.

SEVENTEEN

In which Captain Persson and Major Nye consider the State of the Nation

'It's cold enough for snow,' said Major Nye, rubbing his thin blue-veined hands together. As he ushered her past the guards he hummed a few bars of 'White Christmas'. His offices, bare and poorly furnished, had, now that most of Whitehall was demolished, an uninterrupted view of St James's Park and the refugee camp in the bed of the drained ornamental lake. 'It's a great shame we can't get up some sort of entertainment this year. You know how much I enjoy your songs. "There was I, waiting at the church . . ."'

'I haven't done much singing lately.'

'And a great shame it is. Perhaps we could celebrate the season together?'

'I must be on my way, I'm afraid. I came to apologize.'

'You did your best, my dear. You always do. My regard for your courage and your determination remains as high as ever, Captain Persson.' His yellowed face broke into a trained smile. 'We cannot control this, any of us. The best we can hope for is to retain our personal,' he shrugged, 'integrity.'

'You think your people will stay in power here?'

'Power?' His smile became spontaneous. He attempted to straighten his stooped, thin shoulders. 'Oh, indeed. We'll try to keep things running, you know. There isn't anyone who wants the job. Not in London, at any rate.' There was no heating in the old suite and draughts seemed to blow from a dozen directions at once. He crossed a stretch of parquet flooring to close a connecting door. He wore his battle-dress, his balaclava helmet and a long grey scarf wound several times about his wrinkled throat. 'All we do is look after the refugees. The naked will has triumphed. Civilization is destroyed and most of those who would destroy it are now gone themselves. Their disciples scarcely know why they are still fighting. Who has the will to re-build? I feared anarchy, but this apathy is much worse. They are sitting down to die. Out there!'

He waved at the window behind him. 'English men and women – sitting down to die!'

'Too tired to dream,' said Una. 'That is why someone who will do their dreaming for them has the means to move them to action, as a voodoo man controls his zombies. What about the fighting in the West?'

'Of course there's fighting still, but it's in the nature of a ritual. You'd be hard put to find any real anger. But they won't stop for a while – it's like an unconscious spasm, I suppose. It carries on under its own impetus, like an overshot bowling ball, eh? The jack has long-since been missed.' He offered Una a copper-coloured tobacco tin containing small hand-rolled cigarettes. 'Smoke?'

She shook her head.

He lit one for himself. The tobacco smoke was sweet. He puffed as he sat down on the edge of his desk. 'Take the armchair.' He motioned.

She had not intended to talk, but she was tired. She had lost most of her initiative since her two abortive attempts to bring back order.

'In the twentieth century,' said Major Nye, 'free will has come to mean pure will. The juvenile imagination triumphs and the Civil Service can no longer maintain the balance – a thousand busy, conscientious rabbits are no match for one confident fox. This has been a century of reaction, Captain Persson. All that has come of our hopes, our attempts to bring great justice to the world, is that robber-barons have become more powerful, better able to justify their huge, crude romantic ambitions, more able to convince once rational men and women of the reality of their ludicrous visions. Bad poets, Captain Persson – bad romantic poets. It is awful, the power they held towards the end. Bards should be blinded, so that they can never become soldiers.' He rubbed his eyes. 'I'm rambling.'

'When I was a little girl,' said Una, 'I was convinced that God was German. Every night, out of respect, I used to begin my prayers "Dear Herr God", and if I did wrong I expected the Archangel Gabriel to turn up to punish me. He would be dressed in field-grey, wearing one of those spiked helmets. He had a waxed moustache, sometimes, too.'

'And if you were good?' Major Nye put his head on one side, his expression affectionate.

'Nothing,' she said. 'To some people authority can only punish. It can never reward. Perhaps if one has the kind of temperament which responds to praise from authority or expects rewards from authority, then it has no need for free will.'

'I see.' He re-lit his cigarette. 'Such a person has no interest, then, in the nature of that authority?'

'Not really. And one who trusts no authority is in the opposite position. Irrespective of the nature of the authority, he mistrusts it, must forever be in a posture of resistance. It is, perhaps, because it is so attractive. Probably that is why I admire only revolutionaries who are powerless.'

'I should have thought the problem more complicated than that.'

'Which is why you are a civil servant and I am a political activist, or was.'

'Oh dear, oh dear,' he shook his head from side to side. 'It could be part of the reason, I'll grant you. At any rate, you've helped us considerably. Don't we constitute some kind of authority?'

'You were losing,' she said. 'Weren't you?'

'Yet if we had won . . . ?'

'I should have been on my way. Or joined your enemies. To keep the balance.'

'Perpetually in opposition.'

'It's the easier role to play,' she said. 'Free will is the curse of the twentieth century. I can choose to be anything: wife, mother, businesswoman, poet, politician, soldier – all of them. And if I am successful in these roles, all of them, have I any clearer sense of my own identity? Someone else might have, but not me. I refuse to relinquish that freedom, but I have no idea what to do with it. Not really. So many options confuse a person. You had the army and then the civil service. I had unspecific revolutionary fervour – a sympathy for the underdog, a romantic admiration for wild-eyed orators, a hatred of injustice. And I could choose to be so many things – a helpmeet, partisan, leader.'

'Of course, it has been hard for women . . .'

'It is not only women who suffer from the burden of choice. So many of us, faced with free will, experience a huge desire towards enslavement. Any creed will do. The threat of freedom forces us to fling in with any passing flag, rather than be our own men and women. I have the same yearning, Major Nye – and I am not the only person to yearn for Robin Hood, an outlaw leader. We cry out for a commander. We pine for princes. And who is the leader who betrays us worst? The one who turns around and tells us that the power is in our hands, that we must tell him and his councillors what we want. What we want! As if we know! Lobkowitz was that sort. A traitor to his people. Him and his Civil Service! Oh, if I could only give myself up to slavery – to a cause, to another individual, to enmesh myself so deeply that I could blame all ills, all frustrations, on a specific government, a particular sex, a class, a phenomenon.' She spoke lightly, with self-mockery. 'Once, Major Nye, I had the theatre. It was perfect.'

'And so were you,' he murmured. They had first met at the theatre where she had been playing.

'It was a shallow world,' she said, 'A world of ghosts.'

'Aha.' He turned, significantly, to look out at the shanties in the park.

'This seemed more substantial.' She spoke almost with defiance. 'I had to keep trying.'

'But you, of all people, should have known that the result was inevitable.'

'I can't accept that. Besides, efforts I have made – in the past, as it were – have had better results. And who knows what good might eventually come from this complete collapse? You mourn only the civilization which conditioned you, Major Nye. Society does not collapse, it modifies. In a generation or two, something magnificent could come crawling from that pit over there.'

'So you remain an optimist.'

'I have seen far too much, been involved in far too many failures, to be anything else.'

He replaced the remains of his cigarette in his tin. 'I've fought in four wars, served three political parties, and I can see little hope now for the future. Barbarism triumphs. We return to the Dark Ages.'

'I've fought in a thousand wars,' she said, 'and have served many individuals and have been as depressed to witness the behaviour of those individuals in periods of enlightenment as I have been impressed by the nobility of men and women during periods of darkness. I cannot believe that temperaments are changed by conditions, only that they are modified.'

'Very well. It is the same thing if those temperaments are radically modified, Captain Persson.' He seemed impatient. 'My forefathers were soldiers, scholars, politicians, all serving their society as best they could – my descendants will be savages, serving only their own ends.'

'You're simply talking about what you fear, Major Nye, not what you know to be true.'

'I'll grant you that.' He cleared his throat. 'I'm a bit off-colour this morning. My chest was affected by the smoke.'

'This would be a good time to give them up.'

'What?' He looked down at his cigarette tin. 'Oh, no. Not these. The smoke from the furnaces. We were burning papers. Files and so on. Mainly personal dossiers. There didn't seem much point in keeping them.'

'There never was,' she said. She got up. She was anxious to part from him amiably.

'Where are you off to now?' he asked.

'I had thought of leaving altogether, but I'm curious to follow things through for a bit.' She was, in fact, wondering if there might be a convergence before the century was out. 'You never know, do you? There could be a sudden reverse. Some new development nobody could anticipate.'

'So you'll stay in the country?'

'In England? Yes.'

'You could, in fairness, leave. I stay on because it's all I know. But you . . .'

'Oh, it's all I know, too.'

'There are parts of America, I hear . . .'

'Yes. There are little pockets of "order" in many parts of the globe. But the price of enjoying them is too great for me. At this moment, anyway. Civilization involves too much self-deception for me, too much hypocrisy – at least, the sort of civilization I am likely to find these days. I'll continue to take my chances amongst the savages for a while longer.'

'You remain a remarkable young woman.' They shook hands.

'And you are still a virtuous old man.' She smiled at him to disguise her sadness, her sympathy.

EIGHTEEN

In which Catherine Cornelius enjoys her Silver Days and Golden Nights

'Well,' said Mrs Cornelius amiably, giving the huge cafeteria the once over, 'I don't know abaht this.' The place was reserved for the performers, the journalists and photographers, for management. Outside, visible through the walls of transparent glass, was the empty asphalt of a car-park. Around the fringes of the cordon could be seen knots of young people in Afghan coats, embroidered jeans, feather boas, long Indian skirts, floppy felt hats, beads, buttons and glowing skin-paint; the ones who were still hoping to get tickets. The people inside the cafeteria looked much like their would-be audiences, only the materials of their patched and embroidered velvets, silks and satins tended to be richer. Here and there were journalists in Burton and Cardin suits, managers and publicists in very clean jeans and tan jackets, cafeteria staff in black and white dresses and aprons.

'Where d'they race the dogs, then?' Mrs Cornelius clutched her port and lemon.

'That's the White City, Mum. This is Wembley.'

'Oh, the football.'

'That's right.' Catherine looked down as a three-year-old boy, in a patchwork jacket and tiny jeans, pulled at the folds of her scarlet skirt. 'Stop it, you little bugger.' She bent to give him her glass of wine. 'Want a drink, then?'

'Nah!' The boy glared at her as he backed off.

Terence Allen, the manager, appeared and kissed her on the cheek. 'Hello, Cathy, love. Seen Jack?' He had on a dark denim suit.

'He's in the dressing-room,' she said. 'I couldn't stand it in there. Did you know Graham's turned up?'

Terence slapped his furrowed forehead. 'That's all I need. How many with him?'

'Only five or six.'

'Five or six will do it. I hate those fucking Angels.' He glanced around him to see if he had been overheard. 'Don't worry. I'll handle them. Who invited them?'

'Dunno,' said Catherine, though she knew it could have been Jack himself, in a euphoric moment. 'Probably nobody. You know what they're like.'

'Don't worry,' he said again. 'I'll handle it.' He sped off in the wrong direction and was almost immediately tackled by two angry roadies, with long, matted dark hair, who appeared to want him to settle a dispute they were having.

'Listen, Terence,' they kept saying.

'Don't worry!' Terence's voice was cracking.

' 'As it started, yet?' asked her mum.

'You'll hear it when it does.' At the moment it was just Jimi Hendrix records, played at the side of the stage by Mike, who travelled with the band as a permanent DJ, doing the warm-up before the live show actually got going.

'You goin' aht there?'

'Not me,' said Catherine. 'I've heard it before. I've brought my knitting, as usual.'

'Knitting? Really?' Mrs Cornelius was pleased.

'I always take my knitting to gigs,' Catherine told her. 'It's something to do. And Jack doesn't like it if I stay at home when they're playing in London. Besides,' she waved at a passing acquaintance, 'this is a special occasion, isn't it. Biggest gig of the year.'

Terence reappeared. 'We've sold out,' he said. 'There must be sixty thousand people out there.'

'Blimey!' Mrs Cornelius was impressed as she watched him scamper towards the dressing-room. 'Sixty thahsand!'

'Say twenty and you'll be closer.' Catherine accepted a drink from a tray one of the waitresses offered her. 'He always doubles it, at least, by about this time. Since it's a big gig he'll have trebled it, probably.'

Mrs Cornelius didn't listen. She preferred Terence's estimate. 'Blimey!'

There were tables scattered about the cafeteria. Catherine sat down at one and pulled a chair towards it, for her mother. 'That's better,' said Mrs Cornelius. She peered contentedly around at the war-painted faces, the brocaded beauties, the worn-out boys in Texan boots and studded leather toreador pants whose pale chests were littered with silver crosses, swastikas, ankhs and medallions, whose flimsy shirts seemed fixed to their bodies only by the sweat of their backs and armpits, at the sharp-featured, gloomy girls whose eyes would become suddenly eager when they saw someone they recognized, at the fat teenagers in moumous who held babies in their arms and chatted good-naturedly to old friends with big belts and wistful smiles and long, lank, hennaed hair, who handed on joints or tiny containers made of silver foil. There was an enormous amount of movement, of people leaving tables, sitting briefly at tables, striding slowly about, while managers and roadies raced through the throngs. 'Have you seen Dave?' 'Have you seen Stoatsy?' 'Have you seen that bitch Beryl?' 'What's going on, then?' Nobody paid attention to them; they might have been noisy, playful dogs. Terence went by again, like the White Rabbit. 'There's going to be trouble. I know there's going to be trouble.' He vanished up a flight of stairs.

' 'Ullo, Cathy. Long time no see.' A familiar hand reached under her hair and fondled her neck. Long fingers pushed a joint between her lips, a head appeared to kiss her on the nose, dark drugged eyes regarded her from the depths of an almost fleshless skull. 'How are you love?' It was Zonk. She had been his chick for a couple of months before he had gone off to Wales on his own, to live on a farm, to get his head together.

'Oh, Zonk! I thought you were in the country!'

' 'Ad to come up for this, didn't I? Social event of the year.'

'This is my mum.'

He bowed. The action caused him to stumble and almost fall into Mrs Cornelius's lap. His body was even thinner than ever. He wore a green velvet waistcoat and muddy Levis, patched on the knees and seat. His arms were tattooed, with War on one arm and Peace on the other; they were as muscular as ever and hard as they gripped her round the shoulders, more for support than in affection.

'This is Zonk,' she said to her mother.

'Pleased ter meet yer.' Mrs Cornelius smiled up at the swaying newcomer.

'Yeah,' said Zonk. He nodded profoundly several times. 'Enjoying yourself, then?'

'Oo, yes!'

'That's great.' He fell towards her again, kissing and patting her jowls.

'This is so sudden,' giggled Mrs C. 'Are all your friends like this, Caff?'

'The best of them,' she said.

Steadying himself by means of the back of Mrs Cornelius's chair Zonk scratched himself with a blue fingernail. 'Seen Jack?' he said after a moment's thought.

'Probably in the dressing-room,' said Cathy.

'You his old lady now, eh?'

'Well,' she said, 'I was before, wasn't I?'

'Oh, sure. Sure. No, that's good. Where is he?'

'Dressing-room,' she said.

'Yeah. Right.' Zonk took a deep breath and shoved himself off into the crowd. 'See you, Cathy. Take care.'

'See you, Zonk.'

' 'E seemed a nice enough bloke,' said Mrs Cornelius. 'Sailor was 'e?'

Catherine took her knitting from her big denim bag.

'Wot you smokin'?' asked her mother.

'Oh.' She had been automatically drawing on the joint.

'Reefer, is it?'

'It's only . . .'

'Give us a puff,' said Mrs Cornelius adventurously.

Catherine handed the joint to her mother who drew on it deeply and coughed her heart out. 'Rough bloody stuff, innit?'

Catherine began to knit.

'Don't feel any different,' said Mrs Cornelius. ' 'Ere, ain't that the butcher's boy? 'Enry.' She pointed. 'You know, Caff. 'Is eldest.'

Catherine looked up. Her mother was indicating a group of Hell's Angels who were swaggering sheepishly towards the bar, their helmets and goggles under their arms. ' 'Enry! 'Enry! Yoo-oo!' One of the Angels turned, grinning with recognition. He came towards them, his mates following.

'Well, well, well,' he said, 'Mrs C! 'Ow you doin' then, love?'

'Pretty good. Ya know Caffy, doncher?'

'What 'o, Caff. Wouldn't a recognized ya in that gear.'

Catherine laughed. 'I wouldn't have recognized you in that gear, either, Henry. How long have you been with the Angels?'

'All me life,' he said seriously. 'We come up the M4 from Bristol this mornin'. Give us a drag, then, Mrs C.' He removed the joint from Mrs Cornelius's fingers. 'What is the older generation comin' to, eh? This is me brothers – Rotty, Bern, Carno and Swish. Old friends o' mine,' he explained to the other Angels, handing Swish the joint. 'Watch it. It's a bit manky. Well, well, well.' He fell into an awkward silence, shared by his brothers. 'So . . .'

'Shall we get that drink, then?' said Rotty.

'Yeah. Right, then. See ya later, maybe.' He raised his gauntleted hand in a clenched fist salute and led his friends once again in the direction of the bar.

' 'E must 'ave a motor-bike now,' said Mrs Cornelius.

'Yes,' said Catherine, casting off.

'Is it tomorrow – or just the end of time?' asked the late great Jimi Hendrix over the speakers.

Catherine began a new row.

She saw Jack striding through the crowds, scowling to keep the people at bay. His method of moving was to aim straight for the spot he wanted to get through, ignoring friends and strangers alike until he had arrived. Already journalists had sighted him and were beginning to circle, while acquaintances were left gasping 'Hello, Jack,' in his wake.

Jack's black hair was damp with sweat, it curled around his swarthy, sullen face. He wore a Wrangler denim shirt and yellow velvet trousers. His feet were bare. As he approached their table, his scowl began to vanish and by the time he reached Cathy he was giving her a weary smile. 'You all right, then?'

'Fine,' she said. 'It got too crowded in the dressing-room.'

' 'Alf of London's in there,' he said. 'Wotcher, Mrs C. Finding all this a bit strange, are you?'

'It's smashing,' said Catherine's mother. 'I'm glad I said I'd come. I could stay 'ere forever. Everybody's so nice.'

Sighing, Jack sat between them. 'You seen what it's like out there?' He indicated the hall.

'Terence says there's sixty thousand.'

Jack was amused. 'What? Fleas?'

'It's packed out,' said Catherine.

'It'd 'ave to be, to pay for all the free booze Terence is givin' away.' Jack expected his career to collapse at any moment and he resented anything he considered unnecessary expense. He already had a fortune invested in property, but he continued to be as insecure as he had always been. He was the only member of Emerald City to take any interest at all in the book-keeping.

Already some journalist had arrived. He wore a black plastic wind-cheater and grey flannels, with a pink open-neck shirt, and his shortish fair hair was unkempt and greasy. The journalists were always the graceless ones. 'Have you got a moment, Jack? I don't want to break into a private party? But if we could get a photo. Is this the family?'

Jack ignored him, rubbing his left eye, his hand half-covering his face, his rings flashing on his fingers.

'How does it feel to be the greatest guitarist in the world?' the journalist went on.

Jack grabbed a handful of little sausages from a passing tray and began to cram them into his mouth. Journalists always made him act as crudely as possible. It was about his only protection.

'That's what our readers have just voted you. It was overwhelming. Did you see it?'

Jack had spent most of the morning laughing about it. He licked his fingers.

'Don't bother him now,' said Catherine. 'You know he won't speak to you.'

Catherine heard the journalist mutter to his photographer, even as the flash-guns went off, blinding her. 'Arrogant sod. Manners of a pig.'

'I thought Terence said there wouldn't be any press people back-stage.' Jack took the paper tissues Catherine handed him and began to wipe his fingers.

'He lets them in and you let the Angels in,' said Catherine. 'That's fair.'

Jack put his tongue in his cheek and smiled, relaxed again. 'I hadn't thought of it like that.' He cupped his strong hand behind her head and drew her to him for a kiss.

'Watch the bloody knitting,' she said.

'Bugger the knitting.' He whispered in her ear. 'I got a present for you.'

'Oh, thanks, Jack.' They shared a grin.

He sat, rocking his chair on its back legs, looking out at the crowd, whistling to himself. A couple of young girls approached holding pieces of paper and Biros. Without warning, perhaps not even conscious of their presence, he leapt up and set his face back into the scowl, heading for the dressing-room, body stooped as if he pushed a plough. 'See ya.' He was gone.

'Cor!' Mrs Cornelius wheezed as she hunted in her bag for a cigarette. 'What 'appened to 'im?'

'It's all the fans,' Catherine explained. 'He gets embarrassed.'

'Go on! 'E enjoys it! 'Oo wouldn't?'

'I don't think he does, Mum. The more famous you get, the less you're sure of yourself. He hardly knows his own name sometimes.'

'Too many drugs.'

'Maybe.'

'You gonna marry 'im?'

'Maybe.'

She continued with her knitting. She could guess what Jack's present would be. It was something to look forward to. She wished that she wasn't quite so tired, so that she would be able to enjoy it better tonight. Still, a short line of coke would solve that one.

She watched as two security guards entered and stood staring disapprovingly around them, arms folded. They wore white caps and navy-blue uniforms, with armbands printed in red: SECURITY. She became depressed. The two men talked together for a while and then moved off in different directions.

'I'll 'ave anuvver o' them, darlin'.' Mrs Cornelius reached for a drink. The waitress paused to let her take one from a tray. 'What abaht you, Caff?'

'I'll have a glass of red,' said Catherine.

The waitress's mouth tightened.

The music which began to come over the speakers was disorganized and unpleasant. Catherine realized that it must be live. The concert had begun, probably starting with Better Off Working, who were friends of Jack's. A high voice was singing. *'Sweet paranoia, well, it's melting my brain. Can't get away from that narcotic rain. Don't let it wash me right down the drain. Girl, won't you help me get back on my train . . .'*

Realizing that she had missed a stitch, Catherine began to unravel the line.

Terence reappeared. 'I told them they should do a sound check. Oh, Jesus, it's horrible.'

'They always were horrible,' said Catherine. 'It was your idea to book them. Jack said you'd regret it.'

'Jack didn't say anything to me.'

'Well, he knows them, doesn't he?' Catherine reached for her wine. She had a headache. It might be worth going to the dressing-room, now that the first band and its followers would have left, to get something to make her feel better. She put her knitting away. 'Will you be all right here for a bit, Mum?'

'Don't worry about me, love.'

Catherine stood up, shaking off her dizziness and trying to get on top of her depression. She drew a deep breath of the incensed air. It seemed cold, suddenly.

Reaching the corridor to the dressing-rooms she was stopped by a middle-aged security guard. 'What d'you want, love?'

She looked beyond him, spotting one of the roadies chatting outside the door of Jack's room. 'Bob!'

The roadie saw her there and shouted, 'It's okay.' The guard let her through.

When she got into the room there were only five or six people there, sitting in the chairs or on the floor, all rolling joints. Jack sat on a table chatting to Zonk who appeared to have fallen against the wall and let himself slip to the ground. A very young girl, with long, straight, dark red hair, a beautiful oval face, wearing a dark blue sari, a headband, and little silver chains on her wrists, ankles and throat, stood close to Jack, looking at him as he spoke. She was lovely.

Jack saw Catherine enter but finished what he was saying before greeting her. 'It's better in here now,' he said. 'Cathy, this is Marijka.'

'Hello, Marijka.' Catherine admired her body.

'Hello.' She spoke with an accent.

'She's come all the way from Amsterdam to see us,' said Jack.

'Far out.'

Marijka moved a fraction closer to Jack. She was the loveliest present Catherine had ever had.

'You really ought to start another band, you know, Zonk,'

Jack was saying reasonably. 'I mean, you're off the junk now. You'll be happier working.'

'No, man. I can't stand it,' Zonk mumbled. They had been together in the first band Jack had formed and Zonk had played bass in Red Harvest before it became Emerald City, but he hadn't been able to keep it going; mostly, then, it had been downers. They had wrecked his sense of rhythm.

Terence came in. 'Get these people out of here,' he said weakly. Nobody moved. 'Has Steve turned up yet, Jack?'

'No, man.'

'Then we won't have anybody to do the mixing, "man"!' Terence sounded almost triumphant. 'And you need someone to do the mixing. You really need someone. Have you seen the state Alan's in?' Alan was their keyboard player.

'Don't panic, Terence. It'll be all right.' Jack took a swig from a bottle of wine and made to hand it to Marijka, who shook her head. He reached under his dressing-table and pulled a can of lager from a big cardboard box. The floor was littered with empty cans, bottles, roaches, cigarette packets.

'And you're not in any better condition,' continued Terence.

'Oh, fuck off, Terence.'

A young man in a pink leather suit covered in silver stars came in behind Terence. 'Evenin' all,' he said. He pushed past Terence. 'Evenin', Terry.'

'Piss off, Denny,' said Terence. 'There's a good lad.'

Denny's girlish features showed mock astonishment. 'What? What? When I've brought lovely goodies for everybody?' Denny was a dealer who attended most of Emerald City's home counties gigs, supplying good-quality drugs at moderate prices.

'What have you got?' asked Terence.

'Some genuine Nepalese Temple Dope,' Denny told him sensuously, spreading his hands to frame his face. '*Far* out!'

'Did you get those five grams, Denny?' asked Jack.

Denny put the tip of his left forefinger against the tip of his left thumb and winked. 'Almost a hundred per cent pure. You'll love it, man.'

'How much have you got?' asked Jack. 'Dope, I mean.'

'About four ounces.'

'I'll have the lot,' said Jack reaching into his back pocket.

Denny seemed disappointed. He was a dealer who loved to deal.

'You been in England before?' Catherine asked Marijka softly.

'Oh, yes, many times,' said Marijka. Plainly she did not want to be distracted from her contemplation of Jack.

Denny was handing over the coke. Five silver paper packets wrapped in a plastic bag. Catherine reached out and took it from Jack. 'I've got a rotten headache,' she said.

'This *is* for everybody,' Jack said, adding significantly: 'Marijka would probably like some, too. Why don't you two chicks go somewhere and have a quick snort?' He tended to be mean with his drugs. He snatched the packet back from her and separated one of the silver paper envelopes, handing it to her. 'Save some for later, eh?'

'I just want a little bit for now,' she said. 'Come on, love.'

Marijka looked at Jack.

He nodded. 'You go with her. Come back later. She'll give you some coke, mm?'

'Come on.' Catherine put her hand on Marijka's exposed right shoulder. 'Haven't you got lovely skin?'

Reluctantly, Marijka let Catherine lead her from the dressing-room towards the lavatories at the end of the corridor. 'It'll be nice and private in here,' said Catherine, entering a cubicle and letting the plastic seat cover down. She put the cocaine on the seat and began to take her mirror, razor blade, spoon and straw from her bag.

Marijka watched passively, as she had watched Jack, while with the razor blade Catherine began to prepare two lines for them. She made her own line about twice as long as Marijka's. 'Shall I show you how to sniff it up?' she asked kindly.

Marijka, kneeling now, on the other side of the lavatory seat, nodded.

Catherine put the big glass straw into her left nostril and

sniffed up half the first line. Denny had been right about the quality. As the stuff numbed her nose she got a fantastic buzz almost immediately. It seemed to open up the back of her head and let the headache out. She sighed with pleasure. 'Oh, great.'

She snorted the remainder of the line through her other nostril. 'Too much.'

She watched tenderly as Marijka imitated her. The girl had trouble getting the line up properly, but the coke brought her to life. Suddenly she was beaming at Catherine.

'It's wonderful.'

Catherine leant over the seat and kissed her.

NINETEEN

*In which, once again, Captain Persson finds
herself helping the wounded*

There was thick, grey smoke rising over the tops of the
tall rhododendron bushes. Una noticed that the red and
purple flowers were blackened around the edges, as if
on its way past something had singed them. She could
think of no explanation as to the cause of this curious
effect.

She had stayed in 1973 longer than she had needed to, but
still she had not managed to get to Cambodia. She rather
wished now that she had checked at a Time Centre before
coming on to England in 1979. She wasn't used to horses.
The big sorrel colt kept tossing its head back at her as if it
had not been ridden for a while. She controlled it as best she
could, yanking at the reins and clapping her heels against its
flanks to make it go up the hill so that she could see what
had happened on the other side of the rhododendrons. The
colt's hoofs slipped in the wet, loamy earth and she thought
they would both fall, but eventually the horse had reached
the top and she could look out over what was left of the
North Devon countryside. The smells were confusing —
sweet, rich forest and bitter ash. It was an odd experience to
come out of that oak wood to the sudden sight of such absolute devastation.

The trees were like the black bones of charred beasts,
clearly defined, like specimens on white paper; the hillsides
smoked and were also black, and where there were villages
or houses a little dash of colour came from a red or yellow
flame still guttering on, though it had been three days since
the Brigante planes had been over. She had seen the jets, of
course, since then; they were easily identifiable by the red

and white roses they used for insignia. They had been heading back to their Pennine bases.

What disgusted her most was that this area had possessed absolutely no anti-aircraft cover. The crashed C-130E she had seen earlier had come down purely as a result of inexpert flying (it had never been designed as a bomber in the first place) and she had regretted the waste of the four young crewmen – all with long blond braided hair and fair moustaches, all handsome – whose bodies she had found inside. She had gained something, however. She now possessed a good Polish-made AK-47 rifle (how it had come into Brigante hands she could not guess) which, because of its lightness and lack of kick, she had always preferred to longer-range assault rifles, and this one had the added advantage of the folding metal stock. It fitted neatly into the hand-tooled scabbard strapped to her saddle. She wore her old EM-3 on her back, together with a bag of scarce .28 cartridges which went with it. The AK-47 accepted the far more easily obtained standard 7.63 ammunition.

Una could not believe that anything survived in that landscape, but she had been told that Craven would meet her here and there was nothing for it but to take a deep breath of the relatively clean air and urge the colt forward. As she rode she checked the map she held in her free hand, trying to make out which of the ruined villages was Cattleford. She went slightly to the south east and found the remains of a major road; the horse's hoofs skidded slightly on the asphalt, but it was easier than trying to ride over the burned scrub.

She was lucky. A sign for Cattleford, the metal singed and slightly warped, was still standing. She rode into a mess of masonry which had been so badly hit that there was scarcely a piece larger than the ragged straw sombrero she wore to protect her over-sensitive eyes from the sun.

'Craven?' she called.

Something rose cautiously from what must have been a cellar; it stood there, its M-16 held at the ready. The figure was tall and its gaunt features were covered in soot. It wore an old flying helmet which had been painted silver and it had a cracked leather jacket covered in patches bearing cryptic but not particularly interesting designs.

She knew Craven would not recognize her. He was, in turn, only a dim memory – something that was no longer real.

He was thinner than the men she normally found attractive and she wondered if he had changed physically, if it was merely the name that was the same.

'Craven?'

He smiled, still not sure if Una were an enemy or the courier he was expecting. 'Captain Persson?'

She nodded and dismounted. The sadness in his face attracted her. He seemed to be one of the few who had not been brutalized by this ferociously petty war. A weary veteran, an experienced fighter, like herself.

'Well.' Craven removed the flying helmet to reveal a shock of thick, red hair. 'We really don't need to know about reinforcements now.'

'So I see. How many of your people left?' He reminded her of a poet she had admired in her youth – Wilde, Swinburne; someone like that.

'Two,' he said. 'Both wounded. I had to shoot two others. The bastards were dropping nerve-gas towards the end. They're lucky to have it to waste. The wounded ones are down there.' Craven jerked his head back at the pit from which he had just climbed. 'Have you any medical kit? Anything?'

She reached into the pannier on the left of her saddle and drew out a basic kit. 'There's morphine in here. Not as much as there should be. I used some last night on a civilian.'

'Seems a pity to waste it.' Craven made no other comment but stepped forward to take the kit. He replaced his helmet, slung the M-16 over his shoulder and slid back into the hole. Una did not follow him. She stroked the nose of the horse, glancing around at the ruins, listening to the faint murmurings from the cellar.

Craven came back very quickly. He was shaking his head. 'One had died. I don't think the other will make it, but maybe we could get together some kind of stretcher. There's planks down there which didn't get too badly burned.'

Una sighed. 'You don't want to leave him?'

Craven shook his head. His smile was crooked, a trifle dishonest. 'This is the loser division, Captain Persson. We look after one another.'

While finding the statement a bit peculiar, Una's response was sympathetic. 'We'll use the horse, then. We could make some kind of travois.'

Craven frowned, momentarily abstracted. He looked at her and he smiled again. Then he straightened his back, his eyes becoming slightly hooded, making Una wonder what private rôle he was adopting to get him through this particular crisis. He was the first person she had met for some time who attracted her, whom she wanted to know better. He seemed to be a brave man, hiding a natural dignity behind what appeared to her to be something of a posture of dignity. Perhaps he was doing it for her. She glanced at the blasted ground so that he would not see the private humour in her eyes. This was no time to feel randy.

The deep stone cellar had, as Craven had claimed, hardly been touched by the fire-bombs. Through the gloom Una made out two figures, one moving faintly and muttering, the other quite still. Craven had already found two suitable planks and was clumsily trying to lash them together with a long piece of oily rope. Una put a hand on his shoulder.

'Let's get the bloke up first.'

Craven thought this over and nodded. He propped the planks against the wall and they toppled down, narrowly missing the wounded man. This time Una grinned openly and got her arms under the body of the soldier, through whose fresh bandages blood was already beginning to seep. He had been hit mainly in the right arm and leg, probably by shrapnel. Craven's bandaging had been almost completely useless.

'Take his legs,' said Una.

Craven followed her instructions and they made their way slowly up the slope formed by earth and rubble until they could lower the man to the ground. Craven went back for the planks and watched admiringly as Una, using the rope and her canvas cape, quickly built the travois. Then she re-bandaged the wounded man and they carried him to the travois, making him as comfortable as possible. He was grateful. His morphine-numbed lips formed a few words which Craven seemed to understand. He gave the man a thumbs-up sign.

'We'll be back in no time. There's a hospital in Taunton.'

Una felt that this was not the moment to mention what had happened to Taunton.

Later Una and Captain Craven lay in the shade of a large oak tree watching the horse cropping the grass near the grave which they had dug for the soldier, who had died five or six hours after they had set off. They were relaxing, smoking a joint, fairly sure that the CLF ground troops were nowhere nearby. Craven had removed his helmet and flying jacket and was stripped to the waist.

'So the Brigantes have occupied Leeds,' he said. 'Not bad. No wonder they suddenly started concentrating on the West country. We really didn't expect that strike. We were sitting ducks. We hoped that the war might be over. It looks as if we can't count on a settlement now. We're finished, wouldn't you say?'

'We were finished years ago,' she said. 'It's the foreign interference that's kept everything going. I thought that when the French suddenly rediscovered their old Celtic affiliations it might create a fresh spurt of trouble but so far they don't seem to be supplying the Celtic Liberation Front with anything more than normal support. You should see their newspapers. Full of anti-Anglo Saxon propaganda.'

Craven drew deeply on the joint. 'What about the Normans, then? Where do we fit?'

Una loosened the top buttons of her fatigue jacket. 'You're beginning to talk in their terms. That's never a very good sign. How did you come to get involved?'

'It was something to do. A cop-out, you could say. I used

to be a writer. This, by and large, is a much easier life.'

'You must have been a very sentimental writer, if you can say that.'

'I don't think I was. Well, not about myself, at any rate. Maybe about technology. I was very interested in technology. That, too, is the attraction of the army. I originally applied to the air force, but I'd had a breakdown and apparently they think that's a bad qualification for a flyer but a good one for the infantry.'

Una accepted the joint as he handed it to her. It was Nepalese. She had rescued almost half a pound, along with the rifle, from the crashed C-130E.

'And what did you do before you joined up, Captain Persson?'

'A lot of things. Basically I was in the entertainment business. I took war pictures. I was on the stage for a while.' Una waved one of her beautiful hands. 'Boredom is what gets me.' She was surprised to find herself adopting a posture, perhaps in response to his.

'I can't think of anything much more boring than this fucking war,' he told her. 'It's a fantasy war. Who wants to fight it?'

'People who want to fight. Where did this one start? Perhaps in Belfast. The Irish problem. Of course, there wouldn't have been any Irish problem without England, would there?'

'Don't ask me. I've never had much of an interest in politics.'

'It's always been my weakness. We find our different forms of escape.'

'You like politicians?' He was not looking at her.

'It's glamour, you know, which keeps a woman going. Perhaps it's wrong, but that the truth of it. A dreadful instinct. Stronger than any sex-drive, Captain.'

His mind wasn't apparently on her words, but he turned his head politely back, his eyes half-closed, his fingers (longer even than hers) stroking the faded bracken. 'Sex-drive?'

'Romance. Without it I doubt if the race would have gone on so long. Not if women had had anything to do with it, anyway.'

'Romance?' He smiled slowly at her and reached out to touch her cheek.

She lay back and watched as his face came towards her. There were little scars on the pale skin; there was a piece of tobacco on the upper lip; she noted one last flicker in the eyes before they shut and his lips breathed against hers and she shut her own eyes and put her arms around him so that her fingers closed on rib-cage and muscle, on his lean shoulders; and she opened her lips to his teeth and his tongue, and she felt his tired legs against her own legs and she knew that almost certainly he would not be able to fuck her and, there and then, she loved him.

It had to be the uniform, she thought.

TWENTY

In which Catherine Cornelius enjoys a personal experience of Entropy

Catherine lay in bed listening to Trevor swearing in the next room. If he slept an hour or two longer, she thought, he'd be a lot better off. And so would I. But sleepers and tranquillizers rarely had much effect on him these days. He appeared in the doorway, glaring down at where she lay under the patchwork duvet. His hair was spiky. He had a towel around his thin waist. There was blood running along his neck from a small cut.

'You've been using my razor to shave your bloody legs again. You are a fucking sloppy bitch, aren't you?' When he raved like this he tended to spit.

She felt despondent. 'I haven't shaved my legs in weeks.' She pulled back the duvet and waved her right foot at him. 'Look.'

'Oh, fuck off. Anyway, somebody has been using my razor. Who was here while I was in Holland?'

With a shrug she put her leg back under the blanket. 'About three thousand friends of yours. People you said could crash here while you were away.'

He sneered. 'How many of them did you fuck?'

She remembered Richard. 'You think I'd fuck any of your manky friends? Bloody speed freaks, covered in sores?'

He wiped his neck with the towel. 'All you do is criticize. If I'm not good enough for you, if you don't like me or my friends, why don't you get out of here? I'm pissed off with supporting you. You just lie there all day doing bugger all. How long is it since you cooked me a breakfast?'

'You said you didn't like me doing domestic stuff.'

'Yeah. Well, you don't do anything else nowadays, do you?'

She began to get up. Her body ached with tension. 'I'll cook you a breakfast.'

'There isn't anything to eat.'

'You never eat breakfast, anyway.'

'I might. Shut up, for Christ's sake! I don't need your bloody sarcasm on top of everything else. I should have been at the studios by now. It'll be another bummer, thanks to you. I can't play after one of these scenes. You know that.'

'You ought to save yourself up. What's left of you. Why don't you stop making them?'

'I don't make them, darling. If this place was run a bit better – if I didn't find my bleeding razor fucked every morning – if you kept this place even reasonably tidy – maybe I wouldn't have to lose my temper. Think of that.'

She said: 'You used to accuse me of being too houseproud. Besides, I don't give a shit about your razor or this bloody flat. I came to stay with Mary, remember? You wanted me to. I didn't want to live with you. You asked me to, after Mary got killed. Remember?'

He turned away. 'Sure. I was a sucker.'

She sank back on to the pillows. 'I set out to ruin your life. To lead you on. To make a fool of you. Because I like it.'

'You're closer than you think, darling. I should have listened to Bob. He warned me about you. Why don't you piss off?'

'All right.'

'Oh, great. Now you're going to blackmail me.'

'Make up your mind.'

'It was fine, wasn't it, when I was in the money? When I brought plenty of chicks and drugs home. But it's not so good now, is it?'

'I told you to stop bringing anything home. I told you to get out of the band. Anyone could see Bob was ripping you off. I even told you not to sign that contract, and that was while I was still *with* Bob.'

'I told you so, I told you so. Thanks for nothing.'

'Do you want me to go out and get you something for breakfast?'

'Oh, fuck off.'

He left the room and she listened to him clattering about in the kitchen. She heard him muttering. She knew he was finishing off the rest of the formal accusations. She could no longer feel sorry for him; she could no longer feel guilty. She waited for the silence that usually came after a few minutes of this. Then she prepared herself for his re-entrance.

He came back holding a mug of tea.

'Want some tea?'

'Thanks,' she said.

'I'm sorry about that.'

She sipped the tea. It wasn't worth replying. He never seemed aware of the pattern himself and she couldn't bring herself to go through the ritual, even though it would mean a quieter life. Besides, this was probably only a pause, while he got his breath.

'Well, I am sorry,' he said.

'Good.'

'Well, it's shitty to find your razor fucked.'

'Yes.'

'I'm sorry.'

'Okay.'

'You understand?'

'Oh, sure.'

'You don't sound too convinced.'

She sighed.

'Oh, you fucking bitch!' He was off again. 'You lousy, sloppy, lazy cow! You—' He advanced to the bed and stood looking down at her. 'You bitch.'

'Hadn't you better get to the studio?'

He seized her naked shoulders. He leaned forward to try to kiss her. Instinctively she turned her head away.

'You bitch.' Half-heartedly he slapped her across the cheek. She wondered why she feared physical violence so much when it was accompanied by anger. He crossed the room to the mountain of giant cushions on which his jeans and shirt lay. He began to dress, pulling beads, bangles and medallions expertly over his head and wrists, adjusting his huge belt around his hips, pulling on his stackheel denim boots, one eye on the mirror. He always seemed to dress as if he were getting ready for the stage. 'You come on all lust and rolling eyes and you're really as frigid as a bloody nun.'

'You frighten me,' she said quietly.

'Baby, you frighten *me*.' He pointed a finger at her in much the way he had once pointed it at crowds of screaming thousands. 'You conned me, Catherine. What the fuck do I get out of this one? I lay bread on you, drugs on you, chicks on you, buy up the sex stores, and whenever I get home you're too tired or you're feeling funny or – I don't know!'

'I'll leave, then.'

'Don't threaten me.'

'You don't love me.'

'I do love you.'

She hadn't the courage to say what she wanted to say, that she had never loved him, only felt sorry for him when Mary had been killed when the van hit a lorry head on.

'When will you be back?' she asked.

'Day after tomorrow. If the roads are all right we're going straight on to Newcastle. We're doing a gig for the big base up there.' Most of his work was for the armed forces these days.

'I'll get your washing done for you,' she said.

'Look, there's no need to come on like a martyr, Cathy.'

'I said I'd do it.'

He sat down at the dressing table and began to pour cocaine from a plastic sachet on to the glass surface, carefully breaking down the white crystals with a razor blade. Through a rolled up ten pound note he sniffed the long line into his right nostril, a single snort. He held his nostrils together, still sniffing. He drew a deep breath. 'Nothing. This must be fifty per cent speed, twenty per cent soda, twenty per cent floor-sweepings and ten per cent coke.'

'It seemed all right to me,' she said.

'Maybe it was you cut it.'

'You only gave me about a hundredth of a gram.'

He was in better spirits. The coke was working, though he didn't know it. He went to get his coat and his guitars. He came back into the room, pulling on his Afghan coat. 'I'm sorry, Cathy. You know what I'm like when I'm going off early in the morning. I haven't had a lot of sleep.'

'You don't need to be there for a couple of hours,' she said.

'Yeah, I know, but I've got to score first, haven't I? Before we go, you know.'

'You'd think the army would supply you with that as well.'

He winked. 'They do, these days, but never enough. Those soldiers can keep going on less than a gram a day, some of 'em.' There was a rumour that the army was paying entertainers entirely in drugs, but that was probably the top acts who didn't need the bread.

He glanced around the bedroom. 'Try and tidy this place up a bit before I get back.'

He disappeared.

'Have a nice day,' she said.

'Bitch.' He went out of the front door and slammed it so that everything rattled.

Catherine turned over on her stomach and began to masturbate in the hope that it might relax her.

Later, she packed her things and went to see Richard. He acted as if he had expected her, kissed her and told her to put her things in the bedroom and get undressed. At least he was positive, she thought.

Richard came in and took some of his special gear from a drawer. 'All right?'

She nodded. She was remembering her first pair of high-heeled shoes. She had been fourteen. She remembered how difficult it had been to walk in them, how self-conscious and put-upon she had felt when, lipsticked and perfumed, she had tottered down the street on the way to the party at Sammy's. She had grinned, however, when the two boys on the corner had wolf-whistled her. Then her mum had shaken her arm, telling her not to be so bloody vain. She supposed it was a silly thing to be thinking about, really, while Richard hand-cuffed her hands behind her naked back and told her what a disgusting whore she was and how he was going to fuck her sore. By and large, she reflected vaguely, he wasn't much of an improvement on Trevor. Richard wasn't even working now. He hadn't picked up his guitar in six months, Trevor had said, and before that he had only done a couple of sessions in a whole year.

The time passed slowly, but at last she was massaging Vaseline into her wrists while Richard held her shoulders in his manly left arm and told her how she was the only girl he had ever loved. She stared into the gloom of the basement room and wondered why the glittering rails of the brass bedstead reminded her of home. They had never had anything like a brass bedstead. She counted the bars. There were five. The knobs on the outer two had been replaced with glaring Chinese theatrical masks Richard had been given by some girlfriend. Richard's clothes hung over the top rail; brightly patched dirty Levis and a T-shirt that said Assassinate Frodo. She realized that she liked him even less than Trevor. It was probably this sentimentality which put her off him. Sadists were only worth living with if they were consistent. Her own clothes were folded, as usual, neatly on the chair. Richard reached over her and found his Valium bottle. 'There's only about a hundred mills. left.' He shook four of the yellow five-milligram tablets into his hand and swallowed them down. 'I'll have to get a new script tomorrow. Remind me, will you, Cath?'

She had decided not to stay, after all. 'Yes,' she agreed.

With Richard's history of breakdowns, he had had no difficulty scoring downers from the local GP. When they had first met she had told him that Valium made you speedy and untogether and only calmed you down if you didn't do many drugs (it didn't always work, even then). As it was he had been living off Mandies for years. He wouldn't accept her explanation that the reason he kept falling down and dropping things was not exhaustion, as he claimed, but the effects of the tranquillizers and sleeping pills. He'd told her that she knew shit all about it and that Valium was the only thing that kept him from going over the top, that if he didn't use it he would get violent.

She put the lid back on the Vaseline jar, turned on her side and tried to get comfortable on his constricting arm. The poor sod had served his time, she thought. He had been famous at nineteen. When he was twenty-one he had already been in two expensive mental hospitals. At twenty-two he had gone to the country to get himself together, had got bored one day and gone into Torquay where he had freaked out in a pub when four policemen had been called to ask him to stop talking to the barmaid because she had to go to bed and they wanted to close the pub. The police had brought on his anxiety with a vengeance and he had fought them for over twenty minutes before they got him into the car, into the nick, and from the nick to the local loony bin, where he had been filled up with Largactyl and sent, after two weeks, into the world, knowing himself to be a fully accredited manic-depressive, because that was how they had classified him. After he had stopped the drugs they had prescribed and lived through the subsequent withdrawal, he had come back to London, joined two or three bands for a few gigs, started going up under his own steam and the euphoria of working again, had become so speedy that no one had been able to stand him for more than an hour at a time, and his best friends had told him to go back on downers for his own sake. They hadn't made a lot of difference. He used more and more every day and every day got stranger, which proved to him that his manic-depression was becoming increasingly difficult to control. He had given her as an illustration of his great self-control the fact that he never used speed because it made him worse, that he never, now, dropped acid because too many bummers had tipped him into his established madness, that he never did coke because it made him paranoid, junk made him only depressed, dope made him too self-aware. His point had been that he only used the Valium and Mogadon for keeping himself from doing harm to himself or others.

It was familiar drug-logic. Catherine had heard similar rationales a hundred times before. Some drugs worked for you; some didn't.

She smiled. They started out such nice guys. And so innocent, most of them. She wondered about the housewives and the politicians and soldiers and businessmen whose doctors were helpfully speeding them along through life, keeping them calm, active, happy while every single decision they made was made, as she made her decisions, as Richard made them, in what was rarely better than a semi-conscious condition, whatever it felt like at the time. About the only thing that could be said for the drug culture was that a lot of the people in it at least knew what was happening to them. Her brother, who had in the mid-sixties spent most of his time seeking out new drugs to try, had referred to the 'fantasy quotient'; he believed that the world was becoming less and less rational every day, that the increased reliance on the drug and electronics industries was like Rome relying on charms and omens when she could have been sorting out her economic problems. Nonetheless, she could have done with some coke. She was going to miss it a lot. It was the sort of drug that once enjoyed you missed for the rest of your life. She thought of it as a drug of invulnerability. It was the only substitute for sex she had ever found. She began to think of going back to Trevor, if only for the coke. She didn't know anyone else, these days, who could get hold of it easily. Maybe a soldier? She dismissed the idea. It had become so expensive, coke. It made up for a lot of things. She wondered why she had bothered to see Richard again. Her instincts were shot. She had an urge to return home. To see her mother. But she couldn't face the tension she would find. Perhaps she should get away from the rock scene. It had all gone sour, anyway. Everyone was dying or falling apart.

Richard gave his familiar, peculiar lurch against her buttocks. She relaxed as best she could, hoping that this would be his last effort of the evening to get it up and that, even if he failed, he would not begin one of his inquests. They always revolved around his efforts to give her the kind of sex life she wanted (he had never accepted her claims that it had little, really, to do with sex). He always said at some stage, 'Well, it's what you want, isn't it, you bitch?' She wondered whether it was, perhaps, what she wanted now. It didn't give her the release she had come to expect. Maybe she had to be in love. Maybe she lacked self-respect.

Richard's hands clung to her breasts as if for support while his wasted body pushed desperately against her and then slowly, somewhat apologetically, she fell asleep.

TWENTY-ONE

*In which Una Persson considers the problem
of personal loyalty*

'We're going to have to get out of England, Una,' said Craven. They had reached the Atlantic. They stood together on the cliff looking down towards Tintagel Bay, now an abandoned coastal installation. 'The Brigantes don't usually bother to collect heads. Apparently a warrior can win a lot of esteem if he brings in ours. Are you flattered?'

She was too introspective to bother to acknowledge this poor attempt at humour. Her original plan had been to steal one of the motor boats at Tintagel and head round the coast in the hope of contacting a friendly tribe. All the boats had gone.

Even in the sunshine Tintagel had a gloomy, seedy look, in common with many other once glamorous places like Haight-Ashbury or Prague or Bangkok. The small beach and the sea of the bay below the castle ruins were spread with every sort of litter picked over by dirty gulls. Una was anxious to be on the move and she separated from Craven, plodding along the cliff-edge, holding her long coat so that it would not be snagged by the rusting barbed wire. Soon it was possible to take note of the broader sweep of the ocean; it was blue and only slightly turbulent. The sun struck the cream of the surf and was reflected towards the land. A hint of a memory. She drew her brows together, shading her eyes.

Craven rejoined her. 'I don't think Arthur will be much help.' When she ignored him he added: 'You'd like to be shot of me, wouldn't you? I'm hampering you.'

'I don't think it's you,' she said.

He was displeased with her reply. He made a petulant

sound. 'I thought you knew all the angles. You gave that impression.'

'I'm afraid inertia is taking over.'

'What are you looking at?' He was slightly short-sighted.

'It could be a ship.'

'Hadn't we better get off the cliffs before they spot us?'

'They've already seen us, if those flashes are from binoculars.'

'What sort of ship?'

'Not a warship. I've seen it before somewhere.'

'Friendly?'

'Possibly not. I can't remember.'

The ship was a fore-and-aft rigged steam-yacht; a schooner, white-painted, its brasswork shining, its sails filled with wind. It approached in a curve, turned clear of the wind so that the sails went quite suddenly limp. She saw men furling canvas. She saw an anchor drop.

'Who the hell are they?' Craven started to laugh nervously. 'Pirates? Smugglers? The revenue men?'

Una nodded without listening to him. She saw the longboat go down, heard the clear sound of its engine starting. All the sailors were dressed in white, but the uniforms were not familiar. The longboat was heading for the bay.

She moved quickly, running back along the cliff. 'What's happening?' cried Craven. She shook her head. 'I don't know.' She found the broken concrete of the steps leading down the cliff. She controlled her haste and tested each step as she clambered down.

The longboat rounded the headland. She reached the beach, taking cover behind one of the weed-smeared bunkers. She watched the boat's approach. Craven skulked beside her now, his machine-pistol in his hand. 'Would we have a chance,' he whispered, 'if we rushed them? We could steal the boat.'

'Wait.'

The longboat was beached. The sailors adjusted their clothes. They wore white baggy smocks, baggy trousers. At their throats and their wrists were huge red ruffs and instead of buttons there were red and blue pom-poms on their smocks, shoes and pointed hats. Only one of them had black and white pom-poms and black ruffs. He appeared to be the leader.

'Pierrots,' said Craven. 'This is ridiculous.'

As the pierrots drew the boat up the shingle Una could see the words on its side: *Tintagel Concert Party*.

The leading pierrot wore a black domino. He stood looking about him on the filthy beach, stripping off his mask. Una had already guessed who he might be. She was not entirely relieved; she continued to be suspicious, but she showed herself, wishing that her coat was not so tattered and muddy.

Jerry Cornelius seemed pensive. He screwed the domino in his left hand. 'There you are, Miss Persson. I thought we might be too late.'

'Not at all, Colonel. You arrived just in time.'

Jerry regarded Craven with the cocked eye of a suspicious vulture. 'Who the fuck's this?'

'Craven. He's with me.'

'Any experience?'

'None.'

'Oh, sod. Why do you always have to introduce complications just when I think I've got everything neatly sussed ...' He was not particularly querulous. 'We've no conditioning facilities on board the *Teddy Bear*. She's completely stripped down these days.'

'He'll have to risk it, then, won't he?'

'You've warned him? It's best to be prepared for an identity crisis.'

Craven began. 'Did you know all along about these people coming, Una? Hello, Jerry. A Colonel now, are we?'

'I'm Gilbert the Filbert, didn't you know?' For Craven's benefit Jerry produced a silly smile. Craven missed the reference. It was obvious to Una that Jerry Cornelius didn't recognize Craven. Evidently he had been shifting about and his memory had been at least partially replaced.

One of the pierrots, a pale, anxious man, consulted a

watch, the third in a row which stretched up his arm. Una had seen him once before at a Time Centre. 'We're behind schedule, Mr C. There's not much margin.'

Jerry acknowledged him. 'Okay. Everybody back in the boat.'

Craven showed reluctance. 'Are you sure this is wise, Una?'

She was already seating herself in the forward part of the longboat, feeling better than she had done for a long while. There was something reassuring about Cornelius. It must be part of his attraction. 'Up to you,' she said. 'The only thing I can guarantee is that very shortly we'll be out of this zone altogether. I'm not saying the next zone will be any better. On a straight time-line, of course. Nothing fancy. No hopping about.' She looked to Cornelius for confirmation. He inclined his head.

'Zone?' Craven climbed in beside her. She did not elaborate. The pierrots unshipped the oars, to push the boat away from the shore. In the stern, Jerry started the engine. 'You'd forgotten how to get out, hadn't you?' he called to Una. 'It's been happening a lot lately. Everything's fragmenting, as usual.'

'I thought you liked it like that.' The noise of the engine half-drowned her voice.

'It depends what sort of shape you're in.' He ran a hand over his features, scratching at a faint stubble. 'And what shape they're in, too, of course.'

They left Tintagel behind and had soon reached the yacht. Una was surprised by the freshness of the air. The whole of England must be stinking of rot, she thought. Jerry helped her to climb the rope ladder up the white side. At the rail Shaky Mo Collier, clutching a huge sub machine-gun which dripped oil down his costume, awaited her. 'Glad to have you aboard, Captain Persson,' he said. She winked back at him. The little man still resembled a decadent Eskimo, his movements were still nervous, and excitement still burned in his eyes. He was the only one of the ship's company who sported a weapon.

Una was relieved now that she stood on the deck. She recognized a number of faces but could not name them. She looked around for her best friend.

'Catherine won't be with us on this shift.' Jerry spoke confidently. His spirits had improved considerably since their last encounter. He gave her hope as he put his arm around her, kissing her firmly on the forehead. 'But I expect we can find her, if you're keen. You're not looking well, Una.'

'I'm a bit tired,' she said. 'Were you hunting for me, then?'

'It was obvious you'd gone to pieces. How about the boyfriend?'

'Craven wants to escape. I couldn't leave him.'

'A bit clinging, is he?'

'You know what they're like.' She felt no guilt.

Craven lurched into earshot, swearing. He had lost his footing.

'Frank?' said Una.

'Below. Sulking as usual. He misses his mother.' Jerry watched his men swing the longboat aboard and fix it in its davits. 'Do you remember this yacht? I've probably had it cleaned a bit since you last saw it. It's fitted with my latest engines.'

Una looked back towards England. 'I shouldn't really have left it in that mess.'

'Well, it wasn't just your fault, you know. Everybody had a hand in it.'

'How many of the others are still in there?'

'Just a handful. They'll make their own way out.'

'I didn't.'

'They're not in such lousy shape.'

'Where are we going?' Craven demanded. 'Why is everyone being so bloody mysterious?'

'Because it's a mystery tour.' Jerry always adapted his jokes to his audience. 'Take it easy, Mr Craven. Just enjoy your holiday. It'll be over soon enough. What mysteries would you like to experience today?'

'Easy,' Una warned Jerry carelessly, 'I have certain responsibilities.'

Jerry refused to listen. 'You're on holiday, too, Una. You can forget all about your responsibilities and relax for a while. I'm in charge. You'll find quite a lot of your old wardrobe in your cabin. Have a bath. There's a comfortable deckchair waiting for you as soon as you've changed.'

'What about me?' said Craven. 'Can I change, too?'

Jerry looked him over.

'I doubt it,' he said.

TWENTY-TWO

In which Catherine Cornelius bids farewell to ancient glories

'Few people,' said Constant, stroking Catherine's cheek as he moved his pawn, 'understand the trials and responsibilities of the committed sadist.' He pinched her ear-lobe in his nails.

Marius, his friend, scratched his long nose, glancing casually to where Catherine sat passively on the floor, her shoulder resting against Constant's worsted leg. He swept his queen the length of the board. 'Check,' he said.

Constant scowled and let go of her. His expression became boyish as he tugged at his little beard, studying his method of escape. He was Greek, with the weak, slightly furtive features of the typical antiquarian book-dealer. He was just what she had needed. He moved his king and put his hand against her face again.

'Good,' said Marius. He was a very old friend of Constant's. They had only recently met again, when Marius's regiment had been stationed in the Knightsbridge barracks. Their previous meeting had been in Rome, five years before. Marius hated wearing his uniform and was now dressed in a dark blue sweater and light grey slacks, but his grooming betrayed both his occupation and his race.

Catherine was glad to see that Constant was losing. It would give him the impetus to take his frustration out on her. While she enjoyed the waiting she was feeling a twinge or two of impatience.

The room was lit with dim lamps, mostly *art nouveau* oil lamps supported by draped Mucha nymphs in cast iron and bronze. Along one wall ran the locked, glass-fronted bookcases which held Constant's special collection. By taking one or two books from it a month he was able to live well. He believed that the collection and the other things he had locked in the trunk in the bedroom would provide an excellent income for the rest of his life. Marius was the only soldier who came to the house who was not a customer. Marius refused to be stimulated either by Constant's insinuating references or by the profusion of late-nineteenth- and early-twentieth-century erotica decorating walls, tables and mantelpieces. He showed a mild interest in Constant's Pre-Raphaelites, his Burne-Jones, his two Hunts, his late Millais, for he enjoyed collecting paintings, but his taste was more for Rembrandt and Hals.

'Check.'

Catherine took a keener interest in the game.

Constant said: 'It is weary work, wielding the whip.'

'Oh, true,' replied Marius. 'You should have my job, Constant.'

'They are not dissimilar, I suppose.'

Marius refused consensus.

Catherine, to relieve her boredom, kissed Constant's knee. He smiled affectionately down and slid his fingernail along her shoulder blade.

'I believe it's stalemate,' said Marius.

Constant fell back into his chair, caressing Catherine's face once more. 'Oh, very well.' He gave the appearance of magnanimity. 'My mind isn't on the game. This could go on all night.' He reached to grasp her left breast. 'And it would not be fair to keep this beautiful creature waiting.' He stood up. 'Let's call it a draw, shall we?'

Marius was amused. 'I have to phone Rome, anyway.' He was still nominally head of the family firm which specialized in canning luxury foods. 'It was a pleasant game. Thank you for the dinner. For the drinks.' He stared at Catherine as if he felt he should make some remark to her, perhaps to thank her for her decorative presence. He seemed to disapprove of her. Or perhaps, more likely, he disapproved of Constant's flaunting of his power over her. A man with as much personal power as Marius could afford to regard such displays as vulgar. He accepted the topcoat Constant handed him and began to button it up.

'Goodbye, Colonel,' said Catherine sweetly.

But he was already in the hall. She heard Constant laugh and slap his thigh. She heard Marius clear his throat and murmur some remark.

Constant returned to her. 'Did you say something?'

'Only goodbye.'

He stood over her, his legs slightly apart. 'You can remove that dress now.' She wore the peasant frock he had found for her. Her own clothes were in the bedroom. She began to stand up. 'No,' he said, 'stay there.' She pulled the frock from her body, kneeling. Constant's breathing became deeper and his eyes, focused intensely on her body, had the sudden appearance of strength. 'Good girl,' he said. 'You are a good girl, aren't you, Catherine?'

'Yes,' she whispered, 'oh, yes.'

'And you want to please me?'

'Yes.'

'You shall.' He moved past her. She heard him enter the bedroom. 'Stay in exactly that position,' he told her.

She guessed that he was fetching one of his whips, but when he came into her field of vision again his hands were empty. He had changed into a kimono which reached to his knees, revealing his thin, hairy legs. He wore a pair of dark leather slippers on his feet. As he moved closer the kimono parted. He was naked. His penis was half-erect. She anticipated the effort needed to make it as stiff as possible. As a sadist he was excellent but, in common with most of those she had known, particularly the Greeks, he was never very far away from impotence.

'Take it in your lips,' he said.

Obediently she took his penis into her mouth, rolling her tongue around it, scraping it gently with her teeth, her body supported on her hands. 'Good,' he said. 'Slowly. Good.'

Deliberately, she tried to hold off his full arousal, even as his groin thrust against her face. She knew that he was unlikely to come, but tonight he might be satisfied only by this and she wanted more from him, for she had to leave early if she was to catch her plane. She pretended to cough, pulling free of him. For a moment he continued to move against her face. 'That wasn't right,' he said. 'You're wilful tonight.'

'I'm sorry,' she said. 'I think I've got a cold coming.'

'Hm.' He was mildly angry. 'Now, again.'

She accepted him for the second time and waited until his penis began to swell before she coughed. 'I'm sorry, Constant, really.'

'You are a bad girl, aren't you?' he said.

She bowed her head. 'Yes.'

Impatiently he put both hands under her chin and pushed his by now limp penis between her lips. Almost immediately she started to cough. He dragged her head back by the hair. He glowered down at her. 'Naughty child.'

'Yes.' She was beginning to get her lift. 'I'm sorry. I'm so sorry.' This time her cough was spontaneous. He slapped her across both cheeks. Her face glowed and she stopped coughing. 'Naughty little girl!'

She pretended that she was eager to try again. She bent towards his penis but he drew away. 'No. No more.'

'Please.' She crawled towards him.

'No.'

'I'll try not to—'

'Go into the bedroom,' he said sternly.

Again she began to get to her feet, but he pushed her down. 'No. Crawl.'

She crawled around the furniture, across the Persian carpet, into the gloom of the bedroom. It was lit by candles. 'Get on to the bed,' he said.

She obeyed, lying face forward, arms spread. She heard him open the lid of his trunk. There was a clatter as he took something out, closing the lid. Then he stood staring down at her.

'You have been a particularly bad child tonight,' he said. His accent grew thicker. 'Haven't you?'

She could only nod.

The tip of his whip touched her backbone. He drew it

down to her bottom, he pushed the tip between her legs so that she felt it against her vagina before he moved it down the back of her legs, stroked her just behind the knees with it, caressed her calves with it, slid it around her feet and her ankles. By now she had lost her tiredness entirely and had become acutely conscious of her body, its smoothness, its beauty.

'There will be six strokes tonight,' he said, 'at least.' The whip hissèd. Her buttocks flamed. She did not let him hear her groan. She held it from him. She owed him only a little generosity. He moved methodically down her bottom, placing each stroke expertly, one below the other. On the sixth stroke her whole body sang with white fire and, for her own pleasure, she screamed.

He had not finished. He fell on top of her, biting her neck, her shoulders, pinching the flesh of her waist, scratching her pubis, brutally clutching her clitoris. She groaned and, as methodically as he had whipped her, she began to recite a familiar litany, begging him to stop. He would not. He took her by the hair once again. He made her kneel on the floor while he sat on the edge of the bed with his legs spread.

'Now we will try again,' he said. 'Now you will not cough. You will do better, yes?'

She nodded. She was completely out of her head with pleasure. She sucked him hard, pretending desperation, she rubbed his penis against her cheek as she licked and nipped at his testicles, she took him into her mouth again, using her teeth so that now he groaned and shivered, tangling his fingers in her hair, until with a little feeble movement he ejaculated his drop of semen into her throat. She lay back on her heels, her eyes shut. She wiped her lips. He had collapsed on to the bed and was smoking one of his cheroots by the time she rejoined him, taking her own cigarettes and matches from the jet and mother-of-pearl table beside her. She found her watch. A few more minutes and she would have to be on her way. She hadn't told him of her plans. She became all at once aware of the welts on her bottom and again her whole body came alive. She would regret parting from Constant. He was about the best she had managed to find and had required little training.

He spoke unexpectedly. Usually he never spoke at this stage. 'You look very dignified tonight,' he said. He was praising himself as much as he praised her. 'So completely feminine.'

She smiled around her cigarette.

'And it has only just begun,' he added. She had left him thinking that he was the first; she had enjoyed the fantasy.

'For you,' she said.

She had puzzled him. Again his expression became boyish, petulant. 'What?'

'I've got to go in a moment,' she told him, as if in explanation.

'To your boyfriend?' He was contemptuous. 'To your rock-and-roll hero.'

'I'm leaving.' She was deliberately uncommunicative.

He said, as if to excuse her behaviour: 'Are you still taking drugs?'

'Oh, yes.' She gave in to her impulse. 'Would I be here, otherwise?' Before he could demand enlightenment, she continued: 'But I'm giving them up after tonight.'

'You are wise. You don't need them. You might think that you know what you are doing, but they could destroy you in the end.'

'True.' She sat up, straightening her fine back. She stretched. 'Ah!'

He said, not altogether seriously, 'I will be very angry with you if you go now.'

'You're tired.' She smiled. 'You've overdone it. You should sleep. Shall I get you a cup of cocoa before I leave?'

'No.' He was sulky. He didn't look at her.

She climbed into her underclothes. She pulled up her long, golden skirt. She buttoned her shirt and over this she put her short, quilted jacket.

'You look lovely.' Either he had relented or he hoped to

flatter her, to make her stay. She ran a brush over her hair. 'I feel wonderful.' She could give him that.

'You have your pride again.'

'Yes.'

'When shall I phone you?'

She hesitated, looking down at his odd body. She felt affection for him. She bent and kissed his little cock.

'When?' he said. She picked up her handbag.

'Whenever you like.'

'He won't be there for a while?'

She wondered, momentarily, if she should tell him that Viv would answer the phone to him, for she would have already left the country, if Marius's second-in-command was as good as his word. 'Don't worry,' she said. With a bouncing step she made for the exit.

'I won't phone.' He attempted firmness, but his desire had left him. 'You come here tomorrow. At seven o'clock.'

'Okay. See you then,' she said.

She reached the front door, opening it on its chains to peer outside. The best part of Smith Street consisted of neatly stacked rubble. Marius's men had cleared most of the roads soon after they had arrived. Up at the corner of King's Road she saw the dark outlines of a vehicle. It was waiting for her.

Closing Constant's door behind her, she began to stride up the street. She was whistling. 'I'm Forever Blowing Bubbles.' It was almost her theme song, she thought.

TWENTY-THREE

*In which Miss Una Persson witnesses at last
the restoration of order*

The man who had built the gibbet had taken pains with his work. It was an exact reproduction of the kind once seen in cowboy films. Against those wooden houses still standing in this section of Umeå the gibbet did not look out of place. Craven, on the other hand, hanging there in his flying jacket and silver helmet, looked incongruous. It was inevitable that he had tried to convince the soldiers that she had been involved in his stupid plot to steal the only sea-worthy gunboat in the harbour. Una turned her back on her dead lover as the Finnish major cleared his throat to attract her attention. He was seated at a trestle table on which all the many papers were secured by a variety of heavy objects, including his Walther automatic pistol.

'Could we continue, Mademoiselle Persson?' He spoke Russian. 'A few more of these questions,' he tapped the documents, 'and you can go free. The pacification of Sweden is accomplished. They have already released most of the civilian prisoners in the south.' He was anxious to reassure her. 'A new autonomous parliament is in the process of being convened.' He studied the form, his felt-tip pen poised. Then he glanced up, his eyes amused. 'You agree to recognize the authority of the Emperor of Russia?'

She nodded.

'You are a Swedish national?'

'I have dual nationality. My father was Swedish. Mother was English.'

'They are resident in Sweden?'

'They are both dead.' A sad pout.

'Aha. Occupations?'

'He was a doctor, a missionary, an explorer. She became a missionary, too. They met through the Church. Mother was very devout (although not without a sense of humour).'

'Natural causes? Or . . .?' He meant to ask if they had been killed in the fighting.

'They were killed some years ago.' Una lifted the collar of the mink. 'A ballooning accident in China. It was horrible. They were climbing aboard when the mooring ropes slipped too soon. Clinging to the ropes, they shot into the air. They could be seen trying to reach the basket, but it was improperly attached to the gasbag itself – mother swung into it, it tipped sideways and down Mother fell, with the Peking ducks, the binoculars, the trunk of tropical clothing. Father remained. When he saw mother go, he gave a shrug and released his hold on the rope, plunging after her . . .'

'Tragic.' The Finn wrote 'Killed abroad' in neat Cyrillic capitals.

'Indeed!'

'Your occupation, mademoiselle?'

'I am an actress.'

'Last place of employment?'

She hesitated.

He tried to help her. 'Here, in Umeå?'

'I have been resting,' she told him.

His smile was sympathetic. 'Can you remember your last engagement?'

'Entertaining the troops in England.'

'That will do. A great shame about England. And yet it was inevitable.' He reached for a rubber stamp.

On the other side of the square a group of civilians were dragging a large hand-cart full of coarse red blankets. They all wore Russian army greatcoats and their breath was white in the sharp October air. Apparently with relief he stamped a document and signed it. 'Here is your passport. You still intend to go on to St Petersburg?'

'I have friends there.'

'You are lucky.' He spoke without irony. For a moment

his eyes rested on the hanging body of Craven. 'A few more hours and he would have been free, anyway.'

'Yes.'

'And next year the new century begins, or the old one ends. Nobody seems to be quite clear. It is strange how peace brutalizes some people and ennobles others. It is the same with war. I wonder if there is actually any difference. Many people seem to feel more tranquil when they know there is nothing to do but fight.'

'I know what you mean, major.' She accepted the passport and tucked it into her ermine muff.

'You will be appearing on the stage in St Petersburg?'

'I hope so.'

He stood up and saluted. 'I will come and see you.'

She inclined her head, the mink shako falling a little so that it almost covered her elaborately masacaraed left eye.

'You are a very beautiful woman. You will find many admirers in St Petersburg.'

'Oh, certainly.' She laughed. She was touched by his innocent enthusiasm. 'It is a wonderful city in which to be admired.'

'You must come to Roveniemi some time. My home. The Paris of the North. The Gateway to Lappland!'

She knew the city. 'It is a lovely place,' she said. She felt uncomfortable. The handing over of the passport seemed to have reversed their positions. She was embarrassed. She would have preferred his condescension to his admiration. She turned to take one last look at Craven, her heavy furs swinging. It was odd, she thought, that now she had capitulated she had more power than she had ever possessed when she had been a fighter. The knowledge shocked her, as it always had done. She caught the heavy odour of her own perfume. This was no time for self-examination; she must let herself go, fall into her new role with all the old thoroughness. A good actress, she thought, is a contented woman. Too many rôle options and one became confused. It was much better to let oneself get typecast. And that, she reflected not for the first time, was the trouble with the twentieth century: there was far too much choice for comfort. Well, not any more. The war was over. The Tsar ruled the world (what was left of it) and, with luck, would continue to do so for a long while. Perhaps Jerry had been right, after all, and one big war was preferable to a lot of small ones.

From somewhere the Finnish major had commandeered a hovercab. The driver wore one of Umeå's many municipal uniforms. He saluted self-consciously; the major opened the door for Una. The machine rocked slightly on its air cushion as she boarded. The door was shut.

'The airfield,' said the major in Swedish. 'Good luck, Miss Persson, and *bon voyage*.'

'Next year in St Petersburg.' She blew him a kiss. A rôle is a rôle, she thought. She was already remembering the old lines.

The taxi took the short, privileged route through the city and was soon in the suburbs, driving along streets lined with pines and birches, the timber houses of the rich, set back from the street, consciously built in the Swiss chalet style beloved of Edwardians who had settled in the English Lake District. These streets reminded her of New England and she felt a pang of loss.

The airport came in sight. She rubbed at the misted windows of the taxi. There were several gigantic airships moored there, most of them military craft, drifting at their masts in the wind. She saw the only civil vessel with its Cyrillic inscriptions, its black imperial eagles on their yellow backgrounds. In the semi-darkness its cabin lights were already glowing. Masses of lambent grey clouds swelled on the horizon. She anticipated the warmth and the luxury of the ship.

The taxi crossed the grass. Porters came forward to remove her trunks as the hovercab's engine stopped and the machine sighed to a halt. A loading derrick had been manoeuvred into position. The porters fitted her trunks on to its platform. An officer, in the dark green of the civil air service, politely took her papers. It was obvious that he had been expecting her, for he hardly looked at the documents before handing them back. He was quietly admiring. His nose wrinkled as her perfume reached him. 'We are honoured to have you with us on this flight, Mademoiselle Persson.'

'You are kind.' She gave him one of her endless smiles.

He led her to the passenger derrick. Unlike the other one, this was covered in sheets of aluminium, decorated with the insignia of the Swedish airline. She entered the lift. He pressed the button for her.

'You are holidaying in Russia?' he wanted to know.

'A little pleasure, a little work,' she told him.

The lift stopped and the door slid open. The short covered gangway between the derrick and the ship moved very slightly as she crossed it to be greeted by a steward in white and green livery. 'Good evening, ma'am.' He was English and seemed glad to welcome a fellow national.

The officer said: 'Will you show mademoiselle to her cabin?'

'With pleasure.' He led her along the narrow companionway. Tiny bulbs lit it, set into the slightly curved roof. With a key he opened a door about half-way along. He switched on a light for her. 'There is a bedroom through there,' he said. The cabin was quite small, but comfortably furnished. She would have been glad of a window in the far wall, but the only porthole looked out on to the companionway and the observation window beyond it. No airship cabins looked directly out into the sky.

She took her tiny purse from her muff and tipped the steward. He thanked her enthusiastically, showing her where she could find the service bell, the telephone if she wished the wireless operator to connect her with a number. When he had gone she shrugged off the furs and lay down on the wide bed, reading the standard literature, which was in Russian, smoking one of the cigarettes from the box the company had provided. She slid her hand over her silk dress, pulling the material up so that she could scratch her leg where her stocking met her suspender. She felt wonderful.

A little later she sensed the ship shudder as it freed itself from its mooring and turned slowly towards the east. By morning they would be over St Petersburg.

She undressed and got into her black pyjamas, putting on a matching cap to protect her elaborately waved hair, removing her make-up. Then she got into bed, put out the light and let the distant sound of the motors, the gentle swaying of the ship, send her to sleep.

She was awakened by a juddering, by gunfire. She ran to the porthole, seeing nothing but darkness on the other side of the observation windows. She put on her dressing-gown, opened the cabin door, went out to peer downwards through the perspex. She heard the booming of big guns, saw their flashes below. Searchlights suddenly blinded her. Her steward ran up. 'Best get inside, ma'am.'

'This is horrible!' she complained, as if he was at fault. 'The war is over!'

'For most people, ma'am.'

'The airline should have warned us of any potential trouble.' She retreated and slumped on her bed. 'Oh, it's too bad!'

'Don't worry. We'll soon be out of range. We're making very good speed, with the wind behind us.'

'But we are losing height!'

'It'll be all right.'

She knew enough about the handling of airships to realize that his assurances were meaningless. The ship lurched. The steward fell against her, clutching the rail above the bed. 'Beg pardon, ma'am.' He tried to steady her with his free hand. She shook him off. 'Well,' he said, 'I'd better ...' He staggered through the door and she slammed it behind him. She began to dress and make-up. Her old instincts were coming back. If the ship did go down it was as well to be ready for whoever might have won her.

The cabin tilted from stem to stern. All her belongings slid along the floor into a heap against the wall. The ship righted herself slightly, but then came a terrifying scraping from below, a trembling bump. Quite suddenly all motion ceased.

Una got her door open, swaying on high heels. The steward was still in the companionway. His head was bleeding. The perspex of the observation windows was smashed. They appeared to have crashed in a forest. She saw the outlines of pines. She saw figures moving amongst the trees. Riders appeared in the dawn light, their long hair blowing behind them. They were dressed in wolfskin and leather. They had rifles.

Una returned to her cabin and sat down miserably on her bed. She was far too tired for any more excitement.

There were no more shots, but she heard yells, screams, raised voices. She experienced a passing flash of *déjà vu*. She heard people in the companionway. She went outside.

The marauders who had brought down the ship were gently forcing the passengers back into the cabins. 'I'm sorry,' one of them said, 'we thought this was a warship. We'll do what we can for you.' All the marauders were female. All were good-looking. Some were very young, barely more than ten years old. They had fresh healthy faces. It was as if nuns and their pupils had become long-haired bandits overnight. They all had rifles slung on their backs and had thick fur jerkins, almost as a uniform.

'Don't you know the war is over?' Una asked one of the children. 'Didn't you know that?'

The girl looked at her uncomprehendingly. Una said in Russian: 'There is an amnesty for everyone. The war is finished.'

The girl smiled and touched her dress. 'You are very pretty.' She fingered Una between her legs.

'Oh!' Una was exasperated. 'Who is your commander? Where is he?' She half-suspected Cornelius.

The child pointed down the companionway. A girl, in black and white skins, was marching towards them, her face brightening as she recognized Una. 'Get the cargo off. Hurry, girls!' She was eating a piece of meat. 'Well, well, well. This is a turn up, eh, Una? Were you after this ship, too?'

'I just wanted to go to St Petersburg in peace.' Una realized she was still wearing her night-cap and snatched it off, patting at her hair. 'Are these your people, Catherine? What point is there in shooting us down?'

'We thought it was a military airship, honestly. I'm very sorry, Una. Aren't you pleased to see me?'

'Haven't you heard about the amnesty?'

'No. We're a bit cut off here, me and my gang.'

'Gang? You with a gang?'

'I used to have a gang, years ago. In Whitechapel. Before I got caught and improved.' Catherine was in a jolly mood. Her laughter was hearty 'I haven't introduced us properly. Catherine Cornelius and her All Girl Guerrillas! Aren't you tickled?' She was as bad as her brother, when she felt like it.

But Una was in no state of mind to accept Catherine's levity. Her new way of life had cost her too much. 'You've ruined everything, Catherine. Playing at soldiers.'

'It runs in the family,' Catherine told her. 'Actually, I had a feeling I might be bumping into you soon.'

'How on earth did you turn up in this zone? In this godforsaken place?'

'It suited me. I had to get away from it all.' Catherine studied her friend's face. 'You're not yourself today, are you, Una?'

'No, thanks to you, you silly bitch.' Una simply did not see any reason for disguising her feelings. She had never been more angry, yet already the intensity of her emotion was fading and when Catherine seized her head between her mittened hands and kissed her firmly, Una did not resist.

'I said I was sorry,' Catherine told her, nuzzling her ear. 'You're looking so lovely. And since we managed to hit the ship, we might as well loot it. My kids are starving.'

'Why did you bring them out here?'

'I didn't know there was an amnesty, did I? We'd blown up all these bridges, for one thing. And railways. And there was the garrison we massacred. We were trying to free the Ukraine.' Catherine swept her hair from her face. 'We got pushed back, of course. Oh, don't be so bloody pompous, Una. It's not like you!'

Una sulked on principle.

'Did you say you were going to St Petersburg?' asked Catherine.

'I had everything set up,' Una complained. 'The last thing I needed was another shambles. I'm tired. I want peace. Order. A quiet life with no responsibilities. Have you seen your brother?'

'No. I thought he was with you.'

'He's out. I was getting out. Frank's out. Even Major bloody Nye is out. But you're suddenly right in it, for the first time, doing God knows what damage!'

Catherine was hurt. 'I thought I was helping.'

'It's a fine fucking time to decide to become an activist, just when everything's settling down.'

'That's hardly my fault '

'Oh, bugger off,' said Una. She returned to her cabin and sat on her bed again.

Catherine followed her in. 'I wanted to do something useful,' she said plaintively.

Una scowled at her.

'Look,' said Catherine, taking her friend's limp hand. 'What you need is a holiday.'

'I was just about to have one!'

''Let's have one together, then? Wouldn't you like that? Like old times?'

'Together? Riding about the frozen bloody forest shooting at airships?'

'If the war's over, there's nothing left for us to do. You and I'll go somewhere. I'll tell my girls about the amnesty. They'll be all right.'

Una sucked her lower lip as tenderly Catherine stroked her face. 'I'll look after you,' said Catherine. 'It seems as if things have been rough. I'll keep you safe and warm, Una.'

Una buried her head in Catherine's half-cured skins and began, contentedly, to sob.

Catherine raised her to her feet. 'Come on, then, love.' Una let Catherine lead her through the embarkation doors, down the metal stairway to the ground. A big roan stallion snorted as he recognized his mistress. His breath was white and warm. There was a smell of snow. Catherine climbed into her saddle and reached down to help her friend up. Una sat sideways on the horse in front of Catherine who kicked at the stallion's flanks. The sun was rising as the roan galloped through the frosty trees towards the east. Red light flooded the snow. 'New century soon,' said Catherine, as if to comfort Una. 'By and large, I didn't think a lot of the last one.'

Una felt her spirits rising, for all that the jogging motion of the horse was making her slightly sick. She put her arms around Catherine's neck and kissed her. Catherine supported her back with a strong right hand. 'This won't take long. I've a jeep waiting in the valley.'

'Where are we going?' Una asked. Like a damsel in distress she had been rescued and was reconciled.

'Somewhere nice,' Catherine promised.

'Not the future?'

'Of course not. Somewhere safe.'

The hard earth gave way to grass. The snow had almost melted here, for the proper winter had hardly begun. The horse slowed its pace as they descended towards a number of shacks in the valley below. 'That was our camp,' said Catherine. 'We were almost completely self-sufficient.'

'I've made such a balls-up of things,' said Una.

'Nonsense. I bet you've done wonders. You're the finest Elfberg of them all!'

Una stared up at her friend in astonishment. Then she kissed her firmly on the cheek.

Catherine pursed her lips in a confident whistle.

PART THREE

LIMPING HOME:
THE PROBLEMS OF
RETIREMENT

So you thought silk stockings had had their day. Think again, Besides the male enthusiasts who bemoan the end of the suspender era they now have a new fan. None other than the fashion queen Mary Quant! She believes that 1976 will be The Year of the Sensual Woman and, to celebrate, she has produced a range of beautiful real silk stockings. Mary says: 'Not only will you feel like a lady, but you will have to be treated like one. Things like car doors will have to be opened for you, simply because you cannot afford to snag these stockings.'

DAILY MIRROR, 3 November 1975

TWENTY-FOUR

*In which our heroines, for the moment weary
from their exploits in the world, enjoy the
comforts of peacetime*

It was 1939 on a warm summer day and Catherine Cornelius took Una Persson to tea in the roof garden of Derry and Toms. The garden had only been opened that year and it was to enjoy considerable vogue before the war came to make such places unfashionable. Both ladies were dressed to the nines in the styles they were favouring this summer, Catherine in her rather sporty tweed jacket and golfing skirt and Una in her pale green chiffon frock. Conscious of the other women sitting at the little white tables overlooking the ornamental ponds, Catherine was careful not to touch Una who was, as it happened, in one of her sensitive moods.

They chewed their cucumber sandwiches. They sipped weak tea. Around them came the sounds of lazy bees.

All day Catherine had been trying to amuse Una, to draw her out of her mood of sultry melancholy. 'You are looking so much better, dear,' she said now. 'Has your head gone?'

'It's still there.' Una languidly laid her sandwich upon its plate. 'But it's better.' She sighed.

'And the cinema? Do you still want to go?'

'I'm rather fatigued, after all the shopping.'

'Then we'll go straight home, said Catherine. 'You can relax and I'll cook you a charming supper.'

'You are so good to me, my dear,' said Una raising a wide grey eye. 'If I were only healthier . . .' She uttered a delicate cough.

'You are an artist,' Catherine told her, 'and artists must be nurtured. Ah, look, here is Mr Koutrouboussis.' Mr Koutrouboussis was an impresario who had telephoned Una that morning to offer her the star part in his new West End production. 'Hello, Mr Koutrouboussis.'

The dignified old man sailed up to them, lifting his topper. 'Ladies. What pleasure! Ladies!'

'You will join us for a moment, Mr Koutrouboussis?'

'Oh, ladies! An honour.' He removed his hat and held it with his gloves and cane in his left hand, drawing forth a chair. He seated himself. 'You have had time to consider my suggestion, Miss Persson?'

'Not yet, I fear. Too soon. Too soon, Mr Koutrouboussis.'

'Aha. Of course.' He stroked his imperial beard as he contemplated the menu. 'Hm. Tea.'

'He ...' Catherine hesitated, looking at Una through intense china-blue eyes. 'You ...'

'Who?' Mr Koutrouboussis raised his own eyes above the level of the menu.

'Una. Una,' said Catherine. 'What's the part?'

'Today?'

'The play,' clarified Catherine.

'An excellent part,' said Mr Koutrouboussis. 'Perfect for Miss Persson. From *Victory*, you know. With music.'

'A musical comedy?' Catherine asked. 'How lovely.'

'Based on Conrad,' said Una, without inflection.

'Do you know Conrad, Miss Cornelius?' asked Mr Koutrouboussis.

'The name rings a bell,' said Catherine. 'Once, perhaps. Long ago.' She watched as a large, fat clergyman and his skinny daughter sat down at the next table and ordered pastries.

'He was a sweetie,' said Una. 'A sweetie.'

'All my life,' said Mr Koutrouboussis, 'I have admired his eye, exactitude, his sweep.'

'My brother,' said Catherine, 'has arrived, I gather, and is staying at Blenheim Crescent, while Mother ...'

'He was abroad?' said Una.

'A postcard came. From Pom Pen. In China.'

'What was he doing there?' Una asked.

'Wasting time, as usual, I suppose.' She saw someone she recognized, sitting on her own at a table in the far corner. She leaned forward to whisper to Una. 'Don't look now, but that's our old schoolteacher, Miss Brunner. Hasn't she *aged*!'

'Your brother's *bête noir*?'

'That's the one.' Catherine could not resist a second glance. Miss Brunner was being joined by another amazon. 'She's meeting our old *German* teacher here. Ho, ho! What can they be up to?'

'Very little, by the look of 'em,' said Una with some sudden animation. She relaxed again, studying Mr K as he studied the menu. 'Hm.'

She produced a jade holder and fitted a cigarette. Mr Koutrouboussis hurried through his pockets and found a gold lighter. She puffed.

Catherine giggled to herself.

Una, with a glance at her tiny watch, rose. 'Well.'

Mr Koutrouboussis leapt to his feet.

'Please don't,' said Una. He descended.

Catherine began to gather up their parcels.

'A lift,' said Mr Koutrouboussis. 'Could I offer?'

'No,' said Una. 'Thank you. We have the car.'

'Oh, Una,' said Catherine as they paid at the till, 'you were so haughty.'

Una smiled.

When they arrived at the exit they saw that the sky had clouded. 'Wait here, darling,' Catherine put the parcels into the arms of a doorman. 'I'll fetch the car. It's turning chilly.'

With poise Una waited until Catherine drove up to the kerb. The doorman piled the parcels into the back of the car. Una sat beside Catherine.

They drove through the afternoon streets of Kensington and arrived at last at the house in Holland Park Avenue, borrowed from Catherine's brother. It was high and white. Catherine drove the car into the garage. They disembarked, carrying their parcels to the front door.

Their arrival had been observed. The door opened. Mrs Cornelius stood there, a cigarette in her carmine lips. She was expressionless.

'Well,' she said, 'you got 'ome for right, then.'

Michael Moorcock in Panther Books

The Cornelius Chronicles
The Adventures of Una Persson and Catherine Cornelius in the Twentieth Century	£1.25	☐

The Dancers at the End of Time
An Alien Heat	£1.25	☐
The Hollow Lands	£1.50	☐
The End of All Songs	£1.50	☐
The Dancers at the End of Time (Omnibus)	£2.50	☐

Hawkmoon: The History of the Runestaff
The Jewel in the Skull	£1.95	☐
The Mad God's Amulet	£1.50	☐
The Sword of the Dawn	£1.95	☐
The Runestaff	£1.25	☐
The History of the Runestaff (omnibus)	£2.95	☐

Hawkmoon: The Chronicles of Castle Brass
Count Brass	£1.50	☐
The Champion of Garathorm	£1.50	☐
The Quest for Tanelorn	£1.25	☐

Erekosë
The Eternal Champion	£1.50	☐
Phoenix in Obsidian	£1.95	☐

Elric
The Sailor on the Seas of Fate	£1.95	☐
The Weird of the White Wolf	£1.95	☐
The Vanishing Tower	£1.95	☐
The Bane of the Black Sword	£1.95	☐
Stormbringer	£1.95	☐

The Books of Corum
The Knight of the Swords	£1.25	☐
The Queen of the Swords	£1.50	☐
The King of the Swords	£1.50	☐
The Bull and the Spear	£1.50	☐
The Oak and the Ram	£1.50	☐
The Sword and the Stallion	£1.95	☐

Oswald Bastable
The War Lord of the Air	£1.50	☐
The Land Leviathan	£1.50	☐
The Steel Tsar	£1.25	☐
The Nomad of Time (omnibus)	£2.95	☐

All these books are available at your local bookshop or newsagent, or can be ordered direct from the publisher.

To order direct from the publisher just tick the titles you want and fill in the form below.

Name_____

Address_____

_____

Send to:
Panther Cash Sales
PO Box 11, Falmouth, Cornwall TR10 9EN.

Please enclose remittance to the value of the cover price plus:

UK 45p for the first book, 20p for the second book plus 14p per copy for each additional book ordered to a maximum charge of £1.63.

BFPO and Eire 45p for the first book, 20p for the second book plus 14p per copy for the next 7 books, thereafter 8p per book.

Overseas 75p for the first book and 21p for each additional book.

Panther Books reserve the right to show new retail prices on covers, which may differ from those previously advertised in the text or elsewhere.